★★★★★ "A perfect example of how an author can balance dark humor with emotional depth. It is crisp and engaging, filled with sharp wit and subtle humor that keeps the reader entertained throughout." --The Bookish Elf

★★★★★ "Fans of dark humor will immensely enjoy this story, and those that are looking for action and intriguing plotlines will not be disappointed." -- Literary Titan

★★★★★ "... impossible not to remain intrigued making it difficult to put the book down."
--Reedsy Discovery

★★★★★"This is a book that I know I will read many times over." --OnlineBookClub.org

★★★★★"The conversations that Gil has with the sex workers, his colleagues, and his friends are simply hilarious."
--Readers' Favorite

★★★★★"An insightful yet hilarious read." --Book Nerdection

★★★★★ "Memorable, hilarious, yet poignant and well-written; The Melancholy Strumpet Master is a must-read dark comedy." --Author Anthony Avina's Blog

Los Angeles:
September - 2002

Gilmore Crowell paced from wall to wall, conducting his
thoughts with a raised hacksaw. He might have kept this up till
sunrise, but a cat that lived out of the dumpster below his open
window leapt onto the sill, jarring him into action. He grabbed
his keys, went down the boarding house stairs, and stepped out
into the predawn darkness.

The Isuzu Gemini hatchback was just around the corner
on Eleventh Street. He got beneath it and hacked away at the
wheel brace the Parking Violations Bureau had stuck him with a
few nights before. With each stroke of the saw years of
frustration and resentment poured forth, sweat and muttered
oaths. Nothing but a patch of scratches came of it. He wondered
if he'd bought the wrong blade. There had been others, more
expensive. Or maybe he didn't know how to use a hacksaw.
Also a possibility.

A distant pair of headlights crept into view, advancing
slowly up the street. Gil crawled to the curb to wait it out. A
glance at his watch, four twenty-three. He felt a tingling in his
hands, a tightness to his breathing. From out of the stillness, he
could hear the vehicle approach. A spotlight swept across the
nearby bushes and windows. It settled on the Gemini's frame,
creating a distorted rhombus of shadow where he crouched
beside it. A surge of adrenaline knocked him off balance. His
heart banged away. How he managed not to move, scream, or
vomit he had no idea. It felt like blood was pulsing out his ears,
a stroke to go along with the heart attack. He clenched his teeth.
Just as he was making peace with such a pointless death, a
tunnel of light shone down.

"Whatcha doing there?"

3

"Doing?" Gil repeated.

"LAPD, what's going on?"

"Going on?" The questions struck his frantic mind as remarkably open-ended. He got to his feet.

"He's all right, officer," another voice said. "Just a little shook up."

Gil turned away from the flashlight. A wild-haired woman reclined on the steps of a nearby apartment complex.

"What's that?" the cop asked.

"He tripped on that mess of broken sidewalk there, fell into the gutter. Might be something for the city to look at."

"Just fell in the gutter, you say?"

"That gutter right what he crawled up out of."

The cop toed a chunk of loose concrete, turned off the flashlight. "All righty then. You tell him to stay on his feet now." He returned to the squad car and drove off.

Gil slid back under the Gemini to retrieve the hacksaw and headed for the Koenig House.

"That's how it is, huh?" the woman called after him.

He turned around. "Sorry, do I owe you something?"

"How about a blow job?"

"What?"

"Forty bucks." She lit a cigarette.

He continued walking away. Just then, his entire left side seized up, perhaps an effect of the stroke. He sat on the opposite curb, took off his shoe.

The woman came over. "We could go in the car."

"Another time." He massaged his foot, wincing. "I'm not well."

She looked over at the Isuzu Gemini hatchback with its steel brace attached to the driver-side front wheel. "Little low on cash?"

"Yeah, that too." He got up and limped on, hacksaw in one hand, shoe in the other.

4

He entered the Koenig House and called Rex Healy, a friend and fellow graduate student in the loosest sense of those terms. It went straight to voice mail.

"That insane idea of yours didn't pan out. I'm not sure how I'll get to the border tonight. You're on your own."

Buoyed by a wave of righteousness, he felt the cranial pressure of the imagined stroke begin to lift. Hot showering also helped. As he dressed for work, the stray cat returned. He offered it some cracker crumbs. The cat sniffed his palm and leaped back down to the dumpster. In the still-darkened window Gil caught sight of himself. The eyes, so often narrowed from lost sleep, had retreated deeper into their sockets. For the first time the crescent shadow of a double chin appeared under his bearded baby face.

"What is wrong with you?" he asked his reflection.

No answer.

He headed down to the refectory, the first to arrive. The other men would trickle in as the morning progressed. He took a seat at one of the long wooden tables. Claudia, the middle-aged manager and cook, served him greasy eggs and potatoes with characteristic good morning cheer. He poked at the food, imagined it chewed up in his stomach. In the silence, his mind wandered toward the burden of the work day.

Los Angeles Correctional Academy was one of the state's three incarceration facilities for secondary education. For a change, he was the first sub to arrive. A guard opened the gate of the razor-barbed security fence. Gil headed up the walk to the main building, where another guard cleared him to enter. He went down the hallway to the main office. There was a muted clunk, and a steel door on the far wall slid open.

"Well, look who's here!" Ms. Mott, the elderly office secretary, was returning from the women's staff restroom. Her delight at seeing him was all out of proportion, as though he'd just pulled a live dove from his sleeve.

5

Gil nodded, so much as admitting that, yes, it was he who was here.

"I may have to change your assignment, Mr. Crowell. How would you feel about taking on Mr. Frinkle's old position? There's an increase in pay. Long-term subs fall under a separate wage schedule." She appeared to be taking down information from a Rolodex and entering it into a computer file, a task that produced a range of pained expressions.

"I think I'd be interested, Ms. Mott. Science, correct?"

She nodded.

"I'm about as broke as a person can be."

"You haven't worked here long, have you?" she asked.

"About a year, but not consistently."

"Did you know Mr. Frinkle?"

"I didn't know him well, but I ran into him a couple times." He'd never heard of the man.

"He was on medical leave after falling down the north staircase. Hit his head and lost some memory."

"Terrible."

"Yes, and now he's retiring."

With traces of the morning's shock still playing on his nerves, Gil arrived at some ill-formed idea that he owed someone an amends.

Ms. Mott made a face at the computer screen. "Looks like biology."

"That would be ideal," he said.

"Long term would fit your schedule? You're doing something on the side, aren't you? Acting or filmmaking or...?"

"Finishing my doctorate."

"And what's that about?"

"Anthropology."

"Anthropology," she repeated. "That's one of those words I'm never quite sure what it means."

6

"I'm not quite sure myself at this point. In my case, it has something to do with a microculture of Tijuana street workers."

"People who maintain the streets?"

"More like the people who work them."

"How so?"

He scratched his elbow. "Servicing tourists, that kind of thing."

"Oh, performers and artisans, and so on. Yes, they're wonderful, aren't they? I saw some in Acapulco on my honeymoon. Gosh, that was so many years ago. Well, it must be very rewarding work."

"Mine or theirs?"

She didn't clarify. "Would you like to sign the get-well card for Mr. Frinkle while I set you up with the classes?"

"Yes, I would."

She gestured toward the counter.

While he composed a message of sympathy for a man he'd never met, what he really felt was something like guilt over his cheap luck. As the ink rolled out of the pen, he consoled himself that he did not push Mr. Frinkle down that flight of stairs. He did not cause the man's memory loss. He was not the violent force behind his early retirement. And yet he still felt rather crappy, mostly for himself. What he needed was coffee.

With time to kill before the first class, he took a short walk to a convenience store. The contours of trees and buildings began to solidify as the sky brightened. A flock of parrots screeched overhead, clashing against the roar of traffic. He bought a cartridge of miniature doughnuts and a coffee, and went to stretch out on the front lawn of the correctional facility. Each swallow had an immediate remedial effect. Looking up at the blueness of the sky through the sprawling boughs of a great ficus, he laughed at his ridiculous attempt to free the car. It

7

would have to rot on the street till the agents of parking violations made their next move. He'd miss the easy transportation, though accepted the time had come to part with it.

As traffic jammed to a crawl on Washington Boulevard, the probationary students began to arrive. He got in line with them to clear security at the door, but a guard waved him on ahead. Inside, resident students in gray numbered uniforms made their way from the jailhouse barracks to classrooms, a guard at the front and rear of each line. Gil went into Mr. Frinkle's classroom. Many of the man's personal things were still there, even a cardigan draped across the swivel desk chair. There was no lesson plan. He would have to cook something up out of the textbook. It was then he discovered that Mr. Frinkle did not teach biology or any other science course offered at Los Angeles Correctional Academy. He taught English.

Gil went over to the phone on the wall, intending to clear up the mistake with Ms. Mott. He lifted the handset and pressed the first three buttons of the main office number. Something kept him from pressing that fourth digit. His index finger remained raised before the keypad. It was not adrenaline that brought on the paralysis this time but something deeply wired within his lower brain. He replaced the handset and began digging through the textbook.

As the school day wore on, he discovered that any moderately cunning imposter could pull off teaching high school English, especially to a room full of hooligans. It was not at all like economics or auto mechanics, in which the fraud would be readily exposed. This was something else: a play, a game, a charade. It was teenage daycare with stories to pass the time. The students, despite their petty outlaw status, were rather docile. They mostly stayed in their seats, asked politely to use the bathroom, and otherwise gazed at him open-mouthed as though he had a second scrotum dangling between his eyes. One student even asked a relevant question.

"Why do they call it The Lottery when the winner has to die?"

"You remember when they drew slips of paper out of that box?" Gil asked her. "Well, the randomness of that is similar to a lottery."

"But they don't win anything," the girl clarified. "If it's a lottery, they're supposed to win something."

He coasted through the afternoon's lessons, recognizing with no small measure of comfort that he hadn't had a stroke after all. A text message from Rex Healy came through just before the start of the final period: The brace was off the Gemini. He'd be waiting for Gil in front of the jailhouse as soon as detention camp let out.

"How did you manage that?" Gil texted back. It was the first time he'd ever composed a text message. It took him several minutes.

No reply.

When the dismissal bell rang, he went back down the guarded corridor and out into the light of mid-afternoon. There was old Rex in the Gemini, as promised, his scraggy frame hunched over the steering wheel, long gray-blonde hair shading his face. Gil trotted between passing cars to the other side of the street.

"Hey, there's police all around this place. I get a ticket and we're off to jail for grand theft auto."

"Grand theft auto?" Rex asked, rolling out each word. "For this car?"

"You're in the middle of a crosswalk."

"And?"

"How'd you manage to free it?"

"Some light power tools."

"In broad daylight?"

"I wore my orange reflective vest. Being overly conspicuous acts as a form of camouflage."

Gil pulled out his cell phone.

"Who you calling?" Rex asked.

"The police."

Rex groaned.

"If I report it stolen, that eliminates me as a suspect. And perhaps also you."

Rex laughed. "You're overthinking this, bro."

"Head over to my place. I need to pick up a few things before we leave."

Gil dialed 911. He got a busy signal on the first attempt, then was transferred so many times he wondered if the call was being outsourced to the Philippines.

"Nature of your emergency?" a voice finally asked.

"Someone stole my car."

"Make and model?"

"1984 Isuzu Gemini hatchback."

"What makes you think it was stolen?"

"There's an empty space where I last parked it." He leaned back, observed the sagging cloth ceiling.

"Color?"

"Green."

"Your name?"

"Gilmore Crowell."

"Delinquent on any payments?"

"On an eighteen-year-old car?"

"Standard questions, sir. This is the number at which you may be reached?"

"Correct."

"When did you notice the vehicle missing?"

"About twenty minutes ago."

"Did you see anyone in the area?"

"You mean someone driving my car?" He looked out the window as they passed a series of strip malls, each with its own laundry, liquor store, and check-cashing outlet.

"Location?"

"Eleventh and Alvarado."

10

"And you haven't seen anything suspicious?"

"It's kind of a suspicious place," Gil said.

"What do you mean?"

"Gangsters, drunks, sex workers."

"Anything out of the ordinary?"

"Like someone wearing a suit?"

Rex swerved around a bloody skunk carcass. The odor followed them down the road.

"License plate?"

"J-P-3..."

"I'll send an officer to that location. Please be on hand."

"How long will it take?"

"No idea."

"Sorry, but I can't wait around. I have an appointment."

"Let's hold off on the dispatch. Go to the station when you're able and fill out a stolen-vehicle report."

"That sounds like a wonderful idea."

2

At the Koenig House, Gil picked up a change of underwear, laptop, toothbrush, passport, a couple notebooks, and stuffed it all into a daypack. He ran into Norm, the old resident Buddhist, on the way out.

"You look like you're on your way to *Tia-wanna*," he said, jutting out his dentures.

"I'll be back Sunday, Norm. Keep the peace."

"I can only keep my own peace."

"That's kind of what I meant."

He met up with Rex around the corner, where they switched seats. They drove past the more stable class of

11

homeless in their waterfront MacArthur Park tents and the downtrodden ones on the park's east side. It was just past four, and Friday rush hour was full on. They got on the Harbor freeway, merged into traffic. A CHP cruiser was stopped on the shoulder behind a red Porsche.

"Not a good sign," Gil said.

"No, you hate to see that. What has happened to this town? You can't drive a Porsche on the freeway anymore?"

"We can assume he was speeding."

"In a Porsche? That's not fair."

Gil adjusted the rearview. "I'd ask you to explain but I know it wouldn't help."

"Well, the minute you step onto the showroom floor, you're surrounded by sharks pushing a test drive. Pretty soon seventy-five feels like forty and after a few weeks you're doing ninety on San Vicente Boulevard."

"I'll take your word for it." Gil turned on the radio.

"I went through it back in the day," Rex continued. "After the car came the marching powder and the Grand Marnier and the chicks with the tight white sweaters. Before long, you're waking up on the floor of an abandoned warehouse, half a dozen pigeons trying to figure out how you got there. That reminds me, I had a dream about you the other night."

"What's that supposed to mean?"

"Take it easy," Rex said. "No funny business. I mean, you tried something but I shut it down."

They'd been moving along rather smoothly until traffic bottled up around the Orange Crush interchange. A little farther on, it stopped altogether. Rex lit up a joint.

"Just what we need," Gil said. "Dope smoke trailing out the back of a stolen vehicle."

"Want a hit?"

"Definitely not. And I'll tell you something else. This whole plan is starting to feel very unwise."

12

"Where's the feeling, in your sack?"

"Excuse me?"

"You need to get laid, man. I've been saying that for a while now."

Gil didn't answer.

"Everything feels wrong when you're that uptight. You're not getting any from the whores?"

"I beg your pardon?"

"The *chicas*, baby. Your *focus group*. Christ, you've been studying them for, what – five years now? You never asked them to put a little sugar in your bowl?"

"I don't even know how to respond to that."

"Because you still don't understand that you've got to live it, bro." Rex smacked the dashboard. "That's what Geertz was all about. You're never going to make sense of their world till you get inside it, so to speak."

"That's the most twisted thing I've heard in a while," Gil said. "Do you snort marching powder with the homeless?"

"I've shared a bottle with them, sure."

"You've had your mouth on the same bottle as a homeless person?"

"You think the guys who follow the shamans around the jungle don't chug their miracle mixture on the weekend?"

"That's a sacramental ritual."

"And Red Mountain is a sacrament on Skid Row, baby. What of it? Plus, I thought you went to whores growing up in Yucatán or wherever it was."

"Like three times maybe and that was completely different. I was a horny, misguided youth. I'm not about to screw off eight years of grad school because I'm uptight, as you say. I'll finish up ethically or not at all."

"Maybe that's what's holding you back," Rex said.

"Look, you were clearly too stoned to remember, but I once connected with a family whose standard of living

13

depended on the local sex trade. That they all up and vanished one day was out of my control."

"Right, and you've been spinning your wheels ever since. It's all about the present moment." He flashed the spiky-lettered *Be here now* tattoo on his forearm. "Back to my point, how's anyone going to know if you sample the goods? I mean, whatever gets you through the door, right?"

"Drop it."

"What else have you got going on, man? You never went after Petra Solis when I told you she was available."

The sound of the name tightened Gil's grip on the steering wheel. "Why do you bring her up?"

"Because she's cute in a retro-fascist kind of way, and I think you have something for her. I may even have something for her."

"Why don't you make a move then? Let me guess, because you've completely thrown yourself into the downtown streets like Bourgois took to East Harlem."

"I'm also twice her age and twice divorced. You know I'm only hanging around her because we have the same thesis advisor. His partnering students has ruined so many weekends. But forget about Petra. What you got down there in TJ is all ready for action."

A motorcycle wobbled up between the stalled lanes. The woman riding it was dressed in black leather jacket and pants, wavy blonde hair flowing out of a bright pink helmet. Rex waved her over and asked a bunch of dopy questions about her bike. He finished by handing her his card.

"That's how you do it, huh?" Gil asked.

"If you show any kind of interest in their stuff, they just light right up. I once pretended I didn't know what a pair of sandals were. This chick spent the next twenty minutes telling me all about them, where she got them, what they were made of. Six hours later, we were banging it out."

Gil said nothing, his eyes fixed on the car ahead.

14

"And what's your game? Oh, that's right. You hang around whores but don't fuck them."

"Listen up, asshole." Gil turned down the radio. "I don't pick up women off the side of the highway. I either meet them in the flow of life or I don't. That's my game."

"How's that working out?"

"Hang on, I'm not done. For the hundredth time, do not use the word *whore* around me again. They're called sex workers. Licensed independent sex workers in a profession regulated by the health department. Show some goddamn respect."

A silence kicked in. Gil turned the radio back up.

"You really like jazz or do you listen to it for some other reason?"

Gil didn't answer.

"I'm serious. I could never figure it out."

Gil changed it to an oldies station, a chart-topper about catastrophic heartache.

"You're going to punish me for asking a question?"

"I like this song."

"No, you don't. You think you're being clever, but let me tell you something since you lack any context. This is exactly the kind of seventies crapola that spawned, *by musical antithesis*, the advent of punk rock." He clapped his thigh and finger-pistoled the radio.

"Musical antithesis, huh?" Gil gave it a little more volume.

Rex directed his eyes out the side window like a Labrador riding shotgun. He soon fell asleep. They crawled through Costa Mesa and traffic didn't open up again until they got past Irvine. It took a couple more hours, but they got there.

15

3

They drove past the winding checkpoint lanes at the border and continued several miles before coming to a scorched patch of highway. A long dirt drive led to a set-back auto garage. They pulled in. A number of cars in various states of decay were scattered around. They got out of the Gemini and went up an outdoor staircase to a small apartment above the garage. Rex banged on the battered screen door.

"You know what I've been thinking, Gil?"

"Just go ahead and tell me."

"There must be a male version of the easy chick, know what I mean? The guy women know they can take advantage of. But they don't use him for sex; they get him to move stuff out of their apartment or to listen to their miserable stories. Or maybe they just take a shit on him once in a while in order to feel better. And you're one of those guys, Gil. You really are."

"Good to know."

"I mean it." Rex rapped on the door again.

"That's a keen insight, Rex, but I don't think your friend is here at the moment so maybe we should leave."

"Armando!" Rex bellowed, then opened the door and stepped inside.

"This a good idea?" Gil asked, also entering.

"Yeah, he's cool, though it does seem that he's out, as you so presciently stated."

They went around the small living room, kitchen, and bedroom, turning on lights. A demented-looking dog wagged past. It would last exactly three days in the wild, Gil thought. Rex checked behind doors and inside closets, as though his friend might be hiding out.

"That's it, we're going to have to come back," Rex finally admitted. But as they descended the outdoor staircase,

16

someone was coming up, a heap of unruly black hair jouncing with each step. The man's thin frame and taut brown skin masked his age; he might have been twenty-five or forty. "Let me do the talking," Rex said. Introductions went around, and they headed back down to the Gemini. Speaking in English with just enough Spanish to make believe he knew it well, Rex began. "What we need here, *güey*, is a complete makeover. New paint, VIN, plates, the whole shebang. Untraceable, *¿me entiendes?* You've done this kind of thing before, *¿verdad?*"

Armando replied with perfect unaccented English. "I can give you new plates but no VIN. That's pretty hard to pull off. I can only remove the current one, if that's what you want." He wandered into the garage in search of something.

Rex followed. "Sure, man, but we're looking for a fair price, too. This *payaso* is a little hard up at the moment. He does a lot of charity work down here with the local street girls. What do you call them? *Paraditas?* Flushes his paycheck down that sewer every weekend."

"Entirely untrue," Gil interrupted, "but I guess you know this guy by now."

"Gil, please. Let me finish. He's run into some issues on the home front with *la chota*. Something I know you can relate to. Stuck him with like a grand in parking tickets. Now they've set their scopes on his *carcachita* so he needs a rewrap. I loaned him a few hundred. Hopefully you have the heart to do it for that. Anyway, he's a good man, a good friend of the Mexican people, especially the *paraditas*."

Armando was too focused on his phone to respond to any of this. It was one of those early model smartphones Gil had seen but was far from able to afford. Armando worked it with one hand while sifting through drawers of grimy auto parts with the other. A bit of bartering went back and forth. They came to an agreement, and Armando told them to drop the car off the following morning.

*

Halfway between Tijuana and Rosarito – bordering an enormous paintball battlefield – a Vedantic holy man had established a prosperous ashram and spa. Rex would be spending the night there. He suggested Gil hang out a while and meet some of the characters who haunted the place, but that wasn't about to happen. There was too much chance of running into Petra Solis, who was doing her thesis on the ashram's founder, Swami Tonawanda, and his community of leisure-class American disciples. Despite what Rex thought, Petra and Gil had a bit of a history. It had begun one morning at Caf-Fiend, when they went from comparing field notes to her sharing the experience of coming out as vegan to her parents.

"That couldn't have been too bad," Gil said.

"No, it was a real mess. My father owns a restaurant. He took it personally. *My food's not good enough for you*, that kind of thing. My mother cried. Recriminations went back and forth. It was pretty unpleasant."

As she carried on, Gil became aware of the symmetry of her face and the adorable sweep of her half-hawk hairdo as it spilled out from her Lakers cap.

"At least they didn't cut you off," he said.

"It might have been easier if they had. On them, I mean."

Gil tried consoling her with some of his own family saga. Their conversations till then had been friendly, but essentially all business. They were suddenly now in different territory. Sensing an opening, he invited her to a Laker game.

"You mean for next year?"

"Wait, the season's already over?"

She made a face and gathered up her things.

"I only watch baseball," he called after her, but it was too late. Just as well. He could not have afforded parking at a Laker game, never mind the tickets.

And yet, barely a week later they wound up in bed. They continued winding up in bed. After a few months, things took a turn. He'd made a comment about the boldness of her eyebrows one evening, that they must keep her warm at night. It didn't land too well. A few hours later, they had a charged conversation on the Voynich Manuscript. Had it been an argument? At one point, she rolled onto her side to face the wall. He awoke the following morning with Dizzy Gillespie's *Shaw 'Nuff* bopping through his brain and promptly tapped out the rhythm on the slope of her hip. That afternoon, she tossed him off like an old Band-Aid. The entire arc of the relationship made no sense to Gil, and the thought of running into her at the ashram and having to reprise his role in that truncated drama filled him with dread.

"So, uh, how'd you get to know this Armando character?"

"He's a weekend regular at the holy hacienda. Dude emigrated from East LA. Keep right at the fork."

"You mean he got deported?"

"I'm not sure he'd say that."

"He's a tunnel runner?"

"You have a harsh way of putting things, don't you?" Rex snapped back the seat, rested his huaraches on the dash.

"A subterranean trader?"

Rex flashed his signature sneer, as though he were bothered by the smell of something.

"Just wondered how you met him is all."

"He's a part-time yoga teacher, okay? Studying to become a yoga teacher-trainer."

"A yoga teacher-trainer?"

"I don't know. He's being certified to train yoga teachers," Rex said.

"They figured out a way to regulate yoga, huh?"

It got dark and started to rain. Gil dropped off Rex at the ashram and headed to Zona Norte, the Tijuana red-light district. There was a dirt-cheap hotel behind La Coahuila, the main

19

streetwalker alley. He parked in the street and checked in. The rain faded to mist.

Friday night, prime time. The scene was already raging. Pen and notebook in hand, he went up and down the sidewalk as he had so many times before. Costumed mariachis blasted brass on a corner, drawing a small crowd. Frat boys and old men passed each other on the sidewalk, stepping aside from barkers hawking two-for-one drinks. The colored lights of dance clubs shone off the damp sidewalk. Music spilled out into the streets. Working girls in short skirts and plastic heels lined each side of the Coahuila, chatting away the idle hours. Outliers sheltered in doorways looking pleasantly bored. Men approached. Deals were struck. In pairs they strode off to any number of nearby hotels.

These were the avenues of Gil's long-stalled ethnographic fieldwork. He had made countless attempts to connect with the sex workers over the years, to get his research up and running. There had been lengthy gaps in his efforts, to be sure, and a singular promising lead, but nothing substantial. On this night, though, all that was about to change because on this night he walked up to a working girl and posed a question in Spanish that he had never before had both the desperation and the promise of steady income to ask.

"How much for twenty minutes?"

"*Trescientos pesos.*"

He followed her up the narrow staircase to the room. As soon as he handed over the money, she disrobed. He went through his prepared questions, scribbling the responses in his notebook.

She asked if he wanted to do it. "*¿No me quieres coger?*"

He shook his head. He did not touch her until the end, and then only to receive the complimentary kiss on the cheek before leaving. As he sat on the edge of the bed completing his notes, a hard knock came on the door. His time was up.

20

4

Gil tossed off the gritty bed sheet and crossed the cement floor to the bathroom. The shower's ramshackle plumbing crowed the day. He dressed and returned to Armando's body shop to drop off the Gemini, then took a cab back to Zona Norte to continue his research: three more girls before noon. The first was too reserved in her speech, the second downright hostile, but the third one had something special.

Back in his undergraduate days, at the end of each spring semester, he would take a forty-hour bus ride from Tijuana to Mexico City. It was a way to decompress from the routine strains of college life. Every summer he imagined he would find a girl down there, one he could safely leave after a few weeks but never quite made enough effort. One time, while bumming around the many newsstands near the central park, he picked up a Mexican edition of *Playboy*. The cover model had a remarkable face. Its bold planes and contours invoked the hard-edged look of a young Sophia Loren. The publishers had clearly recognized its singularity and not crowded it with the usual textual clutter. Gil bought the magazine and took it back to his room. There he skimmed over the contrived bio: *Born and raised in Coatzacoalcos, a city on the southern-most point of the Gulf of Mexico, she preferred _____ foreplay,_____ men,_____ attentions....* Wrapped in tattered rags that exposed a bum cheek here, a breast there, she posed the part of a beach-bound castaway. He'd spent the rest of the month looking at those photos, committing her face to long-term memory. The resemblance to this third girl was so striking that he was compelled to ask if she was from Coatzacoalcos.

"You know Coatza?" she replied in English.

"I know a lot about Veracruz. Where'd you learn English?"

"Here and there."

"My father and I lived in Tuxtla Gutierrez for three years when I was younger," he said in Spanish. "He was a lawyer for an energy company."

"That must have been interesting." She turned her eyes away, signaling the free chit chat was about to end.

He asked if they could continue speaking upstairs.

Without another word, she took his hand and led him through a nearby hotel entrance. He followed her long bronze legs up the stairway. Once inside the room she disrobed and got up on the bed, propped herself up against a pillow. She had a tattoo of a hummingbird on one breast that looked as though it were gleaning nectar from the nipple. He handed her the folded pesos, and she tossed them to the nightstand.

"What's your name?"

"Ava."

"Can I ask a few more questions?"

"That's one."

He took out his notebook. "How many more do I have?"

"Till your time runs out, I guess. What do you want to know?"

"How did you get into this line of work?" One of his standard questions. Her answer would guide the rest of his inquiries.

"With my uncle."

"Tell me about that."

"I was eighteen. I didn't like the arrangement so I left for the big city a year later. I got in with a high-end brothel."

"So, you were making money?"

"Of course." She reached out, began stroking his knee. "Why all the questions?"

"I'm an ethnographer studying the profession." He removed her hand from his knee.

"You can study prostitutes?"

"You can study people."

She cocked an eyebrow.

"To understand them better," he said.

"Sounds like a hustle."

"Tell me more about the brothel."

She hesitated a moment, examined the ends of her hair. "Well, I became the preferred girl of some businessmen down there, a few of the local politicians. They paid me well, gave me gifts. They were all in love with me, I think."

"Keep going."

"The man who ran the place became like a father to me. Ricardo was his name. He sent me to school during the day. I only worked two clients in the evening, always booked in advance." She affected a glamorous pose. "I moved out of there when I turned twenty. Tough decision, but it had to happen. The other girls and I didn't get along. I was beginning to feel trapped, unsafe. Since I had some money, I decided to break away."

"How much money?"

"Enough to have a house built in Xalapa."

"That's quite a bit. Why are you still in the business?"

"Planning to get out."

"Do you have any friends here? People who help each other, support each other?"

"Don't you want to do it?" She reached out to him again.

"I need to remain objective." He lowered his eyes to the notebook.

She repeated the question, this time leaning over to the edge of the bed where he sat. She took his hand, removed the pen. "Don't you like hummingbirds?" She led his hand to her breast.

"I'm really not here for that," he said, but the words clattered foolishly off the walls. "I think I should go now."

"Did you like my story?"

"It was interesting and will be useful. Thank you."

"I made it up."

"Ah." He closed the notebook, clipped the pen into the spiral.

"I'm from El Paso, *guapo*. I crossed over ten years ago." She reached out to him again, tousled his hair. In the silence that followed, she got off the bed and slipped back into her panties and bra, the hummingbird returned to its cage. He sat there, notebook in hand, watching her move about the room. She stepped into the mini-skirt, fixed the blouse, studied her face in the mirror. When she leaned forward to receive the complimentary kiss on the cheek, he turned away. Fanning her slender fingers at him, she backed out the door.

It was ninety-eight degrees outside. Slogging down the sidewalk, he could feel the heat rise off the cement. A working girl grabbed his elbow. He jerked it away. Back in his hotel room, he closed the curtains, lay down on the bed, and followed the spin of the ceiling fan as the sweat ran off him to the sheet. He thought back on the morning's desperate transactions. They couldn't possibly continue. There was no way he could afford to keep paying the sex workers for their time. On the other hand, there seemed no way around it. He wasn't about to give up eight years of graduate study to be locked up in a juvenile detention center. Teaching there wasn't the worst job in the world. It wasn't dentistry or scraping barnacles off a battleship. In theory, it was good clean honorable work. But he knew the little hoodlums would get to him eventually. He returned to the dull comfort of his lethargy, falling asleep to the rotation of the ceiling fan and his memory of Ava's face.

An hour later he was awakened by the buzzing of his phone. Another text message from Rex: *What's going on with the car?* His way of reminding Gil he needed a ride back to LA. The interrupted sleep dragged him into more depraved thinking. He should have studied tibia variation in early hominins like his friend Jan Galkin. Very little ethical controversy in that field. Jan would soon be an expert in Lower Paleolithic tibias, maybe the pre-eminent expert west of the Mississippi. When the Sunday morning news programs had a breaking story on tibias, they would trot out Jan. He steered his thoughts back to his present quandary. Too much had happened the last couple days, that was all. Much of it was positive if he could see it that way. It was a matter of reorienting himself to the new methodology. Maybe Rex was right, that he *should* be sleeping with the sex workers. Participant observation. Could he ever get anything true from them – anything *real* – till he'd crossed that line?

He flinched. Had that thought really entered his head? He seized the bed's lone pillow, tried ripping it in half. With a low-pitched howl, he launched it across the room. What would Geertz do? Geertz would not sleep with the sex workers, that much was certain. But would he pay the girls for their time? Gil got stuck on that one and took another shower.

There was a coffee shop on Constitución, one of the few places in Tijuana you could get a decent cup. A tough-looking woman in a faded denim miniskirt slouched out front with her heel against the wall. She was reading a paperback. All the sex work in the city was supposed to take place in Zona Norte, it being illegal everywhere else. Yet here she was, brazenly working it.

25

He asked if he could buy her a cup. She didn't answer. He went inside, got coffee, and sat down at a table in the entry alcove. An endless stream of people walked past in both directions. He began sketching them in his notebook, an amusement held over from his youth. The woman working the street asked him in Spanish what he was doing. He started to explain, but he could see she didn't really want to know. She sat down at his table and pulled out a cigarette.

"All right, buy me a cup of coffee."

He got up from the table, looking back to make sure she didn't walk off with his laptop. She lit the cigarette and tilted her head back, stared into the sky. She didn't seem too interested in stealing anything at the moment. When he returned with the coffee, she asked where the cream and sugar were. He went back to get some, after which she busied herself with the condiments like a chemist in a lab. When she finished getting the coffee just right, she waved the paperback at him.

"This book sucks."

He reached for it to check the title. "Never heard of it."

"Yeah, I'm reading it for school, otherwise I'd burn it." She leaned forward, as though challenging him to counter. He said nothing, and she retreated into the back of her chair. Still eyeing him, she took a drag off her cigarette.

"The Autonomous University?" he asked.

She shook her head, blew away some smoke. "San Diego State."

"Working the streets to pay for college. Very admirable."

She gave the book a little spin on the table. "You know what it's about?"

"I told you I've never heard of it."

"After ten years of marriage, a woman discovers a clitoris between her legs." She took a sip of coffee. "I'm paraphrasing."

He smiled back across the table. "I'm not sure I follow."

26

She cleared her throat. "Well, I figured that out when I was eleven and it didn't take me three hundred pages."

He looked past her, thinking of what next to say. "Maybe the author was trying to expose the sexual rigidness of the times."

"That's the best you can do?"

"I don't know. When was it written?"

"A hundred years ago. And humans have been around – what? – a hundred thousand? What a pioneer." She took another drag off her cigarette.

"It's a good question, though current studies indicate humans have been around quite a bit longer than that."

She leaned back and gave him a hard look. "You're not that bright, are you?"

"I sometimes wonder."

"Is this one of those times?"

Be patient, he told himself. Keep nodding, keep smiling. "What course are you reading it for? Am I doing any better?"

"It's called American literature," she said, in a tone that managed to make it insulting.

"I teach that course at a juvenile detention center. It could be the character is in conflict with the society," he said, pleased with himself. He'd picked that up from a guide to literary terms he found on Frinkle's desk. "If you keep reading, maybe she'll change her views. You know, character development? Or she could spontaneously combust. That's called deus ex machina."

She took another sip of coffee. "Yeah, I don't think you're pronouncing it right, but okay. I'm surprised you've never heard of this book, being a teacher of American literature."

"Tell you the truth, I haven't read much literature. I studied science in college. It's all right. I'm only a substitute teacher anyway so what I don't know doesn't matter to anyone,

27

especially the kids at this school. How are you managing to go to San Diego State and are you Mexican?"

"Oh my, what a rude set of questions."

"I didn't mean it that way. If I'd asked if you were American, would that have been rude?"

She studied his face a moment. "Re-think both questions and re-phrase them if you're still interested in the answers."

"Are you American or Mexican or some other can?"

"Some other *can*? I was born in San Diego, which used to be Mexico, but my parents are from El Salvador, and I live in Tijuana. You figure it out."

"You're American."

"Yeah, I don't think we're having the same conversation," she said. He waited for her to explain but she just snapped her head aside and blew away some more smoke.

"So, you cross the border every time you go to school?"

She hesitated, as though deciding whether the question was worthy of her. "Twice a week. What are you doing here? You come for the coffee?"

"Trying to get a doctorate in sex work."

She shook her head.

"It's called ethnography. Sex work is my specialized field. I drifted into it several years ago. Now I'm stuck."

"The streets can be like that."

"What's your major?"

"Nursing."

"So why do you take this American Lit course?"

She got up from the table, tipped back the last swallow of coffee. "It's a general ed requirement to keep the English instructors employed. Thanks for the caffeine." She went back out to the street.

*

28

He had asked Armando to paint the Gemini a nice safe tan, yet there it was out front of the body shop showy as a stripper's toenails, sparkling emerald green.

"I didn't have the color you wanted," Armando said. "At least, not enough to finish the job. This was left over from a pair of dune buggies I did last weekend. If I'd got anything else, it would have cost you a lot more. I kind of like how it turned out."

Gil walked around the car. He noticed the odd gnat fossilized into the enameled surface. "I didn't think there were many insects in the desert, but you've proven me wrong. And how'd this get here?" He pointed to what looked like a single glittering pubic hair stuck to the hood.

Armando didn't answer, having gotten beneath a raised engine block.

"Here's fifteen hundred pesos," Gil said, holding the folded bills over Armando's head. "That's all the Mexican currency I have. If it's not enough, you can keep the car, the gnats, and the pubic hair."

"I take dollars, too."

"That's all right." Gil opened his fingers and the bills fluttered to the ground. He got into the car and with a defiant outburst of gravel reversed it down the dirt drive.

In the light of midday, the ashram looked like a poor man's San Simeon, a line of architecturally incoherent structures perched on the edge of a bluff overlooking the ocean. A god of good taste would have sent the entire complex crashing onto the rocks in the last big earthquake. Gil parked and called Rex. No answer. He went up the drive toward the visitor center. Some people dressed in ankle-length sheets were playing volleyball out front. It looked like a fun way to handicap the game. Off to the side, a man reclined in a lawn chair, eyes closed. Gil asked where he might find Petra Solis. The man opened one eye, closed it again.

29

"Sorry, didn't mean to disturb you."

"Not at all," the man said. The eyes remain closed. "The journalist, right?"

"She's an anthropology student doing some fieldwork down here. She should be with some other character, a tall riffraffish-looking fellow."

The man held up his hand. "Hang on, I'm getting a signal." Gil took a step back. The man shook his head, opened his eyes. "Nope, false alarm."

"Thanks anyway." Gil walked off, trying on some happy faces to make should he happen to cross Petra's path. He stepped into the visitor center. There was Rex, operating an ATM next to the gift shop. "I have the car. You ready?"

"I have my next idea if that's what you mean. ATM machines for rich folks. Inside their homes, get it?"

"That's the solution, huh?"

"Think about it." Rex gestured toward the machine with both hands as though presenting some new marvel. "They don't have to go to the bank to get cash. It's like a house safe but more convenient and with a built-in record of transactions. One less motion in the course of the day."

"Okay, I'm leaving now. If you need a ride, let's go."

"You didn't get my last text? I'm going with Petra."

"No, I did not."

"It's this Mexican cell service." They went outside. "You know, everyone around this place talks about mindfulness all the time, but detachment is coming on and it's going to be big. Imagine setting up shop across the highway from this joker? Oh wow, is that your car? It looks like a Japanese beetle."

5

The university's college of social sciences divided grad students by level of achievement. Those in the all-but-dissertation cohort were referred to formally as ABDs, informally as Slugs. It was not clear if the anthropology department had more Slugs than history or sociology or psychology, but it sure seemed that way. They were always loafing around the recesses of the social sciences building in their clunky glasses and flannel shirts. It became the department's business to move them along. To that end, a required zero-credit course called Anthro-999 was formed. It met every Monday night for four anguishing hours. Gil had been a student in that class for eleven straight semesters, nearly twice as long as most successful candidates. He was the king Slug, the alpha Slug, the archetypal Slug. The other grad students knew something was off about him, though exactly what had become a topic of shallow debate. One of the more extreme arguments held that he was no longer really a student, just a departmental outcast permitted to remain on campus as a sort of mascot of mismanaged time.

It was not uncommon to fall short of the doctorate. A good many had. Armed with their master's in archaeology or linguistics, they set off into the wilderness never to be heard from again. And, to be sure, Gil was not the first Slug to get snagged in the weeds of the thesis. Writer's block, pecuniary constraints, and any number of family issues held many promising scholars back. In this company, Gil was unique, for while he hadn't gotten kicked out, he also hadn't quit.

In Anthro-999, grad students sat around a boat-shaped conference table discussing at length their chosen fields of research. At the faculty meeting where the assignment of courses was drafted into a master schedule, this one was informally known as Slug-out. To get stuck teaching it was a

31

rite of passage for any incoming instructor, a kind of curse for adjunct professors, and a full-frontal kiss off to any emeritus hangers-on. The Slug-out instructor was expected to do little more than show up for class. Participation was optional. And so, each week Slugs took turns laying out the progress of their research.

Gil played the game with a straight face the first couple years. He had believed in it back then. Now, with his best balderdash behind him, he often had trouble just suiting up for class. He found himself staring off blankly when it came his time to speak. The advancement of knowledge? At this point it seemed like a cruel joke. While the others waxed prophetic, he couldn't quite believe he was still there.

During breaks Slugs gathered in the hallway outside the conference room. Lately Gil had been pulled into a few conversations. These were usually with Srinivas Chakrabarti, Wilson James, and a character named Ebby whose last name Gil didn't know or care enough about to ask. He only thought of them collectively anyway so when he ran into one without the others on campus, it took his mind a moment to recognize the individual in front of him. They were fine young men by university standards, but Gil was thirty-one and they were in their mid-twenties and, yes, there was a difference. Still agog at the rich promise of academic life, they embodied the kind of moxie that made Gil want to jump out a window. It was a sign of his own misdirection that he'd begun hanging around them in the first place, as though he could never quite muster the will to swat them away.

Like most Slugs, these three had shied away from Gil at first, driven back by his vaguely outsider status. Then they looked to be challenging one another to approach him, like jaunty Victorian gents tromping boldly into the bad part of town. They'd seemed to view Gil's failure as a product of his off-center defiance, as though in spite of himself he'd forged his

32

own path. He imagined this portrayal reflected in their faces any time he was forced to speak with them, and had to look away.

Still vibrating with nervous exhaustion from the weekend, he ran into them in the hallway during break the following Monday night, first class of the fall semester.

"I need something to get me through the second half," Ebby said. "Chew on this: We assign one another an awkward term or phrase, something that would never be uttered in an anthro class, like *Marilyn Monroe*, for example, or *rear-window defogger*. As we go around the room, we have to somehow weave the assigned term or phrase into our little share-outs."

"You haven't been laid in a while, have you?" Wilson asked.

"No, listen," Ebby persisted. "This could work. I'll give one to Srini, Srini gives one to Wilson, and so on. The idea is to incorporate the assigned phrase so seamlessly into your presentation that nobody recognizes you're full of shit."

"You think nobody recognizes you're full of shit?" Srinivas asked.

"I'll pass," Gil said and returned to the seminar room. He was there too early, though. The only other occupant was Candace Beswick, who sat down next to him.

"How are the whores treating you, Gil?" She picked a piece of lint off the front of his shirt.

"Sex workers, Candace. They're called sex workers."

"Oh, don't give me that. I'm a woman, I know what they are."

"I just thought you'd like to know what they're called."

"You're cute." She flipped her coiled red hair, leaned a little awkwardly into his space.

"Imagine if I said that to you. You'd probably report me to the administration."

"Oh, I don't mean you're attractive. I mean you're cute. You know, you're a character."

"Ah, I suppose that makes it all right."

33

She laughed as a bunch of other Slugs came through the door. The little conversations they brought with them decreased in volume as the instructor collapsed into his seat at the head of the table. To his left sat Petra Solis. Gil hadn't seen her since the breakup. The half-hawk still perfectly covered one side of her forehead. Wasn't it de rigueur for a woman to change her hairstyle after a breakup? How little she must have thought of him. And Rex? It seemed Rex couldn't make it tonight.

Gil slunk down in his seat. Only ninety minutes to go. A Slug mentioned coming upon a "serendipitous twist" in his research. Gil tuned out the content and focused on the movement of the young man's mouth. The lips seemed asynchronous with the speech, as in a bad movie. It was fascinating to observe. When the time came for Gil to share, it felt odd to say anything after sitting passively for over two hours. And it had been so long since he'd had anything worthwhile to contribute. He sat up straight, took in that first breath.

"I think I've made a bit of a breakthrough. I'm really getting the kind of answers I've been chasing so long. Maybe my subjects have finally warmed up to me. Let it be said that while familiarity may breed contempt, contempt begets its own gains." He didn't know where those words came from or if they meant anything.

A smattering of lifeless chuckles. Candace decided to strike.

"Getting back to this avenue of research you've been channeling from Tijuana, Gil, have you had opportunity yet to probe the economic effects of prostitution on the city? How the local area has been affected by the services these women provide?"

Candace wasn't the first to challenge him. He pressed play on his standard response. "You know, I really bristle at the word prostitution." He paused a moment, allowing its tawdry connotations to stick in everyone's mind. "These women are

34

agents of their own self-empowerment, as I see it. They are empowering, as well, the lives of their families and communities." As he listened to the words spill from his mouth like so much water down a toilet, it took real effort to keep from laughing outright, particularly with Wilson James bugging his eyes from across the table.

"Since you didn't really answer my question, allow me to rephrase it," Candace said. "To what degree is the local economy dependent on this kind of income and how do the prostitutes benefit directly from that? Was that clearer?"

As she spoke, he undressed her with his eyes and carried her into the shower. The steaming water straightened the red ringlets of her hair. He turned her around to lather the freckled crests of her shoulder blades, leaned himself in....

"Mr. Crowell? I asked you a question."

"Yes, Candace. I was just figuring out a polite way to move on from it. I'm less interested in the macroeconomic impact than in the psyche of a community – and hopefully a related network of communities – within the urban sex trade. To that end, it might interest you to know that I once arrived at some essential concepts of purpose and even made inroads into the exchanges of reciprocity among a group of young women. Unfortunately, I lost that connection years ago, but the one I've most recently made holds the same familiar promise."

Empty academic language. It took real effort to keep from gagging on it.

"That's a shame, given the time you've spent down there. What's it been, five years?"

"Eight, Candace." He looked around the room for any other signs of dissent.

"Good answer," Srinivas Chakrabarti said, golf-clapping.

"I'm focusing right now on their individual lives," Gil continued. "These girls – well, these women –"

35

"Ah," Ebby said, rapping his knuckles on the table top. "They are women."

The instructor opened his eyes and peered through the outstretched fingers of the hand holding up his face. He quickly scanned the room, as though jolted from a nap.

"These women are turning tricks, in many cases, just to feed and clothe themselves," Gil said. "It's survival sex. Others are sending money back to families in rural parts of the country. No, I'm not so much concerned with how this affects the downtown economy, Candace. My interest is in the very personal lives formed and deformed by poverty. I'm happy to report that I'm really accessing now a number of narratives to sustain my continued research. It's been tough going these past few years, as most of you know, but gaining their trust has been worth it. I should have something completed by June."

A number of students perked up at this forecast, glancing at one another as though to be sure they'd heard him right.

"Wonderful," Candace said. She teethed the tip of her pen. "I can hardly wait to hear your long-awaited findings, Gil. I'm sure I'm not alone."

6

A man on the other side of middle age came through a door in the wall. His unkempt hair and mismatched clothing advanced the notion that he was living without a woman in his life. He looked like an old boxer; not a pugilist, but a member of the blunt-faced dog breed.

"Frinkle still out?"

"That's right." Gil walked over. "He won't be back."
The man looked Gil up and down as though assessing his threat level, the way dogs do when facing off. "Gilmore Crowell. Just filling in for now." The man kept looking at him, not moving, not saying anything. Gil spoke again just to break the awkwardness. "I, uh…"

"Harlan Wretchler, social studies," the man finally said. "Why you want to teach in a jailhouse?"

"Like I said, I'm not here long-term. Just needed a job." Wretchler took a step forward, looked around. "Ever caught yourself staring down a bottle of bourbon, wondering what hell must be like? This place, that's your answer. Become a guard. They make a lot more money, plus you get to carry a gun."

Gil scratched his beard. "I'm in grad school right now, finishing up a PhD. I probably don't need a gun."

"Is that right? And what have you done with Frinkle? Chopped him up into little pieces and washed him down the drain?"

"My understanding is –"

"Yeah, I heard the story. One of these monsters knocked the shit out of him, now he's suing. Good for him."

Another man came in through the hallway door. Mid-forties, bald, bespectacled. He had the ruddy complexion and puffed-out clothing of a guy who spends a lot of time at the gym. He scanned the classroom as though looking for something he might have left on the ceiling. Gil went over and extended his hand. The man only nodded, returned to the hallway.

"I take it that was your first encounter with Scott Bertram," Wretchler said.

"Seems like an important person."

"Oh, he thinks he's important, all right. He's the assistant principal but he likes to imagine he's the principal."

"I see."

37

Wretchler inhaled, seeming to decide if he wanted to say more. "I would characterize Bertram as a man in the grip of a chronic complex dissociative disorder."

"Excuse me?"

"The clinical term for asshole." He leaned against the edge of the open door like a bear scratching his back on a tree. "See, Bertram spends his time memorizing district bulletins, office memos, the bargaining agreement, all so he can set traps for people like you and me. He thinks we're the delinquents, that we're the ones who are locked up. That's how he stays on top. Behind closed doors, he's the kind of guy who gets off on chimpanzees dressed up in little girls' clothing."

Gil nodded.

"Chronic complex dissociative disorder," Wretchler repeated. "Look it up next time you're in the library."

As soon as school let out, Gil drove the made-over Gemini down to the police station to fill out the necessary forms reporting its theft. The atmosphere of the place gave him the sense the whole thing was only procedural. Nothing would ever come of it. The attending officer twice forgot he was even standing there.

"A stolen ve-a-hi-cle?" she asked. "Is that what you said it was, a stolen ve-a-hi-cle?"

"Sorry to keep pestering you," Gil said. "I just want to know what the next steps are in the investigation?"

"Investigation?" She twisted up her face.

"Whatever it is the department does with –"

"This isn't a department, honey. It's a station."

"Okay, the station or whatever –"

"There won't be any investigation, not on something like this. If we're lucky, this paperwork here will find its way into that basket over there."

"What I mean is, will an officer be conducting a search of the car anytime soon?"

38

"You mean a detective?"

"Whichever policeman or policewoman follows up on this sort of police thing."

"No, no, no. You're totally confused, honey." She leaned forward, squashing her huge chest into the counter between them. Her face opened up and she spoke her sentences slowly, as though clarifying for a child some elementary fact. "Whoever stole it – if they haven't already taken it across the border to scrap – will abandon it downtown as soon as they find a better car. That's usually how it works with a model this old and worthless. Cross your fingers they don't wreck it and maybe you'll get it back some day. Hey, anything's possible."

Exactly what Gil hoped to hear. Nobody knew what was going on and nobody ever would. He thanked her for everything, stopping short of kissing her hand, and left. Things were continuing to look up.

7

He brought his face to the narrow security window and looked out. The sky was a liquid blue, not a ghost of a cloud. In the distance stood the Hollywood sign, sharply in line with the silhouette of the hills. The Los Angeles air looked clear, as it often was following a late autumn rain or overnight windstorm. In such light, the world seemed to make sense, the reality of everything settled and defined. He could see it, believe in it, and feel good. He walked around the empty room, Frinkle's literary guide in hand. Soon the probationary students would trickle in. The residents in their gray numbered uniforms – "the jailed cases," as Wretchler referred to them – would be escorted down by security before the bell. Gil imagined himself as a character in a movie about troubled youths. He was their intrepid mentor, nurturing them to love knowledge and setting them straight on a path to higher ed. Collectively, they resented his rules and stern work ethic, but most took the time to privately thank him for caring so much.

His phone buzzed. Petra Solis. He stared at her name on the screen, delaying the connection, then finally took it.

"Just wondering how you're doing, Gil."

"I guess I'm all right. I haven't thought about it. Funny getting a call from you. What happened to *I'd rather we not see each other again?*"

"That was strongly worded. I apologize. It's one of the reasons I'm calling."

"Yeah, the whole thing was so unexpected, know what I mean?"

"Not to me. I'd been feeling for a while that there had been a drop in my emotional attraction to you. I couldn't see the point of dragging things out. I'm not one to play coy at friendship after something like this."

"Me neither," Gil said. "I was just kind of shocked at such a firmly worded rejection when I didn't think I'd done anything wrong." He tore a blank page from the back of the literary guide, crumpled it up.

"You didn't do anything wrong, Gil. Oh no. It's just that I never really thought of us as a couple. I mean, all we ever did was fool around, right?"

"Every relationship grows in its own way. Maybe we just needed time." He peered back out the window for some more of that sparkling clarity.

"Well, that's the thing. I didn't really consider it a relationship. I mean, I like you and I enjoyed our time together, but I didn't put any feeling into it beyond that."

"Thanks for the update."

"Sorry," she said. "I'm just trying to be honest."

40

"Yes, I can see that. And so why are you calling?" He launched the crumpled-up page to the wastebasket.

"I wanted to be sure you knew it was over, that's all, And I'm sorry I bungled the ending."

"Did I give you reason to think I was confused?"

"Maybe I just wanted some closure then," she said.

"Did you get it?"

"How do you mean?"

"I don't know, how does closure work with someone you didn't have feelings for?" He tore two more pages from the back of the literary guide – severely curtailing its index – and balled them up.

"I didn't say I had no feelings for you, Gil."

"No, that's exactly what you said." He launched each ball of paper to the trash. One in, one out.

"I said I had no feeling about the relationship."

"Ah, I didn't catch the distinction."

"Look, if you're going to be sarcastic with me –"

"Was I being sarcastic with you?" he asked. "I thought I was being sarcastic toward the relationship."

"Point made. So we agree this is over then, and we're both okay with it?"

"You mean if one of us isn't okay, then we have to keep talking?" He tore several more pages from the back of the literary guide, balled each one up, and tossed away.

"Gil, please. I'm trying my best."

"I'm sorry. I'm at work and not in the mood for this right now."

"Understood, and thanks. I'm glad you're doing okay."

While he picked up an errant ball of paper, a second wall door came into view. He hadn't noticed it before as it was obscured by a freestanding bulletin board charting the steps to a successful probation. He moved the board aside and opened the door. An older woman in an otherwise empty classroom made eye contact and came over. Leopard-spotted reading glasses

41

hung from a rosary-bead chain. A number of politically charged pins were tagged to the front of her vest. Like a poisonous toad, her outward colors seemed to have evolved over time to warn others she was approaching.

"How you doing there? I take it Frinkle's out again today."

"Yes, he's been out a few weeks."

"I've been out a few weeks myself. Twisted my chakra."

Gil nodded.

"That's a joke."

"Oh, okay."

"No, my chakras are all in line. Actually, I went in for a hysterectomy. Don't ever get one. Overpriced and overrated. And I still weigh the same. What the hell."

"I hope everything's all right."

"Another joke, sweetie. Try to keep up."

"Ah."

"No, my mother died on the twenty-third. Had to fly up to Portland and put the old bitch in the ground."

This time Gil did laugh.

"That one's not a joke. That really happened."

"Sorry to hear it."

"Don't be. I'm sure she's happier dead."

"Glad it all worked out," Gil said.

"Nothing's worked out. I've got Dan and Stan up there sorting through mountains of trash. The woman was a hoarder. They need to dig through it all to see if she left anything valuable. The whole place is upside down. The barn is a wreck, full of old tools and snakes and horse bones. Just yesterday Stan found an old Buick in there under a pile of chicken coops. You know what I told him? Check the trunk for ex-husbands."

"Nice meeting you. I've got to get back –"

"I didn't catch your name."

"Gilmore Crowell."

"Jeannie Lint, *Esquire*." She laughed. "Oh, I wasn't a bad lawyer, sweetie. I just hated working is all. Here, I get to have fun with the kids. That's what this job is all about. If you survive it, that is. That's a funny name you have there, isn't it?"

"I don't know."

"Gilmore Crowell, Gilmore Crowell." She repeatedly said it out loud, as though giving it a chance to sound better. "Well, I hope you enjoy working here, Gilmore Crowell. The kids are sweet. You know what they say. Dumb as a box of rocks, sweet as a bag of sugar."

"Is that what they say?"

"Listen, do you think something happened to Frinkle? I heard he jumped down a waterfall in the Angeles Forest. Suicide to look like an accident."

"No, he's quite alive. He fell down some stairs and retired."

"Oh sure, that's what the administration is saying. You know, CYA. This job can be awful stressful. When the truth comes out, remember what I said. Would you do that for me?"

Gil couldn't tell if this question required an answer.

"Well, the man had a PhD from Stanford," she said. "An expert on Chaucer or Milton or one of them, and they had him teaching in this zoo? Are you kidding me?"

"I'm sorry, I really have to get back. Nice meeting you."

"Oh, that's all right. Just remember what I told you. If you don't, I'll remember it for you."

43

8

The risks of driving the Isuzu Gemini back and forth across the border were too great to continue. Gil parked on the American side and took the long walk in. He passed the parking lots, duty-free shops, and a coiling ramp that led to a footbridge. Back at street level, a metal gate opened onto a wide and lengthy promenade shaded by a succession of cable-stretched canopies. Desert-camouflaged *federales* stood guard with machine guns hanging off their shoulders, motionless as sex workers posing in doorways. A mad jam of taxis was triple parked along a wide street. A few of the drivers accosted him, hawking rides to the airport and El Centro. He shifted past them to an endless plaza featuring restaurants, cantinas, pharmacies. Outnumbering the other establishments were souvenir shops, all peddling the same margarita glasses, horse blankets, piñatas, and other fare made expressly for American attics and yard sales.

At the end of the plaza was another footbridge crossing the Tijuana River. It was strewn with *palomas*, the dirt-poor Mexican mothers who squatted on the walkway. They sold gum for a peso. Others on the bridge dealt clothing, watches, wallets. Small children ran around, still too young to have any awareness of their social condition. They begged for money, dutifully racing back to their mothers with whatever they'd been handed. In a few years, they would breathe fire and juggle tennis balls at intersections for loose change. Under the bridge by the banks of the foul water, transients raised their arms, calling up to passing tourists for whatever might be tossed down. At night, a few would risk crossing over. Some would make it, and the border patrol would return the others to try again another night.

It was only after crossing this second footbridge that he fully sensed the compound character of the border town: the

44

stylized trappings of patterned brick walkways and gaudily colored shop fronts mixed among the poorer businesses operating out of rusty aluminum sheds. In the dying light, San Diego frat boys howled with drunkenness. A man on a bicycle rode the walkway, trying to decide if Gil could be hustled. He circled around to rattle off his street drug inventory, then rolled on.

The massive chrome arch at Revolución and First stood in the distance. The night took on its bright colors, changing the look of the city. Dance clubs and restaurants came alive with music as Gil drew nearer. The last of the day shift hung on, slouching and stretching, plastic heels in hand. They inspected their fingernails, bored or lost in thought.

He spotted a girl he hadn't seen before. She was a striking beauty, eighteen or nineteen with a round face, wavy black hair, and sad eyes. She had the ramrod straight posture of a newcomer, staring down at her feet as though unsure how they got there. He crossed over, engaged in the obligatory small talk, and followed her up to the hotel room. It was a good interview, filled with the dark shades of pathos he'd long hoped to hear, something he could fit neatly into his projected thesis.

He drove back to LA Saturday morning, having spent all his cash on five girls. He again wondered if he could afford to keep it up. The rest of the weekend he tapped away on the laptop, extracting whatever ethnographic data he could from those narratives. Checking what he wrote against his notes, he could see something begin to come together.

At the reform school the following Monday, Ms. Mott approached as he exited the men's staff restroom.

"Mr. Crowell, good news. The teaching position is yours if you want it. You'd have to enroll in a credential program, but Corrections and Rehabilitation will cover the cost. It meets on Thursday nights at Edison Middle School. In a couple years, you'll be done and on your way to a teaching

45

career. There's a small increase in pay but also an increase in duties. You'd have to submit lesson plans, do grades, check in with probation officers, and attend parent conferences like at any other school. Would you like to continue?"

"I don't think I have much choice."

"I had a feeling you'd say that. I'll start on the paperwork."

He attended the first of these classes the following Thursday. After a few weeks, daily visitors began entering his classroom. The principal, Dr. Lee, would come by, joined by an assistant or some outside expert. They were always escorted by armed security, lagging a few feet behind. He'd look up and they'd just be there, clipboards in hand, observing like primatologists in the field. Before leaving, they'd form a little huddle and whisper back and forth. One morning as he signed in, there was a memo tucked into his timecard. It directed him to meet with Scott Bertram during his conference period later that day.

It took Gil a moment to recall Bertram as the muscled, bullet-headed assistant principal who had mutely popped into and out of his classroom some weeks back. When Gil showed up in the office doorway, Bertram was on the phone. He waved him in.

"I'm on hold," he said, the cell phone pressed to his ear, "but we can get started." His head looked much tighter and pinker than when he'd come into Gil's classroom, as though the blood were being held back from bursting through the skin of his skull. Gil nodded, and Bertram addressed him. "You have any idea why I called you in today?" With his free hand, he stroked his stomach.

"Does it have to do with the assignment becoming permanent?"

"Good guess. How long have you been teaching English, Mr. Crowell?"

46

The question knocked Gil off guard. "Full time, you mean?"

Bertram flared his nostrils. "Let's try this a little different. Do you consider yourself an English teacher?"

Gil took a moment to consider the answer. "I am now."

"All right," Bertram said. He rested the cell phone on the lapel of his jacket. "Reason I ask is anytime someone steps into your classroom, all they see is students reading or you reading to them."

"Okay," Gil said, relieved his cover hadn't been blown.

"And now I'm questioning it. What's it all about?"

"The reading?"

"Yes, what's the purpose of it?" Bertram pulled at his shirt collar.

Gil took a stalling breath. "To improve their reading skills," he said, though it came off like a question.

"See, you're not even sure yourself, are you?" A victorious smirk crept up Bertram's face.

"I'm sure that's the point of reading, yes."

"And I understand the point of reading, as well, Mr. Crowell. I am myself a reader, as you can see." He gestured toward a three-foot high bookcase in the corner filled with educational texts, journals, massive data-filled binders. "I actually did your job before I found my true calling in administration. It is with an acquired appreciation of reading, Crowell – and the craft of teaching itself – that I question not why the students are reading, but upon what learning objective such reading is based." He held up a finger signaling his phone call was about to reconnect. It didn't. "What I'm saying," Bertram continued, "is that I don't see your students engaged in any kind of collaborative learning activities." He shot Gil a look. "Education is about collaborative learning, Crowell, is it not? The students have the right to explore their ideas with one another, not just yours and Tess of the d'Urbervilles'."

"Who?"

47

"Tess of the D'Urbervilles is a novel, Crowell. A novel taught in English classes like yours."

"I'm not teaching it."

"It's sound advice, either way."

"Okay," Gil said. He was starting to put this guy together. Just agree with him and move on.

Bertram nodded. "Don't thank me," he said, bringing the phone down off his ear to check the screen. "It's my job." He clarified further. "It is what I am paid to do, as they say. I'm going to tell you something else, Crowell," but he didn't say what. He just continued studying the phone screen.

"Yes?" Gil asked.

"I'm here to support you. And I'm going to be watching very closely to be sure you get that support." He handed him a business card. "Call any time. During work hours, I mean. Damn it!" He waved Gil off. "Just got disconnected. On hold twenty minutes and just got disconnected."

"Yeah, that's uh, … So, are we done here or...?"

"Yes, we are done, Mr. Crowell. For the moment, we are done."

Collaborative learning, differentiated instruction, equal access to the curriculum, multiple intelligences…. He had heard those terms batted around the credential class, but thought them only the jargon of the profession, not really expecting to apply the concepts in a reform school. As he turned to leave Bertram's office, he caught a glimpse of an illuminated picture frame on the wall, the kind that changes every few seconds. At that instant, it faded from a photo of Bertram, the wife, and the dog in front of a house to one of Bertram and the wife, without the dog, seated in a restaurant. The couple appeared radiant – radioactive, even – in both photos. He thought of telling Bertram what great images they were, but decided it might be taken the wrong way.

9

An earthquake drill brought everyone onto the yard. Gil stood
under the midday sun at the head of a line of students. His only
responsibility was to make sure none of them left, a task that
required no effort on his part with twice as many armed guards
as teachers spread across the warming asphalt expanse. His
mind wandered into the glory days before his academic career
had become a ruin. He thought back on the motherlode of
ethnographic data he'd struck five long years before, welcomed
by chance into a clan of Sinaloense women who'd taken up
residence in Tijuana. Xochitl, a girl he'd met on the Coahuila,
had opened up to him unexpectedly one June evening. He later
met her older, more beautiful sister, who had moved on from
the streets into a strip club. Eager young cousins were groomed
for work by an aunt and de facto matriarch of the two-bedroom
household. Friends from their hometown also worked on the
Coahuila, and half a block away an uncle headed a similar
household.

   Over the following summer weeks, they'd brought Gil
entirely into their milieu. One afternoon the uncle put an arm
around Gil and led him into the master bedroom. From a closet
shelf, he removed his collection of guns, including a Mauser
broom-handle pistol that – he boasted with utmost solemnity –
had once belonged to Porfirio Diaz. As he held the tarnished
piece out in front of him, tears welled up in his eyes. That same
afternoon, in a living room crowded with relatives and
neighbors, they drank beer and watched Germany beat Mexico
in the World Cup. Again, the old pimp wept. A few women

made pozole, and the aunt led the gathering in a simple prayer. Gil closed his eyes. It is the essential nature of the social scientist to identify patterns of human behavior and construct them into narratives. In that moment, he tried to make sense of his place in this extended family's adopted environment. He recalled thinking it was the luckiest break he would ever get.

The next month, a friend had been due to arrive from Guasave, fleeing an outbreak of femicide believed linked to the local cartel. She'd never made it. Three days later, a family member won the California State lottery. In a remarkable expression of communal spirit, she divided the winnings among everyone in the community and – like black magic – they all disappeared. For every day of the next month, Gil had called Xochitl and her sister, the only two from whom he had secured phone numbers. Neither of them ever picked up. One night, he lay in bed and dialed Xochitl's number at least twenty times. He fell asleep with the phone earpiece still attached to his ear.

Early the next morning from the high point of a footbridge over the Tijuana River, he removed from his backpack the copious notes he'd taken over the last several weeks. He leafed through kinship diagrams, exhaustive patterns of reciprocity, economic ties among the TJ inhabitants and their families back in Sinaloa, the syncretism of traditional Catholicism with *curanderos,* and a hundred other notes. He dropped the entire stack into the slowly flowing wastewater.

It was past noon when the signal ending the drill finally came over the PA speakers. They were on their way back to the classroom when a guard sidled up to him.

"I'll take your residents from here. Enjoy your lunch."

Without anything to eat, Gil wandered across the yard to a driveway that looped underground. It led to a small reserved parking lot and delivery dock, but no one was there. He couldn't keep himself from climbing onto the dock and heading into the dark recesses. He slid open what looked like a boxcar door to a hallway lit only by exit signs on the ceiling. This branched off into a complex of old unused cells, many of them now storing uniforms, linens, industrial cleaning supplies. He kept going until he saw another hallway, dark except for a rectangle of light surrounding a doorframe. He pushed the door slightly open, peered in.

"Can I help you?" a voice behind him asked.

Gil jumped. "Christ, where did you come from?"

"Bathroom around the bend," the man said. "You mind telling what you're doing down here? There's no afternoon deliveries."

"Oh, I'm not a delivery person," Gil said. "Just a substitute teacher. I was looking for something."

"All right, but no one's supposed to be down here. What can I help you with?"

"I don't need any help. I'll check with the administration later on. I was just looking around for some … teaching materials." He grinned feebly at the absurdity of this. "Sorry, I didn't catch your name. I'm Gilmore Crowell."

"LeTed Harris, IT. This is my office. Well, I have another up in the computer lab, but this is where I come to freelance, if you know what I mean." He straightened his spine, as though exalting in the few inches of height he bore over a perceived rival. "I was a student at this school, once upon a time. Still locked up when I graduated. How about that? I had the diploma but they wouldn't let me leave."

Gil noted the lingering bitterness in the man's voice and imagined the rest of the story: LeTed discovered after graduating college that all the good tech jobs dried up when the dot-com bubble burst. He compensated for this career disappointment by fixing teachers' workplace computers with as much hostility as the job would permit. The rest of the time he barked at students in the computer lab to put away their food and keep off the social media sites. There wasn't much anyone

51

could do about his logy spirit and underground side projects. They paid him so little he was cheaper to keep than to fire.

"Nice meeting you. What did you say your name was again?"

"LeTed Harris. And, uh, let's try not to run into each other again down here."

Gil stopped at the grocery store on his way home, intending to get some food for the rest of the workweek. For over a month now, he'd been eating bag lunches the Koenig House kitchen staff provided anyone who worked for a living. Tuna on rye, turkey on wheat, egg salad on white.... No choice in the matter; you took what they handed you. By lunchtime, the watery mayonnaise had turned it all to meat pudding suitable for a trash can. When he asked if they could separate the contents into a provided container – that he might assemble the sandwich himself at work – he was met with blank stares.

So here he was pushing a cart through the grocery aisles for the first time in over a year, taking this and that off the shelves. At one point, he left the cart unattended to admire a shapely behind arced over the deli meat case. The high hem of the woman's top exposed Chinese characters tattooed across the iliac crest. He sidled up to her, took a number from the deli ticket dispenser.

"What's the tattoo mean?"

"In English?" she asked.

"Yeah."

"It says keep your eyes off my butt."

"Ironic." He reached for a ball of cheese, checked the price, and returned it to its cold plastic nest.

"What?"

"When something is the opposite of what you'd expect, it's called irony." He waved it off.

"Yes, I know what irony is. What makes it ironic?"

52

"It's like those bumper stickers that say if you can read this, you're too close. Forget it. Look, I'm an artist. I'd like to draw you sometime if that's all right. Nothing formal, just some sketches I could work into a painting later. I could pay you if that makes any difference." He was losing interest in her by the word, but momentum carried him on.

"It's ironic you didn't notice my – what – discomfort." She smirked a little too proudly and craned her neck around the store as though looking for someone to report a crime to.

Without his number being called, he pushed on. He figured he had enough food in his cart anyway. A moment later, he was stuck in a checkout line with three carts behind him and two in front. A youngster squeezed past to take something off the candy display rack. The boy's unzipped jacket dragged across Gil's pantleg, depositing a line of what he imagined to be urine. It was then it occurred to him that he'd walked off with someone else's cart. He tried to get out of line, but was pretty well trapped by that point. It would have caused a great scene to back out of everyone's way, and then what if he ran into the person whose cart he'd taken? He hunched forward and sorted through the groceries, deciding it all more or less agreed with him. The cashier waved him forward. Gil placed everything onto the revolving belt.

"I'll help bag," he said. "I'm late for something." He snatched a paper sack from the hands of the bagger, who looked on with a tragic expression. "It's okay." Gil patted him on the shoulder. "Take five." He paid the cashier and scurried toward the exit, exhilarated by the thrill of each step. It was almost like shoplifting. An old woman without any sense of time or space cut in front of him. He sped up and turned sharply, just grazing her cart enough to knock it out of the way. Two activists collecting signatures outside the door asked if he'd sign a petition to defund prisons and return the tax revenue to public schools. Gil tossed off a maniacal laugh.

"You're part of the problem," one of them called out.

53

He rolled on to the site of the obscenely sparkling Gemini, where he tore into some asparagus stalks. Sifting through the bag for some kind of a dip, he settled on a container of algae-enriched hummus.

This is how some people eat, he thought, and dug in.

10

The reform school had a day off in October for Yom Kippur. It was strange to have the workweek divided that way. Tuesday felt like a Friday and Thursday like a Monday. A week with two Mondays, what could be worse? But on Wednesday morning Gil awoke from such a deep sleep that it felt like a part of him remained in the unconscious world. He was just comfortably lying there, unsure of whether to start the day at all, when the dumpster cat took its place on the sill. It glared at him heavily, drew an enormous tongue-twirling yawn, and looked away as though disgusted.

"The silent treatment, huh?" Gil muttered. "You got a lot of nerve."

The cat did an abrupt spin, waved its tail. Was it mooning him? Gil overcame the forces keeping him bed-bound and sprang to the window. The cat scurried out. Standing there, he noticed a Parking Violations vehicle double-parked alongside the brazenly repainted Gemini. He put on a pair of sandals and flopped down to the street. The vehicle had driven off. No ticket, but what did it mean? He went back up to his room and wrote out a check for five-hundred and seventy-seven dollars to cover the last tabulation of parking tickets and fines.

He placed the check in an envelope, wrote out the address. Seated at the warped particle board desk with the envelope in hand, he tried to picture himself placing it in the mailbox. He couldn't do it. Every dollar was needed to pay the working girls. He tore up the envelope and dropped the pieces into the trash. Later in the day, as he passed the car sparkling in the afternoon sun, he took a moment to wonder about its fate, then went inside the refectory for the penne and beef gravy supper.

His time was now so filled with classes, grading, and other pointless duties that while the days tended to drag, the weeks passed in a mindless blur. When Friday afternoon arrived, he hurried to finish up at the jailhouse. If he left right at three-fifteen, he could get out of LA before the heaviest rush hour and be at the border by six-thirty.

He parked, walked across, and checked into a room, then headed over to Constitución, where the action began. A girl he'd seen once before was working a corner. He hadn't recognized her at first. She'd changed hotels or done something to her hair. As he went by, she pulled at his shirt, turned on the charm. Would he like to get a room? A moment later they were headed up the stairs.

Through a barred window at the top of the staircase he paid the matron for the room. He and the girl went down a dark narrow corridor and through a doorway. He handed over the three hundred pesos for twenty minutes time. Taking the bills in hand she made the sign of the cross, kissed them, and placed the money into her clutch purse. She spent the next five minutes in the bathroom and came out texting. He wondered if they were on the clock yet. She disrobed down to her panties and bra – all the while working the cell phone – then got up on the bed.

He pointed to the phone. "*Ahorita es mi tiempo.*"

She took that as a signal to undress. He asked her in Spanish if they could talk instead.

55

"What do you want to talk about?" She clicked the TV remote to a porn stream.

"Not that." He took the remote and turned it off. "I'm trying to find out about life around here. What it's like for working girls, that kind of thing."

She spoke of growing up in Guadalajara. She'd fallen for some neighborhood boy, gotten pregnant. The boy disappeared and now she was sending money back home to her mother and sister who raised the little girl.

"So your bitterness toward men and sense of emotional abandonment brought you into this line of work, almost like you were striking back at the forces that caused you so much pain in the first place."

"No, I just needed the money."

Outside the open window, the sounds of the city night were at their peak: mariachis playing on the square, the call and response of drunken locals, car horns and police sirens, the music of dance clubs.

He asked how business was.

"I'm not established yet. Standing in a doorway only reaches so many people."

"Good point." He nodded at the far wall, abstracted.

"Some girls post photos on the Internet. I don't know if it does anything."

"Is that right? Maybe you need your own website. Or at least your own web page."

"Sounds expensive," she said.

He stared off into space. She tried making eye contact, then began pulling down her panties.

"Wait a second." He held up his hand.

"What is it?"

He didn't answer, transfixed by the idea unfolding in his mind. If he could do something to really help these women, they'd have a reason to speak to him. He wouldn't have to pry them for crumbs of information, paying for the privilege each time.

She got off the bed and came over, lowered herself to his gaze.

"What if it were free?" he asked.

She gave an off-the-shoulder glance at her reflection in the bureau mirror, arching her back and sticking out her little behind. "How would that work?"

"Never mind the details. Are you interested?"

"Sure." She plopped back on the bed, fully naked.

He stood up, stuffed his notebook into the backpack. "I'll see you next weekend."

"You don't want to do it?"

"Not today. I've got something to take care of."

"We still have ten minutes. How much time do you need?"

"I'm going to need all of it next time we meet. Can you hold it for me?"

"It doesn't work that way."

"You could make an exception. Listen, I'm going to feature you on a website capturing this whole scene, understand? You'll have a web page all to yourself. Photos, promotions, video clips, if you want. A link to your email. You can stare at it all day if you want. What do you think?"

She looked indifferent but lying naked on the bed with her knees pulled up to her nipples, it was a very sexy kind of indifference.

He leaned over, kissed her on the cheek, and charged out the door.

11

His phone buzzed on the passenger seat, which was unusual because most people knew not to call him on the weekends and the others knew not to call him at all. It was his dissertation advisor, Brinda Bagchi, her melodic Calcutta accent as unmistakable as the Isuzu's high-whining engine.

"Gil, I'm surprised to reach you. I figured you'd be in Tijuana till at least Saturday. I was about to leave a message. Do you even have cell service down there? I've never thought to ask."

"I didn't go this weekend, Brinda," he lied. "Had to take care of some personal business."

"The department is having a dinner party at my place. Did you get the invitation?"

"Uh, I think so."

"You didn't respond. Wendel Fripp and John Inmun are leaving for Peru Friday and Alicia Cosgrove had her dissertation approved by committee last week. She's been offered a position at Berkeley beginning in January. Only twenty-five and off teaching at Berkeley, can you imagine?"

"She looks older."

"You can tell her that at the party."

"To be fair, she graduated high school at sixteen so a PhD at twenty-five isn't all that remarkable. You could even say she's behind schedule." It was a revelation to be so insulted by another's success.

"Having a bad day, Gil?"

"Don't worry, I won't bring it up."

58

"Your time will come," she said, though it sounded like she was ending the conversation.

Good old Brinda Bagchi, always in his corner. He recalled the day he sprang his dissertation topic on her. Her big brown eyes seemed to float out of her head. "That's a wonderful idea, Gil! And there are so many avenues you can go down with this, to say nothing of dark alleys," she added, all but winking. "Identity is very happening right now. Postcolonial feminism. You could look into the rituals of sexual exchange as they manifest in the community, the initiations and social structures, arcane politics and semiotics. Oh, it's endless what you'll dig up!" That false prophecy remained etched on the inside of his skull.

At breakfast the next morning, all he could think about was kick-starting the website he'd envisioned in TJ, but the old men at the long wooden table weren't having it.

"How's the job, Gil?" Norm yelled across the clatter of nearby tables.

"Not as good as this coffee."

"That's what you get for studying anthropology," Robert said. "You brought this on yourself, you know."

Gil raised his eyes above the conversation, took in the eclectic look of the place. Part California mission, part Bavarian hunting lodge, the first floor imparted a homely, devotional aesthetic: dark wooden crossbeams, wrought iron sconces, terra cotta floors. Religious art and crucifixes adorned each room. He couldn't tell if it fit the character of the place. Any one of the residents might have stepped out of a Thomas Hart Benton painting, a woeful tale cast in the lines of each face: ex-cons, old vets, alkies and addicts in and out of recovery. Divorce, disease, and minimum wage had brought the others in. Last stop before Skid Row. The young grad student stood out among them, an obvious target of his elders' meddling counsel.

59

"And how's the new car, Gil?" Norm asked. "Running well?"

"Same car, Norm. New paint."

"I don't like it," Brian said. "Why the hell would you paint an old car like that? Looks like what you might paint a dune buggy."

Gil looked across at Javier, the silent old Spaniard. He was the only one who ever left him alone.

Robert went back to his favorite topic. "It's not too late to get into finance, Gil. You're still a young man. Relatively, I mean."

"This type of conversation is a pet peeve of mine," Gil said.

"You know what's my pet peeve?" Brian asked the table. "When actors smoke but they don't inhale. You can tell they don't inhale because no smoke comes out of their mouth. It's bad acting."

"You need a real profession, Gil," Robert said. "Unless you want to continue teaching. It used to be women's work, but the world's changing. I had a male nurse at the clinic the other day. He stuck his finger up my ass. It was all right."

"Like three deranged stepfathers," Gil said.

"Anthropology's not a profession," Robert said.

"Anything that pays is a profession," Norm said. "Group dynamics, human resources. There's a place for all that in the business world."

"You need an exit strategy," Brian added.

"I need to exit this dining hall," Gil said. He got up from the table and turned around.

"Excuse me!" It was Claudia, the manager and cook, bustling past. Her bright morning mood never lasted past noon. "Don't leave your tray here for me to clean up. I'm not your maid."

"Funny, that's exactly what I thought you were," he said. "I was under this impression that I pay to sleep and eat here and you get paid to work." Like a bad dream, he thought. Not a nightmare, just a badly plotted dream.

"I know my job and I don't need you to tell me my job and it's not my job to take up your dirty tray. If you don't take it up yourself, I'll have a talk with Alphonse."

He went back and took up his tray.

The next several hours he spent up in his room sifting through whatever he could find from the Internet on website design and construction. It took him that long to figure out he couldn't possibly do it alone.

The following Monday morning, he went up to the computer lab and stuck his head through the open door. LeTed was playing a video game, feet up. He applied a packet of hot sauce to a breakfast burrito.

"Hey." Gil leaned into the doorway. "I don't know if you remember me. I'm the guy who took over Frinkle's classes. We first met in your underground satellite location."

"Uh huh." LeTed took a loud pull off his beverage.

"I was wondering if you'd be interested in making a little extra money."

"What doing?"

"I need help with a website."

LeTed snickered. "You mean a blog?"

"A little more than that hopefully."

"Tell me about it."

"Ever heard of ethnography?"

"Does it have to do with your website?"

"I'm working on a PhD in cultural anthropology." He took a look around. "My focus is on Tijuana sex workers. Keep that under your hat. I'd rather it not get out."

"Do I look like I'm wearing a hat?" He was that kind of a guy.

"I need a website to keep track of the working girls I'm studying down there."

61

LeTed dropped the act and swiveled his chair around. "Interesting field. Any openings?" He tilted back, dropped the last burrito bite into his mouth.

"Sex work or ethnography?"

"Whatever it is you're trying to do."

"I just want to finish my dissertation so I can get out of this place and teach at a junior college somewhere."

"What are you willing to spend?"

"I wouldn't know where to start."

"Start at thirty."

"An hour?"

"Okay."

"How many hours would it take?" Gil asked.

"Give me two hundred bucks and I'll set it up this weekend."

"I'm kind of low on cash. Could I pay you with my next check?"

"I'll need at least a hundred to start," LeTed said.

"It's also going to need maintenance. I could pay you by the hour for that. Adding girls, updating profiles, video clips, that sort of thing. You follow me?"

"I've been on porn sites if that's what you mean."

Gil nodded, disciplined to not take offense. "Well, hopefully this will be something different."

12

He got roped into carpooling to Brinda Bagchi's with Srinivas Chakrabarti, Wilson James, and Ebby. They had a few drinks at a tavern off campus before heading up after dusk in Wilson's minivan. Her house was in the hills above Westwood at the terminus of a circular dead-end. A two-story Craftsman set back in a wood of pines, it was the kind of place that made Gil wonder how many people had been murdered in it. Two lines of cars were parked in the driveway. The rest filled both sides of the quiet street. Wilson pulled alongside the landscaped island of the dead end, then drove up over the curb and parked in the middle of it.

"This such a good idea?" Srinivas asked.

"At ease," Wilson said. "They don't give parking tickets up here. That branch of government only serves the poor."

A bit of playful trash talk passed among them, shots taken at each other's ethnicity.

"Excuse me, gentlemen," Gil said. "May I remind you where we're going? I've been in these settings a few times before and this kind of chatter is often frowned upon, even more often misunderstood."

Ebby unbuckled his seatbelt and mumbled something about academics.

"No," Gil said. "That's not it. Try channeling your inner adult is all I'm saying. And if you can't manage that, please stay as far away from me as possible."

They got out of the van and headed through the front door, where the sound of polite conversation spilled forth. People were stuck in their little huddles. It took a bit of elbowing just to get a drink. Gil watched Brinda Bagchi's two-year-old daughter somehow manage to flit through the vast grove of legs. She stopped to deliver an incomprehensible speech to a gathering of faculty, who looked down at her, unresponsive. She scanned their blank faces and darted off.

A chaotic assortment of snack foods and wines was laid out across the dining room table. It looked like Gil and the boys had missed out on dinner. In the kitchen, two combat-ready youths – one armed with a ceremonial broadsword, the other holding a four-foot-long wall stud – begged their mother for something while she stood her ground with an upraised scouring pad. Best to walk past without saying anything. Farther back, a Dave Brubeck recording played while halfway up a Queen Anne staircase, three young women – two sitting on the lap of the third – reclined between the outstretched legs of a young man. Their tipsy exuberance hinted at a promising foursome if they could all remain conscious. At the back wall, a sliding glass door opened onto a great yard that two hundred feet farther back fell off into a chaparral-covered canyon. Adolescents, many with glow sticks in hand, engaged in unrestrained horseplay and flirty chasing games. A few pitched empty wine bottles across the yard into a patio tree pot on the one end and a toddler's bathing pool on the other. Another game seemed to involve hurling great heavy sticks through the air with the more reckless participants first setting them on fire.

At the far end of the yard, Rex and a hippie chick sat on the remains of a stone fireplace from some long-ago demolished house. While they sang, an old hobo on the ground accompanied them on harmonica. Petra Solis and a few other young women approached the scene. Gil hadn't spoken with Petra face-to-face since the breakup. He didn't want to now but was already headed for Rex's group and knew he couldn't avoid her forever. He heard Srinivas, Wilson, and Ebby coming up from behind.

"This here's Sunshine," Rex said, indicating the hobo. "He's a regular down at the Row, pulling it together now. And this fair maiden is Magnolia, but we call her Maggie 'cause Magnolia has too many syllables."

"I should clarify that I'm not a card-carrying member of any homeless society, Skid Row or other," Sunshine said, tapping the harmonica against his threadbare denim thigh. "But, yes, I have done my time."

"That's an interesting name," Ebby said. "It mean anything?"

"There's just so much goddamn negativity in the world that I wanted to set myself against it somehow. I've been Sunshine ever since." He spoke in a voice as fragile as the inch-long ash clinging to his cigarette.

People started talking about their lines of research, and Gil sensed the old anxiety coming on. In the company of those specializing in morphology, human variation, and forensic linguistics, he couldn't escape the notion that his streetwalkers didn't quite measure up. The others seemed so knowledgeable in their fields. He felt more at ease around Rex and his ragamuffins. To be sure, there was plenty to despise about Rex, but he didn't make Gil feel inferior. That was something for which he was secretly grateful. It wasn't so important to especially like one's friends as to be comfortable around them.

Someone brought up the subject of academic taboos.

"That term requires some clarification," Rex said.

"Worn out lines of inquiry that aren't supported by evidence. In this case, superior hominin cranial capacity as a natural selector for dominance. I mean, it's probably true, but you got to be careful with that shit."

"Ah," Gil said. "The ones that survived were the cleverest at killing. Yeah, I saw that film."

"Which one?" Wilson asked. "It's a genre."

"Social science fiction," Petra said. "The ritual banter of young men stuck in the minds of teenage boys. It doesn't pertain to my gender."

"But it includes you, my dear," Ebby said. "We ran the tests and you're one of us. We're no happier about it than you are."

65

"Woman's nature is essentially creative," Petra said. "The predisposition for violence is a Y-chromosome thing."

"Somebody's been spending too much time with the mystics down in Rosarito," Ebby said. "How did the bitch gene survive? That's what I want to know."

"Excuse me?" Petra said.

"That's an easy one," Rex said. "They're good in bed."

"And so they produce more offspring, thus perpetuating the gene," Wilson added. "Your thesis makes perfect sense, sir."

"What about the stupid prick gene?" Petra asked, looking squarely at Ebby. "How has that managed to thrive?"

"It's all part of that killer instinct," Gil said, finally making eye contact. "Women are attracted to jerks, whether they want to admit it or not. Loud jocks, paramilitary types, dog-eat-dog businessmen." It felt good saying it to her face. He had often wondered if she thought him beneath her and also what kind of guy she was actually looking for. He remembered once thinking she was unattainable, but what did that even mean? Only that he couldn't date her. That turned out to be only half-true. Still, it amused him to imagine her sense of superiority. In a way, it attracted him to her even more.

In the darkness, Rex's face began to blur beneath the shadow of his long gray-blonde hair and fedora. With his Marfan-like limbs he looked more than ever the scarecrow.

"I used to manage a surf-punk club on Venice Beach back in the Eighties," Rex said. "It was underground, very underground. Hardly anybody knew it was there. I think that's why we went out of business. Anyway, I was all mixed up in the scene for better or worse. I'd check out these local bands on the weekend. The look of these guys on stage… I could never figure it out. After the show, though, always a line of girls waiting around."

"What in god's name are you talking about?" Srinivas asked.

Rex outstretched his arms and mimed falling backward off his crumbling perch.

Gil glanced over at Petra. He thought back on their lovemaking routine: the mood, the sounds, the shape her petite body would take on, the way her half-hawk hairdo rested on the pillow.

"I got to get out of here," Sunshine said. "Work tomorrow."

"Where you staying?" Ebby asked.

"Doing some work at Brighton so, yeah, hanging around there."

"What's Brighton?" Gil asked.

"The private school as you're coming up the hill," Rex said. "Lot of professors' kids go there."

"Does that explain all these little terrorists?" Wilson asked.

"They're not so bad," Sunshine said. "Rex set me up with the job." He gave him a grateful tap on the knee.

Gil recognized the old ethical conflict of meddling with case studies, then thought of the website. Ego permitted all sorts of exceptions.

"I should tell you all how I became so fortunate to work with the homeless," Rex announced.

"By selling them drugs?" Gil asked.

"I think I'm going inside to talk about killer brains," Wilson said. Srinivas and Ebby followed.

"Tell the story," Maggie said to Rex.

"Never mind," Rex said. "I can tell when I'm not wanted. Gil can tell his story, the one that really brought us together."

"My story?"

"About your depraved childhood," Rex said.

"Oh, there isn't time for that," Gil said. Those remaining protested. "All right, I'll tell you just one episode. I sort of grew up on Skid Row," Gil began. He scanned the remaining faces. "I'd gotten interested in street people in the fourth grade. See, both my parents were lawyers and spent a lot of time working. I was about seven when my mom was diagnosed with an extremely rare mutation, almost always fatal. Erdheim-Chester disease. I was addicted to reading so I learned all about it. A couple years later she was gone. As difficult as that was, I felt relieved. For her, but also for me and my father. It was tough watching her die. Soon after, I imagined he was trying to get rid of me, as well. Make a clean break with the past and start over, know what I mean?"

"Not at all," one of the young women said. "That's disturbing."

"Of course it is," Gil said, "but we manage to adjust to our environments. I mean, what choice is there, right? Anyway, the elementary school I went to was walking distance from our home in Miracle Mile, but my father insisted on driving me downtown with him on his way to work every day. He'd drop me off at San Julian and Seventh, a couple blocks from his office building. To get to school, I had to walk over to Fifth and San Pedro and continue west, then catch the bus. It took a long time. At least after school, I could go home directly."

A flaming two-by-four cartwheeled past, briefly drawing everyone's attention.

"One morning after about a week of that, I finally asked him, 'What have you been driving me downtown for? We practically pass my school on the way over here.'

"'Yeah,' he says, 'but we don't spend much time together. I thought it would be nice. This way we can catch up on our lives, maybe even grieve together. It's only the two of us now, buddy.'

"'Yes, I can count,' I say. 'And if you'd come home at a reasonable hour, that would also give us time to grieve. Maybe we could even toss the ball around while we grieve.'

"'I'm talking about quality time,' he says. 'Not after work when I'm spent.'

68

"'I guess you've got some woman set up near your office,' I say.

"'Nothing like that,' he says. 'A lawyer's work is long hours, son. Don't follow in my footsteps. It's a thankless profession.'

"So I say, 'You don't have to worry about me becoming a lawyer, pal. I'd just as soon become a pimp.'

"'What kind of talk is that?' he says.

"'My point is I have no interest in either,' I say.

"'It was the way you said it, like you were comparing lawyers to pimps,' he says."

"I agree," Petra said. "It did sound like you were comparing them."

Gil ignored her and continued on. "So I say, 'Don't flatter yourself. At least, there's some majesty in being a pimp.'

"He gave me a hard look so I changed the subject back to child endangerment. 'Look, you've been dropping me off on Skid Row all week. I'm only nine. Are you trying to have me kidnapped, or what?'

"'You're almost ten,' he says. 'And all this talk about kidnapping is a total hype. It's a media creation to keep people afraid and you've completely bought into it. Fear sells, son. You have no idea.'

"I'm like, 'Are you joking? We live in Los Angeles. Children are kidnapped every day in this town. And violent crime is up for the fourth straight year.'

"'You've been reading too many magazines,' he says. 'Why can't you watch cartoons like a normal kid? And how could someone kidnap you on Skid Row? None of those people have cars or homes. Where would they take you and how would they get you there? Be reasonable for once. If I wanted you kidnapped, I'd drop you off in Culver City.'"

"Good point," Rex said. "I forgot that part."

"I got used to it after a couple weeks," Gil said. "I'd pass the same derelicts, the same streetwalkers. Every now and

69

then, one would no longer be there, and I'd imagine the worst. It was funny. The police presence was strong, and I came to view the neighborhood as oddly safe, even friendly. There was an old bag lady who flashed me every morning. Her idea of a joke, I guess. This old man with a nose like a red potato was always inside one of those portable toilet sheds. The door was ripped off, and he'd just be sitting in there drinking. I'd pass by and he'd raise his brown paper bag at me. 'Good morning, sir.' He always called me sir. There were social services handing out day-old doughnuts and pastries. Little paper cups full of juice on card tables. I'd grab one on the way. It was like looking inside another world without ever having to belong to it."

"This sounds a bit like child abuse or parental neglect," one of the young women said. "I'm not sure how much more I want to hear."

"Keep going," Rex said. "I could listen to this all night."

Gil continued. "I started taking in the scene at Gladys Park along the way to school, which usually meant being late. I'd sit down somewhere in the shade and sketch the weirdness of it all: people shooting up, playing checkers, arguing frantically with whatever demons possessed them. It all fascinated me. That's really where I learned how to draw. One day I was sketching a woman feeding some pigeons. A kestrel or something swooped down and grabbed one of the pigeons off the ground. The woman screamed and threw a handful of bread crumbs as it flew off. Then she sat back down and cried. I'll never forget that. I went over and showed her my sketch. She immediately became absorbed in it, asking me questions about this and that, as though nothing had happened a moment before to make her cry."

Somebody belched. "Excuse me. This beer is really … carbonated."

Gil looked around. He decided to wrap up with a flourish of bullshit. "An idea came to me in that moment, why certain people were forced to live on the streets. No other place

70

could possibly contain the wildness of their spirits. I was wrong, of course, but I was young. My father eventually gave up on the hope of my kidnapping, if that's what it was. The next year I was skateboarding to a different school."

"No kidding?" someone asked.

"I don't know whether to laugh or cry," Maggie said.

"I usually laugh," Rex said, "unless I'm telling it as my own story."

13

They sat in the Isuzu Gemini hatchback drinking free coffee from the Midnight Mission.

"Run it past me again," Rex said.

"It's a website like any other website. I give all the working girls their own page, that's it."

"No, I got that part. I'm trying to figure out the why end of things."

Gil looked out the driver-side window at the packed row of tarps and tents lining the opposite sidewalk. A woman on the curb tapped a vein while a three-legged dog sniffed the blackened soles of her feet.

"This place has changed so much over the years. What's the opposite of gentrification?"

"I thought we were talking about a website," Rex said.

"All right, look, what I'm about to tell you goes in the vault, understand?"

"You started banging them, didn't you?"

"What? No! Just listen for a minute without interrupting. Think of it as a mental exercise."

"Go on," Rex said.

"I've been working full time for a while now at the teen jail. With the money I've made, I started paying the girls, you know, to get the interviews. I've got some openings to work with but I need more and can't afford to keep it up. This is a way of hooking them in, keeping in touch. These little twenty-minute chat sessions we've been having aren't enough. I should be tracking a community over a period of months like snow leopards."

"Comparing women to wild animals," Rex said. "Maybe you're in the wrong line of work. What about ethnomusicology? You could study the link between alternative rock and heroin addiction. Or hip hop and police brutality."

"Jane Goodall has been observing the same community of chimps for over forty years. Just think about that."

"Now you're comparing them to apes. I guess that's a step up."

"Don't get distracted," Gil said. "I need to follow a network of lives – very human lives – over a period of time in order to get anything meaningful. A single interview doesn't mean jack."

"Okay, now it's my turn. You've been at it too long. I've already said you're wasting your time. Let me rephrase that. You *wasted* your time, past tense. Wrap it up. Forget about finding meaning and improvise." Rex dumped what remained of his coffee out the passenger-side window. "Nobody's going down there to fact-check anything. You gave it your best shot, the *chicas* weren't game, and that's it. Now, you can leave with nothing but your empty dignity or gather up your winnings and go home."

72

"My winnings?"

"Whatever, babe. You want to fail with honor, is that it? None of this is your fault. Clean up the mess and get out of there. You're no less of a scholar. Just be smarter about the next thing you study. This website idea is just another way of prolonging your misery. You may not see that now, you know, cognitive distortion and all that shit, but you will eventually. You will when it's too late. That's your style." A homeless man approached Rex's window. He shook his head. "Not now, I'm off the clock."

Gil started the car. "Okay. You've pretty much said everything I need to hear."

That Saturday he drove down to TJ early. There was little traffic and he had a clear view across the Pacific from San Juan Cap to Carlsbad. He parked the Gemini and crossed the border. Rubbish from the night before still littered the streets. Rats scattered on the steps of the footbridge like hurried tourists. He passed over several drunks holding down the pavement. A few all-night girls stood guard on the Coahuila, hanging over from the graveyard to score that last trick before turning in. Others were beginning the day shift. He walked up to one and paid for the minimum time. They climbed the stairs, he got the room, and she went down the hall to make change. He took out his notebook and started fiddling with a camera. On her way back, she stopped abruptly in the doorway.

"What's that for?" she asked in Spanish.

"Just something I brought down..." he began clumsily, then tossed off a pitch for the website.

"What's the site called?"

"It's not up yet. Still under construction."

She asked if there was a charge to join.

"For the girls or the boys?"

She didn't answer.

73

"There's no cost," he said. "It needs girls or it won't fly and it needs guys or it won't keep flying."

"What's in it for you?"

He wasn't ready for the question. "Hopefully banner ads, personal connections. I may run a shuttle down from Los Angeles. With a little luck I'll break even."

She made a face.

"All right, look. I'm trying to connect with people down here. I'm doing a study…."

More questions, more answers, more blank stares. She announced his time was running out.

He held up the camera. "Should we do it then?"

"Sex?"

"No, sign you up and get some photos like we've been talking about."

She made a backhanded sweeping gesture, as though brushing an insect out of her space.

"I don't understand," he said. "This could be great for your business."

"I don't want my face all over the Internet." She gathered up her clothes.

"Excuse me," he said, "but I paid for the time and we still have ten minutes. And nobody searches anyone by face on the Internet anyway, except maybe the FBI."

"Who?"

"Who are you afraid of? No one will even know you're on the site except guys looking for sex in the area. Isn't that what you want?"

The black tights remained halfway up her legs as she stalled in pulling them up.

"Do you want to fuck or not?"

"I want to know what you're afraid of. Is it your parents? You go by a fake name anyway. What's the problem? We can blur your face if that'll help. It would be a shame with such a beautiful face, but –"

74

"Let me tell you something. My parents run a tiny store and restaurant. Four generations. A back door, a few tables and chairs. My grandmother cooked in that place for like eighty years. She started as a child and died last November. At the end, she couldn't even remember people's names, couldn't carry on a conversation. She thought my mother was my grandfather's lover. My grandfather had been dead for ten years. Anytime my mother walked through the kitchen, my grandmother would say, 'Do you have to come around here?' She'd completely lost her mind but somehow, some way, she managed to keep track of all those orders, all those recipes. I moved out and started working here. I'm making real money for the first time, saving for a little clothing shop. But you know something? I can still smell that place on my skin." She looked out the little barred window.

"Somebody told me there are boulevards in Paris named after sex workers. I think they made a few of them saints."

She shrugged. "What are you talking about?"

"Listen, I get it, and thank you for the story. You're trying to escape this intergenerational lockstep of poverty, the dead-end life that kitchen represents. It's really great stuff. I mean, it's exactly the kind of thing I'm looking for. But you don't need to be ashamed of this line of work. It's honorable, really. And I'm not just saying that because I go to sex workers because I don't."

"Too good for that?" She leaned forward to complete the long-suspended act of pulling up her tights.

"What?"

She mustered a tired scoff. "Listen, *güero*, I don't know who you think you are, but this is just a job to me." She turned around, stepped into her skirt.

He grabbed her arm. "Wait a minute."

"What is it now?"

He looked her up and down with something like gall, though he wouldn't have admitted that to himself in the moment. Frustration and a sting of insult are what he felt.

75

"How about sliding those tights back down?"

"Our time is up. You need to pay another three hundred pesos plus the cost of the room."

He took out the money, handed it over.

14

Hangovers come in all shapes and sizes. It really depends on what brings one about. If the drinking started before noon, for example, the aftereffects might come on around four or five the same day. In that case, there are few options: Take a painkiller and wait for sleep, hunker down and just keep on drinking, or cross into the alley behind Chicago Club and pick up a little marching powder, although choice three means a lot more drinking, and not Mexican beer either, which some folks drink to sober up. No, coming out of that kind of hangover often involves relearning some of the basic facts of life, like how to tie a pair of shoes.

In his undergraduate days at UC San Diego, Gil once came down hard from a fierce acid trip, crash-landing naked on the sands of Dog Beach. He awakened as the blistering sun hit the sky and spent the next forty minutes searching for his clothes. A bleach-blonde surfer dude gave him a T-shirt to use as a loincloth and a dollar to take the city bus back to campus. Despite all the painful dimensions of that unforgettable day, this hangover was worse.

He awoke more or less paralyzed, not even sure he was alive. He managed to crawl to the shower and turn on the cold water. All peripheral vision was lost. It was like viewing the world through a foggy tunnel. After showering, he returned to bed to stare at the ceiling and sort through whatever he could recall of the night before. He tracked his way back through the booze and the bars to that fateful moment when he fucked away whatever remained of his academic integrity. But the remembrance didn't last, and he soon fell back asleep. Around noon somebody hammered on the door calling out impossible questions like, "Are you staying? Are you there? Are you alive?" He figured it must be the cleaning woman, though in his reduced mental state, he couldn't possibly answer. She opened the door. Whatever he said or didn't say caused a short thin man with a moustache and oily hair to appear. The desk clerk? A manager? The local police? Whoever it was, he allowed Gil to remain in bed, where he slipped back into unconsciousness and had a vivid dream. Trekking across a barren landscape, he encountered hunger, horniness, and exhaustion. They were not the specimens of allegory he'd read about in Frinkle's literary guide; more like marked stations on a cave dweller's commute.

He awoke again. To his relief, much of the mental fog had lifted. After paying for another night, he went out for coffee. Sitting in the bustling cafe, head in hands, he reflected on his lost life's purpose. A thought came to him. It may have

77

been an insight, it may have been a delusion, but it was most surely a thought. He had to revisit the scene of transgression. On his way out the manager engaged him in a dispute over some vomit on the bathroom ceiling. While there, Gil took another shower, then headed for the hotel where he'd screwed the pooch. He recognized the matron from the night before. She told him the girl wasn't working that night. She'd be back the following afternoon.

"You don't understand. I've lost a very important paper," he lied. "I have to get into that room."

Whatever was left in the room went out with the trash, the woman replied, and furthermore, the room was in use. Come back tomorrow.

"So, it's more likely to be there tomorrow?" His act of umbrage was so compelling, he actually convinced himself this woman had wronged him. The question didn't seem to interest her, though. She closed the sliding window in his face and returned to her telenovela.

A rage seethed inside him, an effect of the incident from the night before, the vomit dispute, the absurd teaching job, the limitations of his fieldwork, the misguided website, the lost imaginary document, Petra Solis and her silly notions of closure. He went down the sidewalk clenching his fists, his jaws, every muscle in his body. He rounded the far corner of the Coahuila. Standing in the shadow of a doorway, glowing like a Marian apparition, was the girl with the hummingbird tattoo.

It was good. It was unbelievably wrong, but it was very very good.

15

The next morning he lay motionless on the scrappy wooden
bunk of his cement-floored hotel room. The dawn light
brightened the only window. Familiar sounds of daybreak came
through: two women laughing, a tamale merchant's resonant
call, the screech of a braking utility truck. He was almost
comfortable. Twenty-four hours before, he'd felt like hell. Now,
something like peace had taken shape in the squalid little room.
So, what had changed? Shocking as it was to admit, he must
have accepted what he'd done, incorporated his missteps into a
revised sense of self, folded them into the reconstructed present
like a wad of yeast-bearing dough. At least, that's what he told
himself.

He elbowed himself upright and called in sick to work.
A reasonable first action. There was no way he could drive back
to Los Angeles in his condition anyhow. Despite his solemn
resolve and the relief it provided, his mind was still a mess.
Like an afterimage of the sun, the blot of his ugly deeds
remained fixed upon it. The thing to do was get up and trudge
forward into the actual light of day. And so, with fewer than
two hundred pesos left in his pocket, he went up and down the
streets of Zona Norte pitching the website to one sex worker
after another. Most of them brushed him off, but a few with
whom he'd secured past paid interviews signed on. It gave him
some dim hope on which to plan the immediate future.

He drove back to LA that night and the next morning
went straight up to the computer lab to check in with LeTed. He
was late, as usual. Gil went down to the dungeon to be sure,
then headed back to the lab during his nutrition break. He saw
LeTed shuffling up the stairs, coffee in hand, a faded leather
satchel looped over his shoulder. He wore sagging jeans, rubber
bath slippers, and a faded T-shirt exhibiting a smiley face on the

front and the outline of a hand giving the middle finger on the back.

Gil approached from behind. "Hey, good to see you." LeTed stopped and turned around slightly. He seemed unsure why Gil would be addressing him. "How's the website, brother?"

"Oh yes, that. It's, uh, progressing. I've run into some minor complications...." His voice trailed off as he took the next step.

"How much longer? I'd like to get things moving." He thought he'd asked the question as gently as possible considering what he really wanted was to throw LeTed down the stairs Frinkle-style.

"By this afternoon." LeTed nodded, as though convincing himself it were possible.

"You'll be working on it here then? Is that such a good idea?"

"Hey, nobody really knows what I do here, pal. Sometimes I'm not even sure. If they walked in on me at any given moment, they might think I was one of the resident thugs. And, to be fair, I used to be one so...."

"Good enough." Gil reached for his wallet, handed off the cash. "Hopefully, this will spur things along. And this," he said, holding up the memory card from the camera, "I'll need back by Friday afternoon. It contains the first set of photos. Here's a piece of paper with names and captions for each, along with some diagrams on how to lay it all out. I plan to take some more this weekend."

"Okay, check back tomorrow."

"And what time do you get in then?"

Because LeTed was wearing the same clothes the following day, Gil thought he must have stayed up all night working on the website, but when he was still wearing them the day after that, he wasn't sure what to think. And yet, by Thursday

80

morning the website was up and running. They sat down in LeTed's little office before school and went over it. It took about two minutes.

"Well," Gil said, "you did the job. It's not quite what I envisioned. I guess it needs some more girls."

"That would flesh it out," LeTed said, "so to speak."

"I'll check in after this weekend."

"Okay, but don't check in too often. I've pretty much shown you how to add them yourself."

"I understand. And listen, if you're ever down that way, let me know. I'll be sure to hook you up."

"Hook me up?"

"Yeah, if you're ever down in TJ, I'll hook you up with a girl. You know, steer you in the right direction. I know a couple friendly ones."

LeTed stiffened his posture, pursed his lips. He seemed to be deciding whether to respond. "Thank you for the, uh, thought, but there's no way I'm ever going to be down there."

"Fine. I guess we're done then."

"I'm taking care of business right here." LeTed pursed his lips again, nodded slightly to the wall behind the computer screen.

"Got it."

"Don't get me wrong, I'm not against your ethics. I just believe there are safer cleaner ways to take care of these things."

"My ethics? Listen man, I'm providing a social service. I already told you, I'm a scholar. I'm documenting what's going on down there, that's it. When I finish, I'll turn that knowledge over to society. And as far as cleanliness goes, they're a hell of a lot cleaner than anyone you're picking up on Slauson and Fig. They bathe and use condoms and have little medical cards they're required by law to get signed off each month by a physician. You know any sex workers in this town who jump

81

through those kinds of hoops? No, you don't because they're all working illegally."

"I don't know any sex workers period, and for you to imply that I do is a bit insulting and perhaps also racist."

"All right, it's just that you come in here each morning looking like maybe you sleep under a bridge. I was thinking if you weren't getting any, maybe I could help out. I apologize. I'm a little touchy on the subject, that's all."

"Good answer," LeTed said. "Now, if you don't mind, I have my own work to do."

16

He left the juvie facility through the parking lot gate as usual. Rex was outside the razor-wire fence talking to a probationary. Gil leaned out the window.

"Everything all right here?"

"Yeah, she was just –"

"I was asking her," Gil said.

Rex nodded, got into the car.

"What is wrong with you?" Gil turned onto the street. "I'm trying to keep a low profile, understand? These kids are all fucked up. There was a fight in my classroom just this morning. Every day some new shit hits the fan. Don't facilitate it."

"Take it easy," Rex said. "She was just selling me a chocolate bar for the girls' soccer team."

"There's no girls' soccer team at this school. It's a jailhouse. Wake up."

"Hey, I don't know. Maybe she's trying to start one. You're getting laid, aren't you?"

"What?"

"I can see it in your attitude, your demeanor. There's some good energy going on there."

"Changing the subject, why are you here?"

"It's the whores, isn't it? You're finally screwing them." He clapped his hands. "I knew this day would come."

Gil hit the brakes and pulled over.

"Cool off," Rex said. "I know you would never do a thing like that. Even I, in all my depravity – in all my moral turpitude – would never do a thing like that. It's a joke, Daddy Ding Dong. Now goddamn it, what's gotten into you?" He patted Gil on the cheek, lit up a joint and laughed. "Oh, before I forget, I need a ride down this weekend. It's my last trip to the ashram, thank Krishna and his blessed mother. I'm done with my thesis and Petra's just finishing up hers. I said I'd go over it with her on Saturday just to work out the kinks."

"Lucky her. And you can't do that here?"

"No, we're celebrating on Sunday. They're having some kind of an all-day puja and paintball tournament. It was just good timing. I don't know all the details, but –"

"Wait, what did you say?"

"About what?"

"You say you finished your thesis?"

"What a relief, huh? You'll get there, baby. Keep on truckin'."

"I hadn't – I mean – I didn't even know you were working on anything."

"Nonstop for three months. It's not in my nature to discuss these things. I just like to plow on through like OCD."

"OCD, huh?"

"Here, let me show you something." Rex pulled out his wallet and removed a photograph. "See this dog?"

"That your dog?"

"No, I cut this out of a magazine I took from the university library. This dog here is some kind of specialized German Shepherd, like a breed within a breed, you know? It was created in the Czech Republic to work constantly. The way it's bred, it can never be a pet. Its genetically modified nature is to either work or go crazy. Can you believe the cruelty of that shit? I guess they wanted to take them to the front lines or something."

"I don't get it."

"Well, when I read this article, it was like a lightbulb went on. I'd finally figured out after all these years what my problem was, why I habitually self-medicate."

"You want to breed these dogs?"

"No, man. I have the same problem they do. If I'm not working at something constantly, I get anxious. That's where this comes in." He held up the burning joint.

Gil broke out laughing, but it was not happy laughter. It was the unhinged mocking laughter of disbelief. "Oh, that's rich, pal. That's really good stuff. You should write this down and take it on the road."

"I'm being serious."

"You're being serious, huh?"

"Yeah, and I've been struggling with this condition my whole life."

"Oh, get off it, will you? If you're being serious, then I'll be serious, too. You're full of it. And I'd like to read this monograph of yours, I really would."

"Monograph?"

"Your thesis, moron. You know, that paper you spent three months writing? I'd like to read it and see what this dissertation committee will finally be treated to. And on the subject of workaholic dogs or whatever it is you think you are, let me say something else. You're bat shit."

"Read it any time. It's already been approved."

"What?"

84

"I got word last Monday. I'm Dr. Healy now. Well, not technically yet but, yeah. It's happening."

Gil threw his head back, closed his eyes. Was this the first stage of madness or was he further along than that? The world seemed to be conspiring in the most screwball manner to disgrace him. Each success of these lesser academics, these charlatans and dilettantes, reaffirmed his lost course.

"I don't know what's going on. Please tell me this is some kind of sick joke."

"Why would I be joking?" Rex asked.

"Because you were arrested for spray-painting a Hitler moustache on a billboard of a child's face, that's why. And now you're a doctor of philosophy? It doesn't compute."

"That was three years ago, baby, and I was protesting for social justice."

"Social justice? It was a public service message. The little girl with the Hitler moustache was a poster child for diabetes."

"Oh, come on, man. This country invented diabetes."

Gil coursed his fingers through his hair, pulled it, rubbed his eyes with the heels of his hands. "I can't believe what I'm hearing. Burn me with the end of that joint, maybe I'll wake up."

"What about that ride?"

"I'm not going down this weekend. You're on your own."

"You're kidding."

"No, I don't have the money and I need to decompress."

"Sure, whatever. Drop me off on the Row then."

"That's not happening either. I'll take you as far as I'm going, which is Pico and Alvarado. You can figure it out from there."

17

Clear Spot was one of the cheapest, darkest, dirtiest places in the city, but they had dollar drafts and live music during the week. Gil had to get back to his room and continue writing at some point that night. He chose Clear Spot because its overall vileness would keep him from hanging out there too long. Customers entering the place immediately ran into a bank of smoky blue air, courtesy of the owner's blithe defiance of indoor smoking laws. Topping that hazard were airborne darts zipping past patrons' heads, thunderous garage punk, and at least one good fight each night. Drinks were served by waitresses with neck tattoos, raggedy voices, and fuck-you personalities.

On his way to an empty stool, Gil saw Harlan Wretchler, the social studies teacher who taught on the other side of his classroom wall. Unsure whether his colleague had seen him, he thought of turning around and heading for the bar. Just then Wretchler made eye contact and nodded.

"The hell you doing here?" he called out, his voice bold with drink.

"I come to soak up the sun," Gil said.

"Let me buy you a whiskey."

"That's all right."

"No, it isn't. You're going to have a shot of Wild Turkey or I'll never speak to you again."

Gil thought that offer almost too good to refuse, but it wasn't to be. Wretchler put his arm around his shoulder and yoked him over to the table. Wretchler sat down while Gil

86

remained standing. He thought of the empty barstool he'd forsaken on the other side of the room. Surely someone had taken it by now.

"You'll never believe what happened today," Wretchler said.

"Don't be too sure. It's been a strange week."

"Two little bitches from my period four class accused me of leering at them. How you like that? *Leering.* I guess they couldn't think up anything better. Lee pulled me into her office. Bertram was there, too, flexing his neck muscles. I threw it all back in their faces."

"Yeah?"

"These are two of the ditziest ..." He stalled, searching for the rest of the sentence, then gave up and started another. "One of them came up to me at the beginning of the semester and offered me a piece of her ass. The other snorts crank off her desktop anytime my back is turned. Now they're pissed 'cause they're failing. That violates probation and they're headed back to court. You realize all the girls at that school are shoplifters and hookers, right?" He pounded his drink back, closed his eyes to the ceiling, and laughed. "You know what I'm going to do?"

"Tell me," Gil said.

"I'm going to send a jolt through that place like –" He burped, hesitated a moment, balanced a thought on a raised fingertip.

A waitress edged in and took their drink orders.

"All right," Gil said. "Lay it on me."

Wretchler leaned forward, his rheumy eyes looking more bloodhound than boxer. He bore in on Gil, the chummy drunk holding a stranger hostage to sudden inspiration. "What I'm going to do is get one of these little shits to plug me."

"One of the girls?"

"Huh?"

"Who's going to plug you?"

87

"Any one of those little buggers," Wretchler said. "Just a little twenty-two in the flank." He spanked his hip. "I get a couple million to retire on, the kid gets his cut, does another six months in juvie, and we're both out of there in great shape. Can you believe nobody's thought of that yet?"

"I can believe it."

"Until they sort it all out, I'll be pulled from the classroom. Teacher jail!" He raised his fists triumphantly.

The waitress arrived with the drinks. Wretchler handed her a five-dollar bill.

"Six fifty," she said.

He handed over another two dollars, waved her off.

"What's teacher jail?" Gil asked.

"What's teacher jail? Oh, my boy. Say you lose it one day and throw a desk across the room or some girl claims you got a little too friendly, right? Next thing you know, you're out of there. You're free." He belched again, wobbled upright on the stool. "Well, you have to report to a downtown office every morning but you can read there, screw off on your laptop, or just stare at the wall. The point is you *still get paid.*" He narrowed his eyes. "After about a year, they complete their investigation and you go back into the classroom, simple as that. Sounds like a winner, huh?"

"A year?"

"It takes that long to fix the air conditioning, doesn't it?" He shot back the whiskey, smacked the empty glass down, feinted a flurry of punches into the space between them. "I knew a guy...." He paused a moment to absorb the last shot. "...I knew a guy who was down there *two* years." He drummed his finger on the table top. "Two whole years doing nothing but getting paid. All for having a magazine and a tube of lotion in his desk. He learned Portuguese in that time. *Fluently.* As soon as they sent him back to the classroom, he said piss off, I'm retiring. How you like that? Moved his ass to the Amazon rainforest, bought a fruit farm, and married a Brazilian woman

88

twenty years younger. I don't think he needs the magazines anymore."

The drinks kept coming. Gil looked for a way out. Finally, somebody cursed the band, the keyboard player threw a bottle, and in the chaos that followed an opening arrived.

18

Gil took the Pasadena Freeway through the hills of Eagle Rock and pulled into the driveway of an old Victorian. The faded porch sign read, "Ronaldo Vasquez, DDS." He pushed the door open. An old woman straight out of a sepia-toned photograph was inside.

"Is there a psychiatrist in this building?" he asked.

She brought him into a converted parlor that served as a waiting area. Nobody else was there.

"Have a seat on the davenport. The doctor will be with you shortly."

He sat down and took a magazine off the coffee table. It was a copy of *Seventeen* from 1983. He leafed past the hair care and acne treatment ads, then flipped the magazine to the coffee table and picked up a copy of *Dental Traumatology*.

A slim fortyish-looking man came into the room. From the front he looked as sharp and square as a television news anchor, but from the side you could see the wispy pony tail hanging between his shoulder blades.

"Good morning, I'm Dr. Bollerup." He had a smile like the grill on a Lincoln Town Car.

"Gilmore Crowell. I think I'm in the wrong place, though. Is there another office in this building?"

"You're in the right place. Have you filled out the medical history form?"

"Not yet, I just got here."

"No matter. They rarely hold up in court. Shall we go down the hall?"

They went to a room at the back of the house. Unopened cardboard boxes were stacked along one wall, all but blocking out the light of a window. The doctor motioned Gil toward a dental patient chair in the center of the room.

"I'm telling you, I'm in the wrong place," Gil said. "I'm here for a psychiatric evaluation."

"Relax and I promise not to drill your teeth." He laughed wolfishly. "The guy I bought this place from was a dentist. I just keep the equipment around as a kind of novelty. You know, a theme clinic – like you have your theme restaurants? The patients get a kick out of it. Sometimes I give them a shot of nitrous to loosen things up. Want some?"

"Do I want a shot of nitrous oxide?

"That was my question, yes."

"I don't think so."

"Why are we meeting today, Mr. Crowell?"

"I don't know where to begin. It's kind of like the world is collapsing around me."

"Are you sure about that?" The doctor nibbled the inside of his cheek. "Or is it more like your mind is imploding? You see, the mind and the external stimuli are one, so it doesn't particularly matter. The idea is to be as precise as possible in expressing whatever you think is happening."

Gil opened up on his scholarly failure, the sex workers refusing to take him seriously, the website, the absurd teaching job, his lost time, lack of money, the breakup, and that moment

90

he crossed the Rubicon separating academic integrity from disgrace.

"Sure you don't want a sip of nitrous?" the doctor asked.

"Yes."

"Yes, you do or yes, you don't?"

"Yes, I don't."

"Reason I ask is you seem overly anxious and perhaps a little resentful. A bit of gas might take the edge off things, bring you within the parameters of the therapeutic window."

"How about analyzing what I've told you or giving me a prescription for some real meds?"

"Some real meds? Oh my, what are we talking about? Xanax? Trazodone? Klonopin?"

"You're the doctor."

"I have benzos if you want. They're not going to help any. Oh, you'll feel better for a few days and then you'll have a real habit to kick in addition to your other self-constructed maladies. Is that what you came here for today, a drug habit?"

"A minute ago you were pushing nitrous oxide."

"Nitrous oxide is not addictive, Mr. Crowell. Moreover, I seriously doubt you'd be able to acquire a tank of it any time soon so I think you'd be safe all around. You want me to tell you what I think your problem is?"

"That's one reason I'm here."

"Let's double back a moment." He stood up, went to the stack of boxes, and looked out the narrow opening of window. "This website, what's the point of it?"

"I'm spending all my money just getting the sex workers to speak to me. Once the website gets moving, word spreads, more women will be willing to talk, and I'll have a solid inroad to the community."

Dr. Bollerup sat down again, drew himself closer to Gil. "Tell me more about this woman who dumped you."

91

"What do you want to know?" Gil reclined into the head rest.

"Were you attracted to her?"

"Of course."

"So, she was good in bed then?"

"You're seriously asking me that?"

"Would you prefer I ask if you were in love with her? I can only assume that you weren't."

"Why do you say that?" Gil asked.

"Because you didn't lead with her today in your lengthy tally of grievances. Thus, the breakup – if we may even call it that – was not the cause of your malaise, only another effect of it."

"Hmm."

"In other words, I suspect she broke it off for good reason." The doctor nodded to himself, nibbled some more on the inside of his cheek. "Yes, I think she did the right thing. I commend her for moving on to richer brighter beginnings. Allow me to confirm one more assumption. Besides these two slip ups in Tijuana, you're not having regular intercourse now, are you?"

Gil looked up into the blinding dental light. "Would you mind turning that thing off?"

"I ask because a breakup is a kind of loss, Mr. Crowell. Even if you had despised this woman – indeed, especially if you had despised her – you would most likely still experience that loss. Your self-worth was unquestionably knocked down a peg or two on that fateful day she packed her bags and left. Now you're striving to function in this surreal little world you've created for yourself, what with the entitled prostitutes and the miscreants at the detention center you're expected to wait on hand and foot. I wouldn't be feeling too good about any of that myself. How about a blood test?" He got up and turned off the dental light.

"What's that going to do?"

92

"Among other things, check your testosterone and Vitamin D levels. Potassium. A deficit in one or the other might bring on a mild depression."

"All right."

"Good answer. Now, the next question is, do you really want to finish this dissertation or is it just something that you would like to see finished?"

"What's the difference?" Gil asked.

"It's a question of motivation." Again, the puckered lips, ruminating. "Logic states you can either finish or not, correct?"

"Uh, yeah."

"Unless there's a third option of which I'm unaware. Let's go over the causal threads. What would happen if you quit?"

"Teaching?" Gil shifted himself on the dental chair.

"No, grad school. Try to focus."

"I have no other prospects."

"You could transfer at some point to a real school, couldn't you? It's a decent profession, all things considered."

"In theory, yes. In practice, it's occupational therapy at a loony bin."

Dr. Bollerup pawed at his flower print necktie. "We call them psychiatric hospitals."

"It's a job for a special kind of masochist. I can hang on a bit longer, that's it."

"Okay, then finish your thesis. You slept with a couple prostitutes, so what?"

"We call them sex workers. And why do you say it doesn't matter? Have you ever slept with a patient?"

"Clients is what we call them, and that's none of your business. What you've done is far less serious."

"What do you recommend?"

"We'll have to check the blood results, but I suspect you need a program of moderate exercise, sound sleep, and vitamin supplementation." He nodded to himself, directed his eyes back to Gil.

"And the sex workers?"

"Finish writing about them."

"I'm concerned that my scholarly sensibilities may have been compromised by –"

"Oh, knock it off, Crowell. Your scholarly sensibilities? Really? Snap out of it and write the paper. Nobody cares that you screwed a couple... What did you call them? Working girls?"

"Sex workers."

"All right, fine. Nobody cares thou hast fouled thine ivory member in the putrid gardens of Babylon. Write your paper and get out of there before I report you to the department." He laughed, the enormous teeth seeming to project monstrously from his face. He tapped Gil on the knee. "Relax, I'm kidding. Nobody but the thesis committee is ever going to read this thing. And hell, they're only going to skim the first few pages and check the footnotes, right? Your real problem, Crowell, is that you've lost your sense of proportion. Not your sense of perspective – that's something else – but your grasp of the size and significance of the matter. Insignificance in this case. That right-sizing won't come back overnight but it will eventually *if* you're able to follow the regimen I've outlined. I apologize for being so direct, but your graduate work doesn't matter nor will it ever matter to anyone, living, dead, or as yet unborn. Isn't there a kind of liberation in admitting that to yourself? That it even matters to you now is a sure sign of an overly scrupulous conscience brought on by acute anxiety disorder. You want a prescription for marijuana? A week of that might speed things along and you won't get addicted as you would with the benzos."

"Telling me my graduate studies don't matter is like saying the last eight years of my life haven't mattered."

94

A gallery wall of diseased mouths smiled down at him. Malocclusion seemed the most empathetic.

"Is that a no on the marijuana?"

"Yes, it's a no."

"If the last eight years haven't mattered, that's on you. And that's not what I said. My point was no one could possibly care that you've slept with a couple slovenly trollops. What's more, they'll never know." He shrugged.

"Don't you see the problem is that I know! It's affecting *me*." Gil jabbed his fingers into his chest. "That's why I'm the one who's here. Get it?"

"It doesn't matter, Crowell. I'm sorry. You want me to write that down for you to read every morning and again before you tuck yourself in at night?" He leaned forward to squirt himself a cup of water from the dental rinsing sink.

"Can you please be serious?"

"I'm being as serious as possible, given the scope of this matter. You'll soon wake up and see how silly the whole thing is, provided you begin taking care of yourself. And quit screwing those filthy rotten whores, would you?" He laughed. "Or keep screwing them. What's the difference? You're hardly the first person to mess up your life, though you'd like to believe it, wouldn't you? Then you'd be a special case and could wallow in the stench of your self-pity. You're not special, Crowell. You're just like every other human who's ever walked the earth. Sure you don't want some nitrous?" He went over to the tank.

"Yes, I'm sure. I'm also sure it's time to leave." Gil slid off the cool vinyl slope of the dental chair.

"Suit yourself. You may proceed to the receptionist. She'll have some things for you to sign." Dr. Bollerup climbed into the dental chair and reached around for the black rubber mask. "Take a sample of toothpaste on your way out. Some dental supply company keeps dropping them off by the truckload."

95

19

At the corner of the Coahuila and Niños Héroes, Gil ate a taco and observed a line of meth heads slavishly awaiting their fix outside the door of an old cargo van. They were as composed as an assembly of moviegoers in front of a theater, a place Gil hadn't been since his father unexpectedly broke on through to the other side.

He was a high school senior – a semester away from graduating – and it was the week between Christmas and New Year's. The two were bound to spend some time together. While Dustin Hoffman and Tom Cruise conspired to rip off casinos, the senior Crowell suddenly pitched forward in his theater seat. Gil rescued the popcorn and asked if everything was all right. Without answering, the fifty-year-old widower lumbered up the inclined aisle to the exits. He collapsed between a concession counter and a parking validation machine, never regaining consciousness. Having witnessed his mother's slow, painful exit, Gil couldn't decide which passing was worse. He had no relatives and so became an orphan of the state for the few weeks until his eighteenth birthday – not enough time to accrue any benefits. The will left him his father's modest assets: twenty-seven thousand dollars and a 1984 Isuzu Gemini hatchback. He spent three hundred on the cremation, paid the rent on the Miracle Mile apartment, and prepared for his next chapter at UC San Diego.

At university, he began role-playing his life: a pretentious know-it-all in class and at the library; a good-humored goof at dinner, in league with the work-study staff; an affectedly detached stoner at night in pursuit of adventure. It was a fun way to pass the time. He disciplined himself to compartmentalize these identities such that when he ran into someone from class while bussing tables in the dining hall or passing a joint at a party, he momentarily froze. Here he was years later, similarly flustered at the sight of Rex Healy, completely out of context on the streets of Zona Norte.

"What in the fuck are you doing here?"

"Ever had a dream where you weren't really a participant in the action? You just sort of hovered through it all like some kind of disembodied witness?"

"I'm serious. Why are you here?"

"Why must you react to everything with such passive-aggressive hostility?"

"No, *passive aggressive* is when you don't respond to an email. I'm being aggressive, plain and simple, because that's the only way to get through to you."

"You understand anger is a symptom of depression in males, right?"

"I already had my analysis," Gil said. "What do you want?"

"I was just in the neighborhood and thought I'd play fly on the wall for one of your little rap sessions. You know, see how this thing works."

"Well, that's not going to happen."

Rex turned to one of the fellows slinging tacos. "*Dos al pastor con todo.*" He reached his freakishly long arm over the people surrounding the grill to hand off a fifty-peso note.

97

Two streetwalkers were posted no more than twenty feet from the taco stand. Rex stepped over to them and began talking. The younger one squirmed coyly. The somewhat older, taller one gazed into the distance, as though holding out.

Gil came over with Rex's tacos. "Here, let me trade these for you getting the hell out of here."

"Easy now," Rex said, reaching for his wallet. "I'll take care of the girls and the room. You just do what you do."

Rex sat in the hotel room's only chair. Gil leaned against the edge of the mirrored bureau, took out his notebook and pen. He was already sorry to be there. The girls began a striptease. Gil got between them.

"Not now," he said in Spanish. "That isn't why we're here."

"What are you guys into?" the older one asked.

"We could start with some introductions," Rex said in broken Spanish.

"I'll handle this," Gil said. "Your job is to sit there and observe, remember?" He turned to the girls. "Okay, let's get everyone's name."

Rex shot back up. "I'm Dr. Healy." He stuck out his hand.

"Sit your ass down, Doctor, or I'm calling this whole thing off."

The older girl quickly figured out the scene, all too eager to uncover the formative story of her sex-working life. The other was in the habit of responding through her friend, as though inhibited.

"What I'm seeing," Gil said to the younger girl, "is that much of your interpretation of this lifestyle has been processed for you. Maybe because of your age you find yourself vulnerable to the influence of older, more experienced, girls. Does that sound fair?"

"Not really," the older one said. "We just didn't like school. You know, afraid we weren't smart enough to do well. I

98

was a sales girl at a shoe store earning twenty pesos an hour. She was working at her aunt's little tortilla shop making whatever they felt like giving her. We didn't know anything about job training for women. I'm still not sure what it is. So, we got on a bus and headed here." She did a little curtsy to mark the end of her story.

Rex nodded. "That's kind of what I understood. Gil, I don't know where that last question came from. It's almost like we're in two different rooms."

Gil flipped the notebook shut, jabbed the pen into the spiral. "Okay, I think we're done. Would either of you like to appear on a promotional website?"

He signed them up, they all left, and he and Rex wound up at an Italian restaurant on Revolución. It was like any Italian restaurant on the other side of the border: checkerboard floor and table cloths; red, white, and green awning over the bar; perennial Christmas lights laced through the rafters. They sat at a dark booth in the back beside a framed placard of Caruso in *Rigoletto*. Rex ordered spaghetti and meatballs, Gil the capellini pomodoro.

"So, you're a vegetarian now?"

"You just saw me eat a taco, didn't you?"

"Then why you getting that?"

Gil sighed. "In Mexico anyone can order off the vegetarian menu. It's one of the reasons I come down. I got a question. If Petra's finished with her thesis, then what are you doing here?"

"Little side business." A waiter set a basket of bread on the table. With a sweep of his hand, Rex brushed aside elaboration.

"I read about that tunnel they found, the one that began under the flower shop and ran a half mile to Otay Mesa. Is that going to get in the way of your little side business?"

Rex made a face. "I've got nothing to do with that. Hey, I just fooled them into giving me a PhD, didn't I? Your words."

99

He snatched a piece of bread from the half loaf. "I'm surprised you don't have any hustle down here, desperate as you are."

Gil drew a slice from the basket with far more circumspection, holding it up as though unsure it was the right one. "The stakes are too small for me. Human trafficking is more my size."

"Got your eye on some *chicas* who need rescuing?"

Gil shrugged, buttered his bread.

"How would their lives be any better in the States, baby? They might be worse. Didn't you hear what those girls were saying? They don't want to go to college. They don't want to do anything."

"Some want to improve their lives; others don't. They're like Americans that way. Hey, I'm just making conversation till the food arrives. I couldn't give less of a shit why you're down here. All I ask is that you stay off my turf going forward and pick up this check. I'm pretty sure you owe me that."

When he got back to the Koenig House, Norm informed him that Brinda Bagchi had stopped by the house for what Gil imagined must have been some kind of intervention. Another encroachment upon his order of things. For the next few days, she took up residence in his head.

At the beginning of the week, a new probationary was admitted to the juvie high school. She took a seat in front. As Gil read aloud, she opened her mini-skirted thighs, directing a pair of blue-striped panties to his line of sight. At first, he pretended not to notice the exhibition. When it happened again the following day, he stopped everything and gave a pop quiz. While everyone was hunched over their paper, he sidled up to her from behind, squatted down, and whispered in her ear, "Cut the shit." She spent the rest of the week in jeans giving him dirty looks. Otherwise, it was just another workweek in a detention center: A probe asked to go to the bathroom and

100

returned a half hour later with a Starbucks in hand. One of the resident thugs stabbed a pencil into another's neck. And for three straight days the fire alarm went off every twenty minutes. He ran out of stories from the textbook and selected an abridged class set of *Pride and Prejudice,* one of the few novels he remembered from high school. Most of the students didn't follow the story. The ones that did offered surprisingly fresh insights.

"Hey, so Lydia's a little ho, right? And Elizabeth is nothing but a cock tease, but this Jane is for reals fine, huh Crowell? You'd do her, wouldn't you?"

"I'll dig 'em all out," another student added. "But tell you what, that Lizzie's got a big mouth on her. I'da bitch-slapped that ratchet back in chapter one."

The class erupted at this hypothetical threat, howling and shrieking and banging their desktops. Jeannie Lint Esquire opened the door between the two classrooms, perhaps to see if anybody was being stomped to death. A guard came in from the hall. He stood in the doorway till everyone got back in their seat.

"Okay, listen up," Gil said. "We can't discuss digging characters out or bitch-slapping them or anything else of a violent or sexual nature, understand? I know you all think you're in jail – and to be fair, some of you are – but this is also a public high school, and we have to behave accordingly."

A couple students nodded. Some others sulked with disgust. Gil picked up his copy of the novel. He was about to continue reading when, like a steam tug whistling through San Pedro Harbor, a tremendous fart sounded out. Again, the class went apeshit.

20

The heavy oak door to Brinda Bagchi's office was a half inch open. Gil ran his fingertip over the recessed name plate, tracking the grooves of the *P,* the *h,* and the *D.* He took a breath and knocked – no answer – then pushed the door open enough to peek through. Bagchi was speaking with a Slug named Magnus Wingate. Both turned their heads at the same moment with identical frozen expressions.

"Sorry, I didn't think…"

"I'll be right with you, Gil."

Wingate looked like he'd been physically violated by the interruption. The descendent of landed nobles, he'd spent the last couple years pondering the influence of Wilshire Country Club members' attachment bonds on the hierarchy of the Hancock Park banking community.

Bagchi opened the door. "Penguin just picked up Magnus' dissertation," she exclaimed. "Isn't that amazing?"

"A classic already," Gil said.

"They must have recognized it was dripping with ingenuity. I certainly did."

"I guess that means the committee approved it." Bagchi and Wingate exchanged glances. "I mean… Never mind. That's great news, Magnus." Gil reached out his hand. Magnus took it limply, clammily, while checking his timepiece, and slid out the door.

Bagchi fell into her chair, eyes bugged, legs splayed, a luster of perspiration on her upper lip. "Can you believe it?" she asked Gil. "I mean, wow. Really, just wow."

"Wow indeed," Gil replied. "It's good to know someone's finally taking rich white folks seriously."

"Okay," she said, straightening her hair, the glow in her face dimming. "How are things with you, Gil? I guess you heard I stopped by."

"Yes, I did. I'm all right. It's a leap of self-improvement for me to hate someone despite their achievements, not because of them."

"Who do you mean? Not me, I hope."

"Forget it."

"How's your thesis coming? That is why you're here, correct?"

"Yes, I've spoken with about forty sex workers in the past two months so...."

"Forty?"

"That's right."

"Wonderful news. To what depth, though?" Her tone indicated she knew the answer. She was only checking to see if he did.

"Not much. I need more of them and more time with each. I've got to strengthen the connections. Six more months should do it. By June, I expect to have something for the committee." He put a smile on it.

"That would be fantastic. What accounts for the recent success?"

"Success?"

"Well, you were set back with all kinds of misfortune there for – I guess it's been a few years now, hasn't it?"

"That's being kind."

"So, why are they cooperating all of a sudden?"

103

"I'm paying them by the hour now. Actually, by the word. Every time they say something useful, I hand over another ten pesos."

"We should have thought of that sooner."

"Yes, well...."

"I'm happy for you, Gil. I really am. I'm your biggest supporter, you know that, right?"

"Sounds like there's more to say."

"There are some things you should know," she said, looking uncomfortable.

"Go ahead."

"It's the department. People are talking."

"They do that, don't they?"

"Your name came up at the last meeting. Some of the folks around here think your time is up. They're looking for an excuse to move you along."

His mind spun like he'd been hit in the head. A light fog filled the room as a pressurized ringing arose in one ear. His chair felt as if it were floating out from under him. He took hold of the armrests and gazed out the window, hoping to identify the source of the change in air quality. For the first time the orange tree looked out of place in the shadow of the sycamore and the eucalyptus ripe for a chainsaw. He inhaled deeply and held it.

"Are you all right?" Bagchi asked.

"I don't know but keep going."

"Their concern is that you might be misappropriating fellowships, that kind of thing. It's not uncommon. Many students get stuck on the dissertation and just keep applying for grants."

The shock of this effrontery cleared his head. "Oh, yes, the great American scandal of living off financial aid. Like welfare fraud, right? I'm not even sure how to respond to that. I can't remember the last time I received a grant for anything."

"Okay, but they don't know that," Bagchi said.

"So, they're concerned but not enough to investigate?"

"A couple influential people have had enough is all I'm saying. I don't think I should keep that from you." She broke eye contact, straightened the sleeves of her blouse.

"Okay, but what does it mean?"

"They want you out of the program."

"I get it, but how much time do I have?"

She exhaled audibly, as though unsure how to proceed. "If you can stick to your plan, things should be okay. It's time to finish up, though, or you're going to have a hard time getting this past the committee."

"That's a chilly forecast."

"Let me know if there's any way I can help."

He headed over to the Warren Andrew Gluck Memorial Library for perhaps the two-thousandth time. A chorus of sprinkler heads hissed at him as he passed. Four newspaper vending machines stood at attention, chests jutted out in defiance of the moment an operations crew would remove them all in the middle of the night. At the apex of the portal arch hung a long-vacant wasp nest. In the lower window panel of the vestibule was scratched a crudely disembodied crotch. Below it, like a name plate engraved in crows-feet typeface, was the word *PUSSY.* Gil wondered what became of the artist, if he had gone on to paint murals of abstract genitalia for the lobbies of statehouses and luxury hotels or was busy managing a Rite-Aid with a teenage son at Los Angeles Correctional Academy. Regardless, here in the entranceway of the Memorial Library, an example of his early work lived on. He passed the same work-study girl checking books, a familiar tramp slouched on the green fabric sofa, and the musty old man behind the glass with the bow tie and suspenders, who looked more each day like a stuffed and mounted chancellor from the university's founding. Did these people remain here in the darkness and dead of night like artifacts in a museum?

105

He went up the stairs to his favorite nook behind the stacks, and there she was, sitting in his chair. She looked the same, although features he once viewed as cute now seemed performatively feminine. She was too cute, stridently cute. She was mocking him with her cuteness. And she still hadn't cut her hair.

"Petra, what are you doing here? That's my seat."

"Gilmore, wow. You're kidding. I've always sat in this chair."

"Well, I'm the one who moved it here eight years ago."

"I've never seen you in it," she said. "We must have different schedules."

"I've been kind of a part-timer the last few years, as you know. I don't really have a study schedule anymore."

"If you want the chair, take it. I'll leave."

"Oh, I don't mind," he said. "You look good in it. Is that inappropriate, to say you look good in my chair?"

"I think it's okay. How are you, Gil?"

"I've been better, I've been worse."

"The answer that deflects all further inquiry."

"What about you?" he asked.

"I'm good. I'm finishing up my thesis. Well, it's done but it feels funny putting it that way."

"Rex mentioned something."

"It's gratifying to conclude working with him." They shared what felt like a fake laugh. It was certainly fake on his end. "And I want to thank you," she said. "I'm not sure I would have finished if you and I had continued together. I needed that tunnel-visionary space to work in."

"Happy to be of service. Let me know if there's anything else I can do." He turned to leave.

"Wait, you're okay, right? What's it been, three months?"

"I didn't mark the calendar."

"I don't see you or speak to you anymore."

106

"That's kind of how breakups work," he said.

"What I mean is I see you around the table at Slug-out and you look kind of lost, like maybe you've given up looking for direction."

"I've got a lot on my mind. I probably am lost, but it's not because of you. My directions were confused from the start, you might say."

"That makes me feel better, I think."

"Would you prefer me saying I miss our fights and your stupefying acumen for pettiness? I'm joking."

"No, I get it," she said. "It's just that I kind of miss us. I miss you, I mean. It's important you know that. I'm not saying I want to get back together. I just miss you is all."

"The whole idea of relationships is so old fashioned, isn't it?"

"How do you mean?" she asked.

"That two people manage to stay together anymore."

"Well, when two people are in love, they want to stay together, regardless of fights and pettiness, because each recognizes that the other is special."

"I can sing like James Taylor. That's pretty special."

"Who?" she asked.

"This guy whose records my dad used to play."

"That's not the kind of special I'm talking about."

"No, I'm not saying I *kind of* sound like James Taylor. I can sing exactly like him. I mean, if I began singing one of his songs right now, people would look around and wonder what James Taylor was doing in a university library. Provided they knew who he was, of course. If I were in the studio with him and he had to take a leak, I could fill in on one of the tracks. He's a damn fine singer, too, which means I'm also a damn fine singer."

"It would be more special if you could sing like yourself. And if we'd really been clicking, I probably would have known about this little talent of yours before now."

"I haven't had any reason to sing in a while."

She brought her hands together. "Okay, I was just saying that I kind of miss you, that's all."

"I think all I miss is having a regular sex partner so maybe your theory has legs."

She got up to face him at eye level. "And so do I. Enjoy the chair." She turned to leave.

"Wait." He put his hand on her shoulder. She turned her head but didn't meet his gaze. "I'm sorry. That didn't come out right. Of course I miss you. What I should have said is I have no lasting regrets about what you decided and at the moment I've got other things on my mind."

She placed an open hand on the side of his face, smiled weakly, and left.

He got back to the Koenig House after dark. As he circled the streets looking for parking, he saw a news crew filming on the entranceway steps. By the time he'd parked, the crew had returned to its wonky van. A number of residents were crowded into the high-ceilinged library off the foyer. There were familiar faces along with those he almost never saw because their work schedules kept them out during communal meals.

"What's going on?" Gil asked.

"Nick stabbed George," someone said.

"Who's Nick?"

The same somebody gave a description that didn't match anyone Gil could recall. He had known George, however, as a sour-faced man of indeterminate age, who struggled to pay his six-hundred-dollar monthly room and board. George had taken to assisting Claudia with the management of the place, busying himself with tasks he executed with misplaced authority.

"What's everyone doing here?" Gil asked.

"Second floor is taped off as a crime scene," someone else said.

108

"Until when?" Gil asked.

"Till the cops finish whatever they're doing. They've been up there since six."

Settled into chairs around the many dark wooden tables, some read magazines, others played cards. Most just sat there, stiffly exchanging fragments of the story: The two men had been boozing all afternoon when George decided that Nick had a drinking problem and began removing liquor bottles from his room. On one of George's return trips, Nick planted some kind of antique dagger in his stomach. George stumbled out of the room and down the third-floor hallway, clutching walls and smearing blood wherever he went. He was now in the hospital.

Gil sat in his usual company.

"Isn't it just like a couple knuckleheads to foul up an evening?" Robert said.

"To stab a guy over a bottle of gin," Brian added. "You got to wonder about that."

"It was a few bottles," Norm corrected.

"Oh, please." Brian said.

"Well," Norm said, "the guy kept coming into his room and taking his booze. Don't overlook the facts."

"One bottle, eight bottles. It doesn't make me feel better about hanging around down here," Brian said. "Those cops could be up there all night trying to figure out how blood drains out a man's gut."

"That right there," Gil said, "is the question at the center of this whole thing."

"Which? Norm asked.

"How long it takes a couple detectives to figure out whatever they're doing. My guess is till the end of their shift, which means I got to find a place to sleep."

The cheapest downtown hotels were only blocks away. After calling a few of the numbers, he quickly discovered he couldn't afford any of them. He found a parking space, put down the back seat of the Gemini, and tried dozing off. Curled up on such an uneven surface with a street lamp blazing through the back window made any kind of rest impossible. He clambered back into the driver's seat, started the car, and drove to the juvie high school. He could sleep on the floor of his classroom. The gate to the campus parking lot was open with an armed guard posted inside. Three shirtless probationaries were in the lot. One of them filmed as the others did skateboard tricks. Gil parked and headed toward the back entrance. The two on skateboards rode up to him, one on either side.

"You guys gonna shake me down?" Gil asked. "The guard's right there."

"Crowell, what are you doing here at night?" one asked.

"I left some papers in the classroom," he said. "Where have you been all week, Freddy?"

"Frankie. I was there today, but you weren't." He somehow managed to tie his sneaker while still rolling on the skateboard. "You got to show up when I'm there."

"Don't you boys have a curfew?"

"We had a sub today. He was crazy."

"Is that right?"

"He was telling us about communism and socialism and how he used to live in Haiti till they tried to poison him."

"That's no good."

"You could hardly understand what he was saying. Where were you today, Crowell?"

"Getting my skateboard fixed."

"Yeah, what kind of board you got?"

"I'm not sure. I found it in the trash." He set his backpack on the asphalt, sorted through the outer pocket for his room key.

"You should skate with us sometime," Frankie said. The other boy did a kick-flip, tossed his hair as he stuck the landing.

"And you should come to class more often or you'll be headed back to jail."

A guard at the back entrance let Gil inside. The hallway leading to his classroom was dark, but he could see a strip of light shining under the door. He unlocked and went in. Sitting on the teacher's desk with his navy-blue Dickies down around his ankles was one of the nighttime custodians. He was reading aloud from one of the classroom sets of novels while another man squatted between his legs. The fellow on the floor sprang up and clutched his chest. He walked around the room in circles, breathing deeply and exclaiming sotto voce. The seated custodian calmly pulled up his trousers.

"Excuse me, I didn't think anyone..." Gil began, before losing his words. He retreated into the darkened hallway.

The man on the receiving end of things spoke up. "It's all right. Come in."

"You sure about that?" Gil asked.

The other man stepped forward. He was tall and handsome with an anthemion headwrap directing his dreadlocks skyward like smoke from a chimney. "I'm Lee Banks," he said, holding out his hand. Gil hesitated a moment, looking down at the outstretched hand before accepting it. "I hope whatever you saw here tonight can remain with the three of us."

"Good idea," the other man said, buckling his trousers. He was much shorter than his friend, also quite handsome, with a trimmed beard and puppy dog eyes. "Brandon Terry." He also held out his hand.

"Lot of handshaking going on tonight," Gil said.

"And you are?" Brandon pointed the book he'd been reading at Gil.

"Gilmore Crowell. I teach in this classroom."

"Okay," Brandon said. He seemed to be processing this new fact while deciding his next move. "Well, Mr. Crowell, we were just finishing our shift. We work the three to eleven, so we were taking a break on a Friday night before leaving."

"I don't have any questions," Gil said. "Just came in to take care of a few things."

111

"So we cool then?" Brandon asked.

"Absolutely," Gil said. He looked down at his shoes. "Are you guys close to being done, though, so I can get to work?"

"Oh yeah, we're definitely done," Brandon said. He turned to face Lee, who had taken a seat at one of the student desks. He looked to be hyperventilating himself down from the shock of the intrusion.

Brandon cleared his throat. "I do want to say one more thing, though, if that's all right. This book you got here..." He waved it out in front of him. "...is a real fine novel."

"I wouldn't know," Gil said.

"You haven't read this book?" He held it up to Gil's face.

"No," Gil said. "It was just in the classroom when I started teaching here. I haven't read hardly any of these books."

"Oh, wow. This is a cold-blooded book, mister," Brandon said.

"I'll consider your recommendation," Gil said.

"Can I add something to that?" Lee asked, raising his hand from the student desk. Gil didn't answer. Lee got up and pulled a copy of another book from a class set on a shelf. "This one here is also a very sick book, my friend. It's a horror story. We read it, just a chapter each night while taking our break over there by your desk."

"Okay." Gil looked over at the desk as though it had betrayed him.

"It *is* a horror story," Brandon agreed, his eyes widening. "Except that you don't *think* it's a horror story when you begin reading it. Pretty good, huh?"

"I suppose so," Gil said. "I don't know."

"But you do see the problem with horror stories is that you know they're horror stories before you even start reading them," Brandon said, his voice rising. "Am I right?" He tapped

112

the book's binding along the heel of his hand. "Now, how is that supposed to scare you?"

"Like I said, I haven't thought much about it."

"Well, that's just it!" Brandon said, his face lighting up. "Nobody's thought much about it, especially the people making horror stories." He turned to Lee Banks and they shared a laugh. "How's a book supposed to scare you when you're *expecting it* to scare you?" he restated. "Come on now. That's why Halloween is a children's holiday."

"You got me there," Gil said, looking around the room. "It is kind of late though."

"That's a really good point," Lee said, "about Halloween. I never thought of it that way, but you're absolutely right."

"I'd prefer we discuss it another time," Gil said, "if possible."

"Oh, we don't have to discuss it at all," Brandon said. "Just *think about it* is all I'm saying. It's about expectation and anticipation."

"And revelation," Lee added.

"That's right," Brandon said, turning to face Lee. He pointed the book at him. "And revelation. Very good."

"All right guys," Gil said. "Is it okay if I just get some things done here so I can go to sleep tonight?"

Brandon Terry and Lee Banks exchanged looks, seemingly confused. "Sure, of course," Brandon said. "Like I said, we're done."

"You know," Gil said with a chuckle, "I was just thinking that you two could probably teach these classes better than I can. I'm supposed to be teaching science. They messed up my schedule when they gave me this job. I'm totally unqualified to teach English."

Brandon nodded thoughtfully, glanced over at Lee. He stepped forward and clapped a hand on Gil's shoulder. "Don't worry about it, brother. Your secret is safe with us."

113

21

Gil was still asleep, face down on a pile of old newspapers in the corner, when he received a single kick on the sole of his shoe. He awoke slowly, righted himself into a seated position.

"What's all this?" Bertram asked.

"All what?" Gil ran his fingers through his hair and beard.

"What are you doing here, Crowell?"

Gil rubbed his eyes. "I came to do some grading last night and must have fallen asleep. What time is it?"

"Are you drunk, Crowell?"

"Wait, why are you here?"

"Why am I here?"

"Yeah, I mean, isn't it Saturday?"

"I am here, Mr. Crowell, because I am the administrator in charge of plant facilities and the plant facilities do not take the weekends off. Further, while you are correct that it is a Saturday, you may not be aware that a group of Korean-

American senior citizens attend an ESL class in this very room on Saturday mornings."

"Old people take English lessons at a juvenile detention center?"

"Stay on point, Crowell. Have you been drinking or are you now on any drugs?"

"No, Mr. Bertram, I'm not on drugs. You want me to piss in that coffee cup?"

"Take it easy." He stretched out his hand, holding the index finger a few inches from Gil's nose bridge. "You see this finger?"

"The one in my face? Yeah, I see it."

"Follow the tip of this finger. Do not move your head. Just follow the tip with your eyes, understand?"

Bertram moved his hand and the tip of the raised index finger went up and down, side to side, then made a series of curls and swirls in front of Gil's bleary-eyed face. With his head perfectly still, Gil followed the moving fingertip. Suddenly Bertram outstretched all the fingers of the raised hand, spun them clockwise and contracted them into a fist. He snapped his hand away, then thrust it – open fingered – back toward Gil's face.

"What was that supposed to be?"

"*That,* Mr. Crowell, was a field test for drug abuse. It's not one-hundred percent accurate, but it's pretty close. Based on the results, I am directing you to meet in my office Monday morning, eight o'clock."

"Did I pass the test?"

"Ah, now a better question might be would a clean and sober person ask such a thing?" He raised his chin, evidently pleased with the retort. "And the answer, of course, is no. Such a person would not ask because such a person would not be drunk or on drugs."

"That's not it, Bertram. I'm trying to figure out where your head is at."

115

"We'll discuss it Monday morning."

"I have a class then."

"Ms. Mott will provide coverage. Now get out of here before the Koreans arrive."

Gil went back to the Koenig House to grab some things from his room before heading to Tijuana. The police had taken down the crime scene tape, restoring access to the rooms on the second floor. The one wall had already been repainted, and the bloody section of carpet replaced. It was shocking how efficiently everything had been put back to normal, except that one man was now in jail and the other was lying in a hospital bed. Somehow it all fit together. A violent act, a police inspection, a crackerjack cleanup, and life at the Koenig House went on as usual. The cop, the doctor, and the custodian all played their parts. Soon lawyers would be brought in to wrangle some sense out of it. He bore his pithy bewilderment down to the second-floor bathroom and, like an abject lower primate, failed to recognize himself in the mirror. His eyes, dried out from sleeping with contact lenses, were as bloodshot as ever. No wonder Bertram had interrogated him about drug use. The only question now was if he owed the mad dunce an explanation. He had his business card handy, but decided against calling him.

On his way out he passed the chapel. There was Norm, the old Buddhist, seated motionless in front of the altar. His shoulders were hunched forward, his head slightly bowed. Gil approached quietly from behind. He didn't want to disturb Norm; he only wanted to observe this ancient rite: quieting the mind, tuning into the rhythms of the breath, practicing presence. Maybe this was what he, too, needed.

"Mother of hell!"

Gil took a step forward. "What is it, Norm?"

Norm held up his laptop. "It's this website. It tells me to put in my password and when I put in my password it asks me if

116

I've forgotten my password. Well, I haven't forgotten my password, but I can't pay the bill because this thing won't recognize my password. I have to change the password just to pay the bill. Do you have any idea how much time I've spent entering and saving and changing and re-entering this password?"

Gil looked down at the poor man. "Life is mostly maintenance, Norm. You should know that by now."

"Maintenance? I'm talking about this goddamn password!"

22

"What's your name?" Gil asked, tracing with his fingertip the outline of the hummingbird tattoo.

"Ava," she said. "I already told you that."

"No, your real name."

"My real name?"

"Yeah."

"Is it going to help your studies any?"

"Probably not."

"Then don't worry about it."

She lay on the bed in a copper cuff bracelet and matching headband, nothing else. He was also naked and just stoned enough to imagine she was the second coming of an Aztec empress warrior. He rolled across the bed and picked up his notebook. She gently removed it, dropped it to the floor.

"I have work to do." He got up.

"What's all that in your notebook?"

"How much time have you got?"

"It's not about my time," she said. "It's about your money."

He pulled up his underwear. "Nothing too important. I haven't found what I'm looking for. What my professors are looking for, I should say."

"What are they looking for?"

"I'll know when I've found it."

She reached up to squeeze his face, stuck out her tongue.

He assumed the lecturer's posture. "Kidnapping, sex trafficking, exploitation of minors, psychological abuse, socially transmitted bejesus. Shall I continue?"

She took off the headband and shook out her hair. "I know a girl who was murdered, but it wasn't a client."

"Yeah, I read all about it." He picked his T-shirt off the floor.

"I thought you weren't sleeping with the girls."

"I've made an exception in your case." He pulled a pant leg of his jeans right side out. "You remind me of someone. I need to trace the connection."

"There's someone like me out there?" She bit her thumb. "I thought I had them all terminated."

"I don't remember her name, but she was from Veracruz."

"That's right, you were talking about Coatza that first time."

"Yeah, and you told a pretty good lie."

She laughed. "She was special, huh?"

"Yes."

118

"But not special enough to remember her name."

"No."

"You were in love?" She took her BlackBerry off the headboard, began fiddling with it.

"I never met her." He squared up to the mirror, pulled up his jeans. "She was a cover girl on a magazine."

"So, I'm the only one you're doing it with?"

He zipped and buttoned up, checked his posture with the gut relaxed, the gut pulled in. "I slept with another, but it was a mistake."

"You were stoned and thought she was me."

He shrugged into the mirror. "She said something and next thing I knew we were doing it." He turned his T-shirt right side out, put it on.

"But you're okay with this?" She leaned forward to meet his reflection.

"No, but I'm doing it anyway. See, I also lie. Mostly to myself."

She laughed again. "If I were you, I'd lie to myself, too."

He dropped back onto the bed. "I need to take my studies less seriously. Doctor's orders." She got on top of him. He reached up to massage her shoulders. They wrestled.

"If you need sex, get a girlfriend."

"I didn't say I needed sex." He rolled her over. "And I definitely don't need a girlfriend. Too often it's a problem."

"What's the problem?" She slid out of his hold, pinned him facedown with a forearm to the back of the neck.

He jolted up. "My conscience tells me if I sleep with a woman, I should care about her. Then I feel bad afterward. The whole arrangement messes me up."

"You must be joking." She grabbed his wrists and wrestled him back down to the mattress.

"No, I'm not. That's another problem. I'm too honest. With others, I mean." He slipped out of her grip, but she pitched

119

on top of him into a straddle. He flopped back, surrendered with outstretched arms.

"You really think I believe that?"

"I can live with it either way."

"Find a girl you like." She made a face dramatizing the obviousness of this solution.

"Maybe I will." He rolled her off. "I'm just not in a rush."

"Okay, but don't pretend you're being noble by sleeping with prostitutes. I mean, you're still really confused about this whole scene."

"Probably, but I've interviewed dozens in the past couple months. That's a start, and they all tell me the same things."

She perked up on the mattress to a seated position. "What do they say?"

"What do you want to know?"

"All of it." She leaned forward, beaming like a college freshman on the first day of class.

"You'd be surprised how many have had their little hearts broken by some guy in their village who knocked them up."

She bit her thumb again. "I wonder if I know the guy."

He hit her with a pillow. She grabbed it, stood up on the mattress and swung it overhead, smashing the ceiling lightbulb. Shards of glass rained down on his head and shoulders. She kneeled down on the mattress, and they looked at each other in the sudden dimness.

"Also, they need the money and don't particularly mind the work."

"I could have told you that."

"Another problem," he said. "Everything I've learned can be summed up in three pages. I need another two hundred. That's the reason I've taken up lying to myself. It's a diversion.

120

A part of me has stopped caring about this whole business." He got up from the mattress, brushed off the broken glass.

A steady knock came through the wall followed by muted wailing. Ava laughed.

"I know that *pendeja*. I even know the guy she's doing it with. They've been at it for years in that same room. She could buy this hotel with what he's spent on her. If I didn't know better, I'd say they were in love."

"Let's get out of here, have some lunch."

"Lunch?"

"A meal in the middle of the day."

"I don't eat lunch," she said.

"But you do eat. Call it whatever you want."

"I just started work." She minced into the bathroom, closed the door.

"Then we'll go someplace later." He stood on the other side of the door, waiting for a response.

"I don't know you well enough for that," she yelled out to him.

"All right."

"Hey, could you hand me those panties off the night stand?"

23

Gil sat in the space outside Bertram's office scanning notices on the corkboard: *The retirement party of Earl Parsons .... Think you've been sexually harassed? .... It is YOUR duty to report child abuse....* He lowered his face to its distorted reflection in

121

the chrome arm support of the chair. The eyes looked okay, but the emergence of a few gray hairs was something new.

The door was ajar and he could hear Bertram and Jeannie Lint, Esquire, bickering inside. "You do realize I'm an attorney, correct? And know what that means?"

"I know what an attorney is, Ms. Lint, if that's your question. I also know the sale of unauthorized food products –"

"Food products? You mean food? It's illegal to eat food around here?"

"It is illegal to sell it, Ms. Lint, but you already know that. You also know that we have a contract through Correction and Rehabilitation's meal program, and that students on campus between the hours of eight and three –"

"That prison food you're serving? Are you kidding me? It's poison...."

It went on like that, the one voice rising with indignation, the other steady with appeals to reason until the moment Jeannie Lint swung the door open and steamed past in a rage. Bertram appeared in the doorway, waved Gil in.

"Mr. Crowell." It was a statement of fact, not a greeting. "Would you like to sit down?"

"That's all right, Mr. Bertram. Hopefully I won't be here long. I just want to explain what happened the other morning. I came in at night to do some grading –"

"I've memorialized the incident, Crowell, and would rather not revisit it now. I've asked you here for another reason." The bulging neck and face were redder than ever. Gil noticed two bristling whiskers that missed the morning shave. From the shadow of a nostril, they pointed at him.

"Okay, but I don't do drugs, Mr. Bertram, and I'd like to make that clear. And even if I did do them, I would never do them here or show up in any kind of –"

"The matter now before us concerns Toby Mackey, a probationary of yours in the tenth grade." Bertram took a sheet of paper off his desk.

122

"What about him?" Gil asked.

"I received a phone call from a Mrs. Wilmington, Toby's foster mother. In the course of that conversation she revealed a disturbing event that allegedly took place in your classroom."

"I think I know what you're talking about."

"Would you like to tell your version?" Bertram asked.

"I think I'll listen to yours first."

"This Mrs. Wilmington stated that another student in the class, a resident by the name of Jimmy Pittman, pulled down Mackey's pants while he was standing at the white board completing one of your grammar exercises or whatever. Does that sound familiar?"

"Something like that."

"When Mackey complained, you told him, quote, that he'd been asking for it. Is that correct?"

"Not quite. I said it wouldn't have happened if he'd been wearing a belt rather than going around with falling down pants."

"Falling down pants? He's a sagger, is that what you're saying?"

"He wears his pants in that urban style, yes."

"And, according to you, that means he's inviting others to pull his pants down? And what else?"

"What else what?"

"Why do you think he wants his pants pulled down? I need to hear you say it."

"I only meant that it could have been avoided."

Bertram circled around from behind his desk, intently studying the sheet of paper in his hand. "Mr. Crowell, I have to be sure I understand your side of this. You claimed Toby Mackey was asking to have his pants pulled down. We've established that. Did you imagine he enjoyed this experience?"

"Not at all."

"Did *you* enjoy it?"

"What?"

"Did it please you to see this Pittman character pull down Mackey's pants is my question."

"Of course not."

Bertram gave one of his knowing smiles. "But you didn't stop it, did you? And you didn't report it either."

"I simply meant by my statement that both boys played a role –"

"Do you think Toby Mackey enjoys having his pants pulled down, yes or no?"

Gil shifted his stance. He was thinking about that seat he'd passed up. "I wouldn't know, but I haven't thought much about it either."

"You wouldn't know," Bertram repeated. "But you know *you* don't enjoy it, right?"

"I already said that, yes."

"I just want to be absolutely sure, Crowell, because this is not a normal high school, as you know. This is a *special* high school for *special* students in *special* circumstances. Understand? These probationaries come from very different backgrounds. They're not like our resident students. Most of them are just punks, if I may be frank. Shoplifters, check-forgers, dope dealers. Something else you know nothing about, right?" He winked. "Our resident students are hardened cases. They need our best care. And they must be watched very carefully around these probationaries, get it?" He leaned back, pelvis thrust forward, directing his eyes to the far corner of the ceiling. "Let me ask you something else, Crowell, and I want you to think very hard before answering. Do you think there are grown men who derive pleasure from seeing boys pull one another's pants down, and if so, do such men belong in a correctional facility?"

"Excuse me?"

"You heard me, Crowell."

124

Gil had heard him, but he could not answer. The air in the room had begun to whiten as though streams of fibrous fog were descending from the ceiling vents. The room itself began to gently spin.

"Mr. Crowell?"

The floor fell away and Bertram evaporated into the mist. The only thing that remained visible through the thickening whiteness was the illuminated photo monitor on the wall behind Bertram's desk. Gil steadied his gaze upon it as though it were the only fixed point of reference available, a means by which to stabilize his senses. The photos continued to change every few seconds as before, just as they did all day and perhaps into the night.

"Mr. Crowell?"

The photo monitor became larger, warping and enveloping the room. Gil found himself standing within the various changing scenes of each photograph. One photo seemed to channel him specifically. It showed a number of teachers seated around a room. Gil was among them, off to the side. The teachers were talking, reading, goofing around on laptops and smartphones. One slept in a chair with his head against the wall, a magazine folded over his face. Another ate a sandwich. Gil could not tell where they were but he could easily discern it was a wonderful place to be.

"Teacher jail," one of them said with a smirk. "We're in teacher jail." He laughed, and the other teachers joined in the laughter. They seemed to be laughing both with Gil and at him. It was the laughter of a richly shared bliss. Gil laughed, too, and then – with the timed change to the next photo – everything snapped back to reality.

"Mr. Crowell, I asked you a question. Are you on drugs again?"

Gil blinked, inspected his open hands. "Sorry, what was the question?"

"Are you on something now? It seems to me that you are."

"No, the one before that."

"Why don't you sit down."

"I'm all right, Mr. Bertram. It's just – Wasn't there a question about perverts or something?"

"I think that's enough for today, Crowell. I have some district guidelines and memoranda I'd like you to look over when you're able. I'll place them with the disciplinary report in your mailbox. Is there anything else? Anything you'd like to ask me?"

Gil pointed to the photo monitor. "Yeah, where can I get one of those?"

"All right, listen to me. Are you listening? Watch yourself going forward. You're on very thin ice, sir. Try to remember where you work." Bertram jutted out his chin and leaned his head toward the door.

24

The long wooden tables of the Koenig House refectory were filled with wizened old men. Gil looked down at his saucer of processed turkey, scoop of instant potato, and dollop of cranberry gel. Was there anything to be thankful for?

The website continued to go nowhere. He comforted himself that he'd meant well by it, that he'd wanted to help the sex workers and give something back to their community. Those weren't his principal aims, of course, but viewed alongside free and easy access to the working girls, they meant win-win opportunities for everyone. If only the girls had shared in that foggy vision. They hadn't, in part, from a lack of imagination over the potential of cyberspace to make clever people rich. To them it was a means of communication: a gateway to celebrity gossip, cute animal videos, and inspiring messages enwreathed in glittery script. If such things provided relief from their dreary lives, who was he to get in the way? Rule number one, never interfere with the culture. The thing to do now was slog through the scene as before. Pay the girls for their time. Go broke perhaps, but at least get the interviews. Write the dissertation, as the aristocratic hippie psychiatrist had advised, and be done with it.

The fall semester ended as it began, with parent-teacher conferences on Thursday night. He went to a nearby diner at the end of the school day to get something to eat before the sessions. As he jingled through the door, some teachers and probation officers made eye contact and looked away. Were they purposefully ignoring him or not yet aware he was one of them? He took a seat in a far corner booth, feeling a bit sorry no one had waved him over, yet also grateful he wouldn't have to make small talk. He didn't so much want their company as to be respectfully acknowledged. He recalled a literary term from Frinkle's guide he'd recently taught the teen convicts: *ambivalent. The teacher felt ambivalent about eating alone.*

A spoon sailed through the air, clattering onto his tabletop. He turned toward the assailant, a chubby toddler with curly black hair. The little boy made eye contact with Gil and held it. He seemed to be assessing if Gil had the guts to return fire. The weary mother got up and removed the projectile.

127

A waiter arrived. Handsome and cool, he inspired the notion that he wasn't really waiting tables but rather sleepwalking through a working-class nightmare till his acting career got off the ground.

"I'll have the Asian pear salad," Gil said, handing back the menu.

"We don't have anything like that."

"Fine, give me an onion sandwich."

"An onion sandwich?"

"Two pieces of bread with a couple slices of onion in the middle. If the cook's feeling reckless, he can throw a little mustard in there."

"Wheat, white, sourdough, or rye?"

"Sourdough, I guess."

"Sourdough?" The waiter's raised eyebrow conveyed doubt over that selection. If it had been a multiple-choice question, *sourdough* would have been the primary distractor. He braved the order and skulked off.

The toddler, now marching in place on the milk-spattered booster seat, started making high-pitched growling noises. He seemed sure he was communicating something of value. The sounds, though phonically meaningless, were complex in their phrasing. Gil figured it out. It wasn't language; it was some kind of primitive music. Not quite song, but definitely music. The toddler conducted the sounds by waving his spoon high in the air. He seemed keenly aware that he was really improvising now.

"All right, man!" Gil said.

The toddler fell silent and went back to eyeballing Gil. The mother reseated her child and tried directing his attention to the goodness of the food before him. The moody prodigy would have none of that. He held his eyes steadily on Gil and again pitched the spoon, this time striking him in the ear. It was a remarkable throw because of both the angle of the high chair and the child's confinement within it. He'd had to throw the

128

spoon across his body like a third baseman taking out a runner at first.

"Pretty good stuff," Gil said. He returned the spoon to the unamused mother.

"Please don't encourage him," she said. "He has a behavioral disorder."

"I think Cab Calloway had the same condition."

"Who?" She wiped the toddler's face.

"My cellmate in prison."

He went back to his classroom. Three parents came in all at once, each wearing a different tragic expression. Their delinquent offspring tagged alongside them. As probation officers rubber-necked from the open doorway, a resident student named Hector Flores and his mother sat down at Gil's desk. Gil opened up the online gradebook and went over the dismal scores. Some talk went back and forth over Hector's indifference to learning and lack of motivation. Then came the moment of truth.

"What do you recommend?" the mother asked in Spanish.

"When they release him in two weeks, throw out all his computer toys and lock him in a closet for three days."

"Lock him in a closet?"

"For three days."

Mrs. Flores began breathing unsteadily, seeming to have lost the ability to speak. Hector looked on, as though unsure what he was witnessing.

Mr. Coche, father of probationary student Kim Coche, was next.

"Her grades are excellent, Mr. Coche, and she's a well-mannered girl, but her style of dress begs for improvement."

"How do you mean exactly?"

"I'm not sure exactly, but this is a correctional high school, not the Bunny Ranch, know what I mean?"

"No, I don't."

"Check out their website. You can thank me later."

Next was Mrs. Wilmington, foster mother of Toby Mackey.

"Mrs. Wilmington, I'm guessing you're here to discuss Toby's wardrobe malfunction the other day."

"That's not how I'd put it," she said, "but yes. I'd like to know what you think happened."

"What I think happened? Okay, not a good start. What I *think happened* is some kid pulled your son's pants down."

"My concern is how you handled it. According to Toby, you did nothing to discipline the other boy and joined the class as they laughed over it."

He sat up straight. "That's not right. I may have smiled but I never laughed. And let's get something else straight while we're all here. He walks around with his pants falling down, showing off his underwear. The other students just got a nice view of the bottom half of his boxers, which – no surprise – was made of the same material as the top half! At no time was his virgin behind ever bared. I stand by my original statement. He was asking for it. Now, go take it to your minister or your therapist or your minister's therapist, but if you really want to get me fired talk to the principal, though I should warn you in advance you'll be doing me the biggest favor of my life."

"The biggest favor of your life?"

"Okay, that was a bit of an exaggeration. Just think hard on your next course of action is all I'm saying. My advice is to forget the whole thing and go buy yourself a nice bottle of wine. Next!"

25

Philippe De Goeuf was pretty famous as French-Canadian academics go. Lured away from McGill University by balmy weather and two hundred thousand a year, he also enjoyed steady profits from *The Civilized Savage,* a required text in cultural anthro courses throughout the academic world. Soon after his transplant to Los Angeles, he married the beautiful television broadcaster, Arianna Routledge. Nine months later, the couple welcomed twin apricot poodles into their home.

As a first-year grad student, Gil had taken De Goeuf's course on pre-Columbian intellectual property. It didn't go too well. Anytime he went looking for De Goeuf during office hours, some hot teaching assistant would be there standing guard, it seemed, to keep students out. The great man was inaccessible, that was the only word for it. He did not take questions in class, did not answer emails, did not make eye contact in the hallways. He just appeared on the lecture hall stage with a microphone wrapped around his head, voice booming through the speakers like the Wizard of Oz giving a TED Talk. One time Gil had stood behind him in line at Caf-Fiend. Meaning to introduce himself, he tapped the great man on the shoulder. De Goeuf turned around but seemed not to notice Gil standing there.

Every December, De Goeuf and his celebrated wife threw a winter solstice gala at their Palisades home. Gil had never gone, but Bagchi strongly encouraged him to attend this year having heard De Goeuf would be sitting on Gil's dissertation committee. Within the gated entranceway, beyond the circular drive and landscaped front lawns, stood two white party tents. Inside one, a salsa band performed on a raised stage while people at round banquet tables feasted on roast pork. The other tent contained a wet bar, salsa dancers, and some decorative woodwork of the Algonquin people with whom De Goeuf claimed to share one-sixteenth of his ancestry. Gil stood just inside the second tent striving, like a good ethnographer, to remain detached from the scene.

"Why, you miserable fraud," a voice behind him whispered. Gil turned around. It was Wilson James, Srinivas Chakrabarti, and Ebby: the three-headed monster.

"Let the insults fly, gentlemen." Gil looked past them and out the tent. "I'd expect nothing less in such surroundings."

"Here's a better idea," Ebby said, handing him a cold bottled beverage. "These were micro-brewed in Nepal at fifteen thousand feet. If you pound two of them fast enough, it'll change your cranial capacity."

A moment later Rex came into the tent. Shadowing him was an apple-faced young woman in a sun dress and matching hat. "Gil, I'd like you to meet Shelly Elkington. She's a linguistics student from Britain paying her way through school as a gentleman escort. Isn't that resourceful? Shelly, Gil hangs out with prostitutes in Tijuana."

"Is that right?" she asked.

"It beats working for a living," Gil said, taking her hand, "though I also do that."

"Where's the host?" Rex asked. "Hiding in the shadows like Gatsby waiting to club some babe over the head?"

"Did that happen in The Great Gatsby?" Ebby asked. "I don't remember."

"Not in my version," Srinivas said, "but I read it in Bengali."

"The drunken floozy he was always stalking," Rex clarified. "Gil, you teach high school English. What was the name of that whore?"

"Sex worker," Gil said. "She was a sex worker."

"You're an English teacher?" Shelly asked. "My mother teaches English in Manchester."

132

"Ah, right from the source," Gil said. "Yes to your question, though at the moment I'm trying to get myself fired, so that complicates things a bit."

"Trying to get yourself fired?" she asked. "Why is that?"

"I can't reach the students, the administration gives me the creeps, and the pay sucks. Also, I'm finishing my dissertation." He tried smiling.

"Gil's not very good with people," Ebby said.

"Or managing his time," Srinivas added.

"Excuse me a moment." She walked off.

"There she goes," Ebby said. "I predict she doesn't return."

"No, she's looking for clients," Wilson said.

"Or a bathroom," Srinivas said, "in which case, there's still hope."

"You need hope to approach a call girl?" Wilson asked. "No, that sounds right."

"She was cute, though, wasn't she?" Ebby said.

"She's still cute," Wilson said. "She's just not here anymore."

It started to rain, and people trotted like circus ponies into the tents.

"Gil, how are you?" It was Brinda Bagchi. With what looked like hastily applied make up, dampened flat hair, and a new facial twitch, she didn't look too happy to be there. "I was hoping to find you."

"Hello, Brinda. I was hoping to find you, too, considering you told me to be here."

"Let's go see Phil."

"Phil?"

"It wouldn't hurt to meet him before your dissertation. That's the point of this, isn't it?"

"Sure, it's just that I almost met Phil once before and it didn't go too well."

133

"Meaning?"

"I think he mistook me for some dog shit he'd stepped in."

"Come on," she said, and charged off into the downpour.

Just as they were preparing to head through the patio door of the main house, the great man was coming out, umbrella in one hand, leash to a poodle in the other.

"Phil, I'd like you to meet my student, Gilmore Crowell," Bagchi said. "He's just finishing up his dissertation on Zona Norte, the red-light district of Tijuana."

De Goeuf scowled into the rain, as though affronted by some quality of its downfall.

"I took your class several years ago," Gil said. "You may not recall."

"Good guess. Did you buy my book?"

"It was required, so yes."

"New or used?"

"I'm pretty sure I don't remember," Gil said. "It was a great book, though. And a great class. And this is a great dog you have here, too. Hey, boy."

The rain fell harder.

"This dog is deaf," De Goeuf said. "You'll have to really squat down if you want to talk to him." He demonstrated. "Who's a good Gramsci?"

"He seems to be responding well to you," Brinda said, her voice raised above the pounding rain.

"He reads lips," De Goeuf shouted. "Come on down, uh, what's your name again?"

Gil bent over. "How are you, Gramsci?"

"No, no," De Goeuf instructed. "Really get down where he can see your face."

Gil kneeled into the rain-soaked sod.

"Now tell him what a good boy he is."

"You're a good boy, Gramsci."

134

The dog wagged his tail.

"See there?" De Goeuf said.

"Yeah, that's terrific," Gil said. "So how long did it take you to, uh…."

"Teach him to read lips?" De Goeuf asked.

"Yeah."

"I was being facetious. He can't read lips. While dogs attach significance to certain sounds, they have no sense of language, per se. As a graduate student in anthropology, you should know that. He just likes it when people get down on his level."

Gil got back up, one foot at a time, brushed some debris off his waterlogged jeans. "Yeah, that makes more sense."

"Our neighbor has a Persian cat that speaks Farsi, though, if you'd like to meet her."

De Goeuf and Bagchi erupted in laughter and walked off with the great man's deaf dog.

26

The sun broke through, lighting up the afternoon sky. Gil noticed handbills in the picture window of Luscious Loins, the Hollywood sex shop, and pulled over to ask about posting one for the website. He'd only been to a sex shop once before, back in his college days. Within minutes, he and his roommate were kicked out for having a dildo fight.

A young pony-tailed woman greeted him. "Need any assistance?" She rocked forward on the balls of her feet. A brief conversation followed, in which she explained that everything in the window was community outreach, not business; she

135

couldn't help him. He headed for the exit. "We have a Christmas special right now on all butt plugs, strap-ons, and anal beads," she called after him.

"What?"

"All butt plugs, strap-ons, and anal beads are half off through the holidays."

"I was kind of hoping you wouldn't repeat it, but okay. No, I'm pretty well stocked up at the moment."

Coming out, he brushed past a man in dark glasses who gave him a side-glance, then spun around and took him by the shoulder.

"Hey, how are you?" The man took off his glasses.

"Dr. Bollerup? How odd to see you here."

"I'm well, thank you." He stepped back and gave Gil the once over, seeming to delight in the sight of him. "It's Gabriel, isn't it?"

"Gilmore Crowell." In that moment, a wave of nausea surged up from Gil's stomach to his mouth and back down again. It must have been the roast pig at De Goeuf's. He thought of charging back into Luscious Loins to use the bathroom but wanted to ditch Bollerup.

"My mistress and I exchange gag gifts each anniversary of the messiah's birth. I thought what better place to find them? And what are you doing here or shouldn't I ask?"

"I'm here by mistake. I thought this was a Walgreens." The nausea took another vicious turn. "I guess my GPS needs a tune-up."

Bollerup affected a laugh. "And how is your condition now, Gilmore? Were you able to access any of my recommendations?"

"Yes, I was able to access them and at the moment I'm hoping to access a bathroom. Sorry to cut this short."

"Not at all. I wouldn't be human if I didn't understand. Be well, won't you?"

136

Gil got to the McDonalds across the street just in time, but the only stall was occupied. Meanwhile, the illness traveled south. He shuffled from foot to foot, alternately tightening his stomach and sphincter muscles, clenching his fists, beating at his rain-soaked thighs. A minute stretched to three, then five. He got down on one knee to peer under the stall. A transient was on the toilet sorting through newspapers, plastic bags, and other rubbish. The sour stench of homelessness knocked Gil back. He almost heaved right there on the floor but managed to get back on his feet. He tapped the stall door.

"Hurry up please."

No reply. A moment later the door swung open.

"What'd you say?"

"Let's go. It's a toilet, not a homeless shelter."

The transient took a step forward. Thinking he was leaving, Gil tried to push past, but the man blocked his way with an outstretched arm. "I'm not done in there, mister. And what do you know about homeless shelters?"

"Some of my best friends are homeless," Gil said. "Now please get out of the way. It's coming out both ends."

Voices rose. A scuffle ensued. In walked a uniformed employee with broom in hand. "You two are going to have to leave," he said, holding the broom out in front of him like a weapon.

"You're joking, right?" Gil asked. "It's an emergency. I've been waiting for the stall."

"No fighting and restrooms are for customers only. There's a sign on the door."

"A sign?" Gil reached into his pocket. "Here's two dollars. Go buy yourself a coke."

"It doesn't work that way."

"Oh, really? You want me to shit in that urinal? Look, I'll buy whatever you want. In fact, I'll buy it for *him*. Does that work for everyone? Would that officially enlist me as one of your paying customers or do I have to fill out a form?"

137

"Everyone out," the broom wielder stated, "or I'll bring in the manager."

"Oh, so you're not even the manager?" Gil tossed his arms in disbelief.

"I'm the assistant manager in training, sir. Now get out."

"No, it's all right," the transient said. "He can use it now. I'm done."

"No, it is not all right," the assistant manager in training said. "This is a family restaurant. You can't be fighting in here. Everybody out. Let's go."

"A family restaurant?" Gil said. "For a family of vermin perhaps. May you spend the rest of your career sweeping this restroom, mister assistant manager in training. May you never become assistant manager! Do you hear me?"

"Come on," the transient said, gently steering Gil from behind. "Let's take it outside. I know a place where you can throw up and shit."

Another man entered the restroom, nodded in passing, and went into the open stall.

27

Gil sat at his desk in the empty classroom eating a mixed-green salad, his stomach still too queasy for anything heavier. In case of another emergency, the door remained open for easy escape. The expected fallout from parent-teacher conferences hadn't materialized. He couldn't grasp why, having gone out of his way to insult over a dozen parents. Maybe the administration was still consulting with the union or working out the transfer to teacher jail. Every organization had its way of confounding the simplest process. He recalled to what lengths the police had gone to bury the stolen-Gemini report.

One of the resident students shuffled himself into the classroom. He was eating a burrito.

"Crowell, you got a minute?"

"How'd you get here?" Gil asked.

"The door is open."

"Yeah, I can see the door is open. I'm the one who opened it. Aren't you supposed to be in the cafeteria or something?"

"I told one of the guards I needed to talk to you. He's waiting in the hall."

Gil took another bite of salad. "All right, what is it?"

"I don't know how to say this except to just come right out and say it."

"That usually works."

The student pulled a chair over to Gil's desk and sat down. "I've got girl problems."

"What are you talking about? You're in jail."

The student looked up at the ceiling, shook his head. He appeared to be holding back tears. "Yeah, and this girl's probationary. I don't feel like I measure up, know what I mean, to her standards."

"What standards?" Gil asked. "She's a juvenile delinquent."

"I don't know, but my lawyer tells me I'm stuck here for the next two months. I just feel like such a loser, know what I mean?"

Gil looked the kid over. Had a fast track to teacher jail suddenly opened before his eyes? Sometimes the universe worked that way. There were a number of things he could say to completely blow the kid's mind, send him racing off to the administration with a vengeance. No, it would never work out. In his vulnerable state, the student obviously trusted him.

139

Anything Gil said, however perverse, would be taken in earnest. He decided to play it straight.

"Most guys feel like losers at some point in life, kid. It's actually pretty normal. It means you know you're better than your current situation, that's all. You messed up, so what? What did you do, rob someone? Steal a car?"

"Shot my stepfather."

"Well, that's a little different."

"No, he's all right. It was a shot gun and the pellets just sprayed –"

"Yeah, I get it. But you learned your lesson, right? I mean, you know you can't go around shooting people and get anywhere with this girl, correct?"

"It won't happen again."

"What's up with the girl?"

"It's Angela Ochoa."

"You like her, huh?"

"Yeah, and I can't do anything about it. That's the thing. They have all the hard cases separated from the probes, know what I mean? I can't talk to her, can't go anywhere near her. She'll probably finish her probation without even knowing I exist."

Gil inspected a salad dressing stain on his shirt, set the empty bowl aside. "Let me tell you what's really going on, uh… What did you say your name was again?"

"Daniel."

"Okay, Daniel. Look, this whole thing has nothing to do with Amber Alonso or whatever her name is."

"Angela Ochoa."

"All right, listen. Your real problem is that you let yourself down. You know you're better than this place and you feel bad about being here. It's completely natural. You look at the walls, and it's like they're closing in on you a bit more every day. At night, you lie awake in bed and can't quite believe your life has come to this because you know you

140

deserve better. But that part of you that feels like a loser is not a loser because real losers never feel like losers. They're almost always just big whiny assholes. You'll be out of here on probation in a couple months and be able to work on your game a little more. And if she leaves this place before you, who cares? She'll still be around. It's not like she's moving to China."

"And how do I do that?"

"Do what?"

"Work on my game. How do I get her to like me?"

"You'll just have to get to know her and find out what she likes and listen to her when she talks about that stuff. Over time, she'll figure out that you like her. It's not that complicated, dude, but there's no guarantees. Just be thoughtful and kind and if that's not good enough then fuck her. I mean, forget her. But if she's nice and you play your cards right you've got a good shot, and that's all any guy ever gets. Now cheer up and get out of here. I've got a stomach ache."

"All right, Crowell. Thanks." The student leaned forward in his chair and the two suffered through an unbearably awkward hug. The kid got to his feet and headed toward the doorway.

"Oh, and, hey," Gil called after him.

"Yeah?"

"Down the road, if she ever says anything like this isn't a relationship or she doesn't think of you as her boyfriend or…. Ah, never mind."

28

The high school's winter break didn't coincide with the university's, but that didn't matter. Gil hadn't taken a class for credit in years. For three weeks he didn't have to bear the students, suffer the administration, or smile at the guards as he passed them in the hallway. No pointless faculty meetings, no last-minute lesson plans, no soul-crushing assignments to grade. He spent the first eleven days holed up in his room staring down a computer screen. The sun would come through the window each morning and die off by late afternoon. He sat at his desk, notes at hand, and banged away on the laptop, getting up only for bathroom breaks and microwave popcorn.

On three occasions old men rapped on his door like mythical messengers. First Norm, then Robert, then Brian. Each time Gil answered the sudden brightness of the hallway startled him like oncoming headlights in a dream. The hours passed, and he retained only the vaguest memory of the visitors and no clear idea why they'd come. His actual dreams were of clawing through the laptop keyboard for an insight, just out of reach.

One night the dumpster cat sprang into view, oblivious to the importance of Gil's work. It got between him and the desk, circled his lap several times as though deciding whether to plant itself there. To Gil's mind – distorted as it was by sleep deprivation and horniness – the feline's movements were unmistakably sexual. The cat raised its hind quarters in the air and tossed its tail with backward glances. The rise and fall of its paws on Gil's lap caused him to stiffen. As he ushered the dirty beast to the floor, an accidental brush of the touchpad caused his website to take over the screen. One of the eleven girls he'd enlisted popped up. He mechanically rubbed one out. The cat looked on in disgust.

On the twelfth day of vacation, he took the train to Old Town San Diego and rode the trolley to the border. He'd be there a week – too much time to pay for parking – so the Gemini stayed in LA. It was the day after Christmas, and most of the working girls had gone home for the holidays. He went to his favorite coffee shop. The stocky nursing student was planted out front. She looked good in her plastic heels and denim mini skirt, leaning up against the wall with another book in hand.

"What are you reading this time?" he asked.

"What's that?"

"I bought you a cup of coffee a while back. You were reading a book about sexual awakening or something. You had some pretty strong opinions about it."

"Oh right, the pornographer."

"Anthropologist."

She held the paperback out between them like a dead rat. "I'm just reading this to pass the time. It also sucks but in a completely original way."

"What's the problem now?"

"It's about these two teenagers with AIDS. They're supposed to be in love, but it's totally unbelievable. They're both beautiful and brilliant and even though they're only sixteen years old, they speak with the sophistication of a couple West End playwrights."

"West End playwrights?"

"That's right, you're stupid. I forgot. What are you doing here? You want to fuck or buy me another cup of coffee?"

He couldn't help himself. "Let's start with a fuck and see if it leads anywhere."

It was like twenty minutes of murder. Gil consented when she asked him to try something new. It involved moving the bed to the bathroom doorway, her doing a handstand, and him holding onto the bathroom sink for balance. She called it the flying wheelbarrow. Things were rocking and rolling pretty

143

well until he got the hiccups and lost his grip. On the descent, he smashed one cheekbone on the sink edge, the other on the bathroom floor. They skipped the coffee. He went over to a bench in front of the Metropolitan Cathedral and lay down on the iron slats. A woman from the congregation approached with religious pamphlets but when she got a good look at both his black eyes she went the other way. Some people aren't ready for salvation.

29

He lay in the lopsided bed, stroking Ava's long black hair, the strains of Ramón Ayala coming up from a car stereo in the street. A coil poked through the wasted mattress. He noted the room was not much different from the one he rented at the Koenig House, wondered about the significance of that, and dozed off.

"Whatever you're doing isn't anthropology. You know that, right?" She straightened herself up against the headboard.

He opened his eyes. "Did you say something?"

"You can't just talk to a bunch of girls and think it means anything." She drew her face to his. "And what happened to your eyes?"

"I had an accident. Yes, I realize I'm not quite where I need to be."

"That's putting it mildly."

"Where's all this coming from?" he asked.

"I know a little bit, enough to see that you're doing things wrong. Hand me those panties, would you? You're supposed to be studying a community. And that bra over there. No, on the floor."

"Well, of course you're right." He rolled over to pick up the bra. "It's just that I'm under some real pressure to finish up. I'm not able to get things done the way I once thought was possible. I don't know what –"

"Here, hook this for me," she said. "You're not seeing the whole –"

"I'm working on that," he said, cutting her off. "I guess you took an anthropology course or read a book or something."

"I went to junior college for a few semesters back in El Paso. They messed up my schedule one year and I had to sit through this anthro course for a week to keep my financial aid. It wasn't a complete waste of time. They taught us all about culture in those first few classes so...."

"Lucky me." He remained in bed, stared at the wall.

"That's how I know you're doing it wrong." She stepped into her mini skirt. "Aren't you going to get dressed?"

"Yeah, I'm just a bit dumbfounded at the moment. I mean, if you can see through my act, then maybe my dissertation committee –"

"You're not connecting to anything."

"Yes, I get it. It's been my problem for a while now. I was making some inroads a few years back, but –"

"Well, if you were, then you'd know about places where girls gather and you could break into that. Over time, it would lead somewhere."

"You mean a brothel."

"Or a house where a bunch of them split the rent."

He laughed. "That's a brothel."

"No, it's a place where they live. No madam, no pimp, no agency. And they don't meet the clients there."

"I can hardly get these girls to talk to me when I pay them. How am I supposed to get into their homes?"

"Come to my place." She faced the mirror, began applying makeup.

"You won't have lunch with me and now you're asking me to move in?"

"They're not the same thing, are they? And you wouldn't be moving in." She turned her head from side to side for the mirror, puckered the lipstick around.

"Explain."

"How much vacation do you have left?"

"Seven days."

"Okay, so a week. If you pay next month's rent, you can stay with us till you go back. No sex, though. I mean, it's not included." She turned from the mirror to give him a look.

"How much is the rent?"

"Five-thousand pesos, split four ways."

"So, about three-hundred dollars. I couldn't pay till next month, though."

"Good, that's when it's due." She dabbed at her cheeks.

"And the other girls would be okay with this?"

"Sure, why not? There's a room in the garage. You can stay there. It's small but there's a bathroom and shower. Come into the house whenever you need to. Use the kitchen. Observe the community."

"And why are you offering this?"

"Because I think you need help." She pinched his bruised cheek. "It looks like it, too."

The knock came on the door.

30

The familiar morning racket in the streets got him up early. He skipped breakfast and gathered up his things, meaning to follow up on Ava's offer while it was still fresh in everyone's mind. The taxi-to-tourist ratio in Zona Norte made it a rider's market. If he walked up any street, there'd be three of them backing against traffic to pick him up. He had Ava's address in hand and caught a cab at Revolución and Third. The driver looked about twelve years old.

"I just got this job," he said in Spanish. "Took over for a guy with cancer of the foot. How you like that? What was the one foot doing that the other wasn't?"

"Maybe stepping on that gas pedal," Gil said.

"What the hell," the driver said, laughing.

"Keep your eye on the road, amigo. I don't mind you getting in an accident, just not on my time."

The driver took those as possibly the funniest words ever spoken, his body unfit to contain the laughter it expelled. "You got places to go, right?" he choked through guffaws.

"Yeah, not now. Maybe another day."

More spirited laughter. They wound up in the hills, the old taxi's engine sputtering against the strain of the ascent. Ava's house was just below the landmark Mexican flag that waves to approaching tourists still miles from the border. The air was clearer than in Zona Norte. A strong breeze rustled some trash in the street. He went up to the door and knocked. No answer. Eleven in the morning. The girls were likely sleeping off their late-night shifts. He went around back into the little garage house Ava had rented him for the week. A nine-by-eleven-foot space, he estimated. It was crowded by a dusty couch, plastic storage containers, wooden crates overflowing with grime-coated gardening tools and electric cords, a four-

147

drawer file cabinet, nine mismatched chairs in a rickety stack, a stepladder, and some kind of outmoded aerobics device. From the only uncluttered wall space, a faded poster of the late screen star María Félix glared at the disarray. Anyone sitting on the old couch was forced to endure her looming cross-eyed visage. He went through a door to the adjoining cinderblock bathroom. An old floater in the toilet knocked him back a step. The sight was almost worse than the smell. He tried flushing it down but there was no water in the tank.

Back in the little room he flopped down on the couch. *I must still believe in this work. It must continue to mean something because I keep coming back to it.* His mind drifted to the tropical fish store on La Brea Avenue that he would stop into on his way home from grade school. It didn't seem strange to Gil at the time, but the old Korean man who ran the place actually lived in the office space by the loading dock. Gil couldn't have known at that young age that the old man wasn't bringing in any money. He only understood the absence of customers as part of the magical tranquility of the place amid the glow of fish tanks and the burble of so many air pumps. The atmosphere struck him as ideal for decompressing after the day's tiresome lessons. It wasn't until many years later that he'd had sense to wonder how the man survived at all. By then the place had shut down.

The door of the small room opened.

"*¿Quien eres tú?*" A tall broad-shouldered trans woman in a pink bathrobe carried a basket of laundry.

"Gilmore Crowell, friend of Ava's," he said in Spanish. "You live here?"

"Yes, I live here, *Papacito*." She took a box of laundry soap from a file cabinet drawer. "I'm Lupita. If you need anything, I'm usually in the house. That is, if I'm not working." She giggled to herself and went out to start the washing machine.

148

He awoke on the musty couch to the sight of María Félix scowling down at him. A bluebottle landed on his T-shirt. With its hind legs, it meticulously groomed its wings. Then, with its middle set of legs, it groomed its hind legs. The place was even too dirty for the flies. His mind wandered back to the toilet, its likely birthplace. He went inside the main house and made a phone call to have it fixed.

The interior of the house made no visual sense. It was fairly clean, yet also spare of contents, as though occupied by a sorority of extremely frugal sisters. The bathroom wastebasket nearly overflowed, but the floor and tub were scrubbed and tidy. Except for a hairbrush and a bottle of eye drops, the medicine cabinet was empty. Not a single cleansing or make-up product around. Did the women not trust one another to leave such items in a common space? He made a note of the inquiry in his legal pad. The kitchen sink contained a single plate. The counters were clean and bare except for a Santa and Mrs. Claus salt and pepper set. In a plastic container on the table was a frog-shaped Christmas cookie missing one of its frog legs. Nothing to report. A young woman wrapped in a flowery bedsheet slept on the living room couch. He took a seat under a painting of a Day of the Dead skeleton woman curtsying on the face of a clown. As he scratched out his notes, Snoring Beauty opened an eye.

"I'm with Ava," Gil said in Spanish.

"Were you drawing me?" She made a performance of covering her breasts and tucking the bedsheet between her legs.

"No, I was just taking some notes," he said. "I could sketch you, if you want. Little hobby of mine."

"Did you touch me?"

"What?"

A moment later, Ava came down the stairs in basketball shorts and a Mexican National soccer jersey. "He's all right, Ginny. He's only here to check out the house. Want some coffee?"

149

"Please," Gil said.

"I was asking Ginny."

"Got it. I just called to have your toilet fixed, but you can't make me a cup of coffee."

"What are you talking about?" Ava asked.

"There's a turd in there from 1996."

"Okay, but you said you were fixing it for me. I haven't been in that garage in I don't know how long. You're fixing it for yourself, aren't you?"

"Sure, Ava. Whatever."

Another girl came down the stairs, dressed for work. She made a face at Gil and started for the door.

"Crystal, this is Gil," Ava called out. "He's here to talk to us a bit, learn about our lives. He's not a cop or reporter or anything like that." To Gil she asked, "You've met Ginny, right?"

"Yes, I've already managed to upset her, though how I'm not sure," he said in English. "Is she on drugs or did you forget to tell people I'd be here?"

"I wanted to keep things natural," she called back from the kitchen. "That man who studied the monkeys didn't get their permission, did he? Or ask them to make coffee?"

"If you're referring to George Schaller, he studied gorillas, not monkeys," Gil said.

Ava came back down the hallway to flash that smile, the one that instantly softens past sassy remarks. "In that case, I'll make you some coffee." She returned to the kitchen.

"I won't tell anyone."

"Crystal works at Angelina's. Have you been there?"

"Not really. Why, do they have a strong community?" She didn't answer. "This study concerns streetwalkers, not club girls," he called back.

"And how's that working out for you?"

*

150

He'd been to sex clubs in the past, impossible as they were to avoid in Zona Norte, but only to use the bathroom or down a quick beer. He thought them especially sleazy venues, dens of unbridled American businessmen, rich frat boys, and working girls spun from the media-driven standard of beauty. Whether he was there now to bring Crystal into his little circle of study or to please Ava, he wasn't sure. It was still early evening. Angelina's wasn't yet ass-to-elbow with slobbering men. He was able to get a seat. Four seconds later, a woman sat down next to him.

"You want to buy me a drink?" she asked in English. She placed her hand on his thigh.

"Thank you for the offer," he said. She looked confused. "Ah, so you don't really speak English. *Sería un placer comprarte un trago.* Better?"

She snapped her fingers at the waiter, who took the signal and continued to the bar.

"My name is Yolanda." She pulled out her phone.

"I'll keep that in mind." Though he'd said it in Spanish, she looked up at him, irritated or confused; he couldn't tell. "Sorry, I'm Desmond Morris." He stuck out his hand. She took it, then surveyed the room for something more interesting.

The waiter returned. "Three hundred pesos."

"Three hundred pesos?" Gil reached for his wallet. "These drinks cost more than my last fuck."

The waiter placed the glasses on the table.

"You can put your arm around me," Yolanda said, "unless you want to get a room."

"Another time."

A woman took the raised platform in the center of the floor, accompanied by some old school hip hop. For the next several minutes she pole-danced, spun, writhed, hung upside down from a suspended metal ring, all while tossing clothes to the floor. After the dance, she walked around the edge of the stage while men placed money into her G-string. Those who

151

paid up got hugs. Most of them eagerly buried their faces in her cleavage.

"Want to buy me another drink?" Yolanda asked.

"No, I think we should call it a night," Gil said.

Without another word, she got up and left. Ten seconds later another girl took her place, began caressing his thigh....

31

He got back to the house just after dark. Ava was on the side porch in running shorts and a tank top, barefoot and braless, painting her outstretched toenails. Her long black hair shone almost blue in the light. He stood for a moment on the other side of that light, obscured by the vine growth in the lattice work and the outer darkness. It was possible he'd witnessed more natural beauty, though he wasn't sure. He asked if he could take her photo in that exact position, seated as she was with one bronzed leg raised above the other. She didn't answer.

"For the website," he added.

"That stupid idea." She shook her head. "What are you doing back?"

"I got depressed."

"I thought you were already depressed."

"This was different." He came up the steps to the porch.

"You started feeling sorry for yourself," she said.

"And others. What are *you* doing here?"

152

She flipped back her hair. "This job comes with a few days off each month."

"Mind if I join you? I might pay to watch you do the other foot." He sat down.

She tightened her expression, bore down on the brushstrokes.

"You don't take compliments very well."

"I've been taking them my whole life."

"There are women who spend a lot of money for that."

She looked over at him. "What an ignorant statement."

"I'll try harder next time."

She sighed. "Picture not being able to walk down the street without the stares, the whistles, the stupid questions, the compliments, as you call them. You have no idea what I'm talking about. Over the years, it wears you down. It becomes the way you relate to men."

He put his head back, too exhausted from the day to argue. "Hang in there, kid. You'll be old and ugly someday."

She laughed. "Hey, you said something clever. I had a feeling it might happen. I just didn't know this would be the night."

"I really wish I could impress you somehow. I mean, I'm not trying to be difficult."

"It's my mood, not you. I'm getting too old for this."

"Twenty-nine, right?"

"Thirty next month. I thought I'd be doing something else by now." She thrust the nail brush into the bottle of polish.

"Well, I'll be thirty-two in March if that makes you feel any better. And we're in exactly the same place."

She rose up in her seat. "Why would that make me feel better?"

"Wow, you're really on fire tonight."

"Here's a question I've been meaning to ask. What attracts you to a person like me? Is it about wanting something you can't really have so that you'll never have to actually deal with it?"

"Does this regard sex workers generally or specifically you?"

"Answer it however you like."

"How much time have you got?" he asked.

"Until these toes dry."

"I was born in Cedar Sinai hospital –"

"Skip over that part; it's quick-drying polish."

"The only child of Skip and Mariela Crowell."

"Keep going."

"My mother got sick and died when I was nine. My father and I moved to Tuxtla-Gutierrez three years later. He was doing legal work for an energy company down there."

"Chiapas."

"That's where it started. There was a place on the edge of the city on the highway to Chiapa de Corzo. A long narrow road forked off. A couple friends and I took our bicycles one day. At the end of the road was an admissions kiosk. They'd check your ID, frisk you, and that was it. It was all fenced around like an amusement park. Inside were paved foot paths that led to these little shacks the girls rented out. They'd stand in the doorway or just leave the door open. You'd walk up, start a little conversation, maybe set up a deal."

"And you were twelve, you're saying?"

"Fifteen at that time. A friend from school had an older brother who worked the weekend gate. We'd pay him to let us in. I only went a few times."

"You lost your virginity to a little *morenita*, then figured out you couldn't really have her." She laughed. "A pornographic fairy tale."

"Not quite."

"What happened?"

"I was just fascinated by the scene, that's all. It was like a miracle. My hormones were tearing me up inside. Then I go to

154

this place that I couldn't believe really existed. We moved back to LA that same summer and went to Magic Mountain. It wasn't the same."

She lit up a joint. "I think I understand."

"Explain it to me."

"You're just like every other guy down here."

"That's all you have to say?"

"Your idea of sex is the same as your idea of eating a meal or going to the bathroom."

He laughed. "Don't I get a little credit for honesty? I mean, I don't think that way anymore."

"You're still down here, aren't you?"

"Oh, come on. I'm studying the most time-honored trade known to man. And woman. It's economic anthropology, for Christ's sake. You of all people should understand that."

"I've understood it for years and now I'm disgusted by it. And if you want to understand it, take a look in the mirror."

"Aw, that's not fair. I once went two years without sex. What's your record?"

"Didn't have the money?"

He closed his eyes, tilted his head back.

"Okay, okay," she said, handing him the joint. "What did Maryann and Slim think of this little hobby of yours?"

"Mariela and Skip didn't know anything about it. You forget my mother was dead by this point. Keep up." He hit the joint.

"Where'd you get the money?"

"Like I said, I only went a few times."

"You discovered that you liked cheap sex and proved you're a man. Congratulations, Gilmore Crowell."

He handed back the joint. "You have a lot of resentment, you know that? I didn't see it at first, but it's there."

"Well, I've made a little money, and I'm getting ready to move on. I don't need to fake my opinions anymore. I can afford to look down on this shithole."

155

"That reminds me, did the plumber show up?"

"Yes, he did, and thank you. I shouldn't have snapped at you this morning."

They sat for a moment without speaking. He became aware of a ceiling fan clacking away through an open door to the living room. "That doesn't drive you crazy?"

"What?"

"That sound."

"Get on with your story. We're almost out of time."

"That's it, there's nothing left to say. You've completely emasculated me."

She looked at him across the clattering silence. He wondered if he saw something like longing in her eyes or if it was only her beauty that inspired him to imagine it.

"You need some new ideas," she said. "That's your problem."

"You want a massage? I give a great massage."

"Five hundred pesos for half an hour."

"You'd charge *me* to give *you* a massage?"

"Why not?"

"Would I have to tip you afterward?"

She stood up. "If it was good for you, then yes."

32

The only problem with time off work is the days fly away like blown cash at a blackjack table. It doesn't matter if the vacation is at a four-star hotel in Vegas or a storage shed in the hills of Tijuana. He looked at a clock on the wall and noticed for the first time all week that it was missing the hour hand. This led to a reverie on the nature of time and the value of tracking it. Before long, he'd fallen asleep on the sofa, no wiser on the subject.

He got stuck at immigration and customs in an endlessly winding queue. A pack of young drunks from the night before were right in front of him every step of the way. The boisterous idiocy of their exchanges, the stench from the street, the lung-stinging pollution of the parallel traffic chipped away at his sanity. Two hours later he was finally at the front, the next to churn through one of the passport control booths. He stepped over the strip of black tape on the floor to approach an officer.

"Did I ask you to come forward?"

"What?"

"Wait till I call you."

He stepped back behind the strip of tape. A moment later, the officer waved his hand for Gil to approach. He remained standing there. The officer craned his neck, waved his hand again.

"Come on, let's go."

"I was waiting for you to call me, like you'd said."

"Ah, a funny guy."

"Was I being funny? I thought I was following orders."

He looked the officer over. The closely cropped hair and clean shave, the muscular arms. Just another face of border politics and bureaucracy, a man who failed the exam to give speeding tickets. He was bringing in real money, though. Making payments on an oversized pick up, to be sure. Contributing to a 401K. A little condo in National City. He could very easily hate this man, but that would be just as foolish as feeling anything about him.

"Open the backpack."

He unzipped it, directed the contents to the officer's eyes. "I finished all the coke waiting in line."

The officer gestured overhead. Two ICE guards in combat attire and protective head gear approached, weapons drawn. They dragged Gil down a series of hallways to a windowless room in the center of the complex and zip-tied him to a straight-backed metal chair. Having nothing to charge him with they turned it into a waiting game, and time began to show its hard edges. When they released him seven hours later, he stumbled out into the dusk. An ache traveled from his lower back to his neck. Light rain fell from a gray sky. He leaned against a wall and observed the streams of people hustling in both directions across the border. They were hunched into their collars, holding any number of objects overhead against the weather, each in a hurry to get wherever they were going.

The trolley to Old Town left every hour. From there, he took a train to downtown LA, arriving back at the Koenig House at eleven-thirty. Before going in, he went down the side street to check on the Isuzu Gemini hatchback. The space under the palm tree where he'd parked it eight days before was now occupied by a truck with a busted camper shell. The car was nowhere in sight.

He went into the Koenig House library, sat down at one of the long wooden tables and turned on the lamp. Calling the police was out of the question. They already had a file on the Gemini listing it stolen four months ago. Something about the long shadows on the walls drove home the point that there was

158

nothing to be done. He went up to his room. The dumpster cat was sprawled out asleep in the middle of his bed, four fist-sized kittens fastened to its underside. He took off his shorts, put on a pair of sweats and a heavy jacket, and lay down on the cold hard floor.

33

Three separate memos were tucked into his time card, each directing him to meet with Scott Bertram on a different day after school. He snatched them up and stormed into the man's office.

"What are these?"

Bertram sat at his desk, hands circled around a mug of coffee. He looked at Gil as though trying to place where he knew him from.

"What are these?" Gil repeated, tossing the memos to the desktop. "And why can't it all be covered at one meeting?"

"Mr. Crowell, who is watching your class at this time?"

"I came in late. I have no idea."

"Exactly, and you weren't here yesterday either. I am directing you now to your classroom to relieve whichever teacher was burdened to cover your tardiness."

"You can't answer a simple question?"

"I'll answer all your simple questions at our first appointed conference today after school. Now go to your assigned location."

As Gil walked in, the students were slouched or standing around with their cell phones. A woman sat at his desk, her bobbed blonde hair tucked behind her ears. She appeared to be shopping for shoes on the Internet.

Gil slung his backpack to the floor. "All right, take out your goddamn books."

The students froze a moment, then scurried to their seats. The substitute closed out the server screen, abruptly terminating the shoe purchase. She got up from the desk and started for the door.

"I apologize for my lateness," Gil said to the class. "The cops stole my car and it took a while longer to get here this morning. Let's get reacquainted around a journal topic. The prompt is…" He held off completing that sentence till he had all the students' eyes on him. "Should prostitution be legal in the State of California? One full page and please skip lines. Regardless of your position, you must clearly state your reasoning."

"I take the missionary position," someone called out.

Almost every student took out their notebook and pen. Two remained sleeping in their gray numbered uniforms. Gil went over to the larger of the two and lifted up the desk on which his head had been resting, then dropped it back to the floor.

"What the fuck, man?"

"No, what the fuck you," Gil said. "You want to sleep, go to the nurse. Better yet, stay in the barracks. When I mark you present, it means both your body and mind are here. The morons who run this place are judging me on your academic performance. You're not awake, neither one of us has a chance."

160

He delivered the speech with little expectation that the young convict would follow any of it. Indeed, Gil half-hoped that he wouldn't and a violent exchange would transpire. Instead the troubled youth sat up in his seat, folded his huge forearms defiantly, and glowered in Gil's direction. He did not take out his notebook, but neither did he go back to sleep. The other resident awoke in the flow of commotion. Unlike his friend, this one took out his notebook, tore out two sheets of paper, and handed one off to the other.

The bell rang and the energy packing the corridors was like at any other high school. Outbursts of joy filled the main floor as the probes left their classrooms. Two lovers embraced, vine-like, in a recessed classroom doorway. A foot chase erupted. And laughter – the glorious laughter of youth in spite of looming authority. The residents, by contrast, assembled in the hallways and shuffled off to their cells single file like a class of kindergartners, a guard at the front and rear of each line.

Gil took the long walk to Bertram's office, tapped on the open door.

"We aren't meeting here, Crowell," Bertram said. "Go to the principal's conference room."

When Gil entered, both the principal and union rep were already there, seated at opposite sides of the conference table, their open laptops positioned like shields against one another. Bertram sat down next to the principal, Dr. Lee. He motioned Gil to the empty chair by the rep.

"David Costa-Price," the rep said to Gil through a mouthful of cookie. He held out his meaty hand.

Bertram began his address, reading aloud from a script on his laptop. He paused to slide his plastic-framed spectacles up the bridge of his nose with the outstretched tip of a middle finger. Most of what he said made no immediate sense, though the legalistic phrasing wielded a kind of severity. Was it happening? Was he finally being relegated to the teacher jail of

161

which Wretchler so infectiously raved? Was this how it began, over three afternoon sessions of somberly-invoked gobbledygook? He'd only been fired from one job before, a pizza place on Dog Beach his freshman year of college. The manager, a bearded fat guy with sailor tattoos on his arms and tomato stains on his smock, had told Gil to get the fuck out. It was a remarkably efficient termination, lasting perhaps five seconds.

"Relax, you're not being fired," David Costa-Price said, brushing some crumbs off his tie.

"This is a memorandum of improficiency," Bertram said.

"You mean nonproficiency?" Gil asked.

"Improficiency," Bertram restated.

"I think it's *in*proficiency," David Costa-Price said. "With an *n*."

"Never heard the word before," Gil said.

"Forget the word," Bertram said. "What's important is the meaning."

Dr. Lee's eyes darted from face to face. "Mr. Crow, whether it is or is not a word is beside the point. We are here today because you are being reprimanded, do you understand? A report of this meeting will go into your permanent file downtown. Now let me say something else. We have a job to do, each one of us. We are trusted with educating the next generation of young people. These students represent the future. Now, ours are very special students with very special needs. Encouraging violence among them, insulting parents, and passing out on the floor of the classroom are not how we meet those needs, Mr. Crow. Think of this as a business. The parents represent our customers. They are not required to send their children here. And when they stop sending them, we will all be looking for other jobs, now won't we?"

"But the state sends these kids here," Gil said. "I mean, they're juvenile delinquents doing time or probation. The only

162

way this school would shut down is if the kids stopped getting caught."

"Not my point," Dr. Lee said. "These students are my guests while they're here, and their parents are my clients, understand?"

Gil laughed and saw something flicker in the doorway. He turned his head ever so slightly. There stood Rex Healy, the hapless old shammer, out of view of the administration. He performed a delirious marionette act: hands and feet rising and falling in herky-jerk motions, head swiveling from an apparently disjointed neck, a foolish grin stamped on his face. Dr. Lee turned around to behold the spectacle. Rex's hands promptly straightened to his sides, the soldier at attention.

"Do you need help, sir?" she asked.

"He needs the kind of help we don't provide," Gil stated.

Bertram crossed his eyes, apparently straining to figure that one out.

Rex leaned into the doorway. "That's all right, ma'am. I need to speak to that gentleman right there when you're done with him." He pointed at Gil with his outstretched lanky limb. "With your permission, I'd like the next shot."

"Ignore him," Gil said. "He's not one of those parent clients you were talking about. He's just a charity case I'm working with on the side. By the way, are we done?" He stood up, his disappointment at not being banished to teacher jail now turned to disdain.

Before he could get away, David Costa-Price grabbed him by the elbow and handed off a business card. "I'm running for school board on a power-to-the-parents ticket. If you want to help out with the campaign, here's my direct number. We need people to phone bank, hand out flyers, that kind of thing."

Gil took hold of the card just long enough to flick it to the wastebasket. As he stepped into the hallway, Rex began clapping.

163

"Don't say a word," Gil said. "There's a lot going on." He took hold of Rex's upper arm and walked him out the front entrance. Parked directly in front of the building was the sparkling Isuzu Gemini hatchback.

"What the hell?" Gil trotted up to it.

"Sorry, man. I meant to call you," Rex said, loping behind. "It's a long story, but it's a good one."

"What a relief. I was afraid it would make no sense." Gil circled around the car.

"I thought you were coming back later, that your little jailhouse gig started up the same week as the university."

"That's how your mind works, huh?" Gil stepped into the driver's seat. "Well, maybe the cops will go easy on you then."

"Sorry, man, I needed to borrow it. I had a job interview in Riverside and did a little weekend camping up in Big Bear with my daughter. I really feel good about where we're at right now. We're in a really solid place, a really safe space in our relationship, know what I mean? I learned all kinds of things about teenage girls that I never even took the time to think about before. I mean, they get just as nuts over the same stuff we do."

"Sure." Gil adjusted the seat and mirrors. He leaned forward, hands at ten and two, collecting his thoughts to say something more. After a moment's pause, he hurled himself across the front seat, seizing Rex's neck with both hands. Rex slid down in the passenger seat and brought his feet up into Gil's stomach, hoisting him to the car's tattered ceiling. The force of that movement snapped flat the passenger seat, jolting Gil upside down and into the cramped backseat. He somehow managed to retain a hold of Rex's neck. Rex brought one leg down and kneed Gil between the legs, slamming him square in the perineum.

164

A knock came at the driver-side window. A Parking Violations officer peered in. Gil let go of Rex's neck and dropped headlong into the rear footwell.

"This is a no-stopping zone, gentlemen. Everything all right?"

"Little misunderstanding," Rex said through choking coughs. Gil clambered back into the driver's seat. "We worked it out."

"You have to move this car before it's towed." He handed Gil a ticket and waddled back to his service vehicle.

The two of them sat there motionless, their heavy breathing the only sound passing between them. Rex took the ticket from Gil's hand. "Let me get this one," he mumbled.

They drove off in silence. When Gil turned around to head west on Washington Boulevard rather than continue toward the Koenig House, Rex kept from questioning the change of direction. The mystery was resolved when Gil pulled into a pet store. It was time for someone to speak.

"You need anything?" Gil asked.

"From the pet store?"

"Yeah."

"I don't know, you recommend something?"

The act of walking into the store made Gil freshly aware of the injury at the back of his balls, accented with each stabbing footfall. He wondered if this was what prostate cancer felt like. He thought about the complex of nerves and blood vessels tangled up in that region, whether he'd ever get an erection again, how he'd sue Rex Healy for every dollar the old hustler had squirreled away if such a condition were to develop. He imagined photos of his pelvic floor passed among jurors in a civil trial, discussed at length during courtroom recesses, and projected onto a screen for everyone to behold while he sat, limp-dicked, next to his grim-faced attorney.

He picked out a bag of cat food. He figured the cheapest brand from a pet store was probably as good as the most

165

expensive stuff from a supermarket. It was only a hunch; he had no nutritional data to back it up.

The woman at the checkout asked if he was a PetFriends member.

He shook his head.

"Would you like to become a PetFriends member?" she asked.

"Is this something I won't be able to get out of?"

"What do you mean?" she asked.

"You know what I mean."

"It's very easy to join and you'll receive coupons with each purchase and special weekly discounts on PetFriends products, as well as other member benefits."

"What are these other benefits or are you forbidden from saying?"

"What?"

"Count me out." He swiped his debit card.

"Would you like to donate a dollar to save an animal's life?"

"What kind of animal are we talking about?"

"A cat or dog."

"I don't think so. I'm already saving cats' lives, and it costs a lot more than that."

"Well, this supports a pet adoption agency." She handed him a five-foot-long receipt.

"What about you?" he asked.

"What about me?"

"Are you up for adoption?"

"I'm twenty-three," she said.

"Age is just a number."

"Next customer, please."

When Gil returned to the car, Rex was leaning back in the broken passenger seat, smoking a joint and sorting through some notes. He held the joint out to Gil, who ignored it and pulled out of the lot. Rex continued holding out the joint, as though seeking conciliation. Gil finally took hold of it. He studied the burning end a moment and took a series of short halting hits before dropping it out the window.

"You just threw away twenty dollars."

Gil coughed up the smoke.

"That was the purest Jamaican sativa ever harvested on American soil, refined by a Rasta in Topanga Canyon whose been isolating the same cannabinoid for twelve generations. Guy made a bonsai forest out of the stuff."

"Fuck off."

"I'm serious. It's on display at the National Arboretum till the end of August."

Gil looked down at Rex lying flat in the passenger seat. "I misspoke. I meant shut up."

"You're angry, aren't you? You're angry because I'm a doctor of anthropology, and you're still lost in the slums of Tijuana."

Gil drove on, saying nothing. They arrived at the Koenig House.

"Okay," he said to Rex, "you can go do whatever it is that you do now."

"Dude, I don't know if this is a good time to ask, but can I get a meal here? They still charge five bucks a plate?"

"Listen to me because I'm only going to say this once. You are not homeless, understand? You were never homeless. What you are is an aging amateur hack, okay? Now, I congratulate you on fooling the idiots who sat on your dissertation committee. I really do, but it's time to give up this act you've been carrying on the last few years. Cut your hair, wash your clothes, boil those huaraches in bleach water and get a place where you can cook your own food. Can you follow those instructions in your present state? It's time to go our separate ways."

Rex laughed. "You're starting to feel this shit, huh? I told you it was good. So how about it then?"

167

Something unusual was going on at the Koenig House. Expensive cars were parked out front. Formally-dressed older couples milled around the foyer, drinking wine and German ale. A larger group of similar folks was seated at cloth-covered tables in the courtyard, waiting to be served. Most of the ragged residents were set apart, eating in the library. Five-hundred-pound Brian Schulze, president of the Los Angeles Chapter of the Koenig Society, addressed the guests through an unnecessary arrangement of loudspeakers. His natural voice projected beyond the reedy amplification. Everything was going well at the house, he declaimed. The residents were eating nutritious meals, working hard, and becoming invested in the local community. God was in his heaven, all was right with the world. He couldn't express that sentiment redundantly enough, though he tried. That, and how grateful he was – in the name of the Blessed Adolphus Koenig – for every one of those here gathered and their heartfelt contributions to the society.

"Who are these old people?" Rex asked.

"These are the wealthy German Catholics who subsidize this place. They show up here every few months and the staff serves a fancy dinner. It must be some kind of fundraising thing. All I know is every once in a while we eat really well, and this is one of those times."

They each had two plates of broiled knackwurst, mashed potatoes with mushroom-onion gravy, some kind of vegetable casserole, and freshly-baked *dampfnudel* with quince jelly. It had been a long time since Gil had eaten so well. A dopey exhaustion settled over him, all but wiping away the residue of the afternoon's conflicts. Rex made the rounds, enchanting some of the older ladies. He came up behind Gil, seated alone at a corner table, and placed his massive bony hands on Gil's shoulders.

"Fucking incredible food, man. Hey, I wanted to tell you I'll be leaving soon."

168

Gil turned around, looked up at him. "Yeah, that's the idea."

"No, I mean leaving LA."

"I'll believe it when I stop seeing you."

"UC Riverside took me on to direct their Center for Religion and American Culture."

"Oh yeah?" Gil jabbed a toothpick into his gums. "You know something about religion, do you?"

"It's a side gig. They need someone to baby-sit in the library a few hours each week, straighten up the stacks. Write an article for the newsletter every now and then, that sort of thing. Maybe teach a couple classes, I don't know. Ninety thousand."

"Whatever."

"Come on, I'm an idea man. You know that. Hey, I got another one while you were picking out your kitty litter. A series of picture books you read to your dog. Another line for your cat, your rat, your iguana, you follow me? Is that a billion-dollar industry just waiting to happen?"

"Okay, good luck. Cup of coffee for the road?"

"No, I'm going to do a few lines with some of these people, then find a place to crash in the park."

34

Two visitors entered Gil's classroom, one a tall, graceful woman in a gun-metal-gray suit, the other a short pompadoured man, attired in the same grim shade. Like a pair of ice dancers, they coursed across the floor, peering over students' shoulders.

They passed one another in the middle and exchanged a whisper, then sat at opposite corners and tapped away on their laptops.

The students were reading the somewhat dated story of a character who murders his friend in a wine cellar by erecting a stone wall around him.

"Okay," Gil said to the class. "That's it for today's reading. If you didn't finish, get it done for homework. It's time for our daily journal. Today's topic is whether a sex worker needs a pimp." He clapped his hands together, solemnly lowered his chin to his fingertips. "Or is that just a bygone trope of some not-yet-forgotten era? One full sheet of paper please, and don't forget to double space."

A few students groaned. "What's a sex worker?" someone asked. "Is that like a whore?" Half the class picked up a pen and started in on the assignment. The others squabbled among themselves.

"It seems there are students who have conflicting views on this subject," Gil said, his arms outstretched dramatically. He sashayed past the female visitor, grimaced down at her. "Okay, listen up. If you prefer to respond to the short story, I'll give you a different topic. The alternative prompt regards the death of Fortunato. The question is, how would you have done it?"

"What do you mean?" a probe in the front row asked.

"Murder is what I mean!" Gil roared. The room fell silent. "Do you really expect me to believe this guy killed his friend by building a stone wall? Ridiculous!"

"Well, the other dude was passed out drunk," a student said.

"Oh, please," Gil countered. "It would have been easier to drop a barrel of wine on his head."

"But then you got a bloody mess to clean up," a resident from the back row stated. "No, he did it the right way."

A girl in the front turned around. "Bloody mess? Who cares? They're in a wine cellar." In one sweeping motion, she rolled her eyes and flipped back her hair.

A spate of debates popped up around the room.

"All right," Gil said. "Your attention please. The revised alternative journal prompt is this: How would *you* murder *your* friend? I can see many of you have already given that some hard thought. Be sure to skip lines and leave some space at the margins for my comments."

The gray-suited visitors gathered up their materials and left.

At the end of the school day, Gil pulled up the website to check out the number of hits it had received the past week. Nineteen. One-nine. Nineteen people out of a denominator of seven billion had checked it out. Or, perhaps one individual had checked in nineteen times. There was no way of knowing. He had fourteen girls enlisted. If each of them had checked it out once, that would bring the total number of hits down to five.

The truth finally dawned on him with blinding intensity. The website wasn't going anywhere. Like many good ideas, it had come to nothing. Bad timing, poor execution, flaws in design, whatever; the point was it had failed. The immense burden of his ethnographic research and all its related setbacks instantly lifted with that single admission. There was nothing left to do but finish writing. The aristocratic hippie psychiatrist had once again been correct: Complete the dissertation and be done with it. Even Rex had advised him to move on. In his relief, Gil chuckled. A warm glow burned within him, surrounded his physical being. It lit up the whole classroom. He could see everything with a renewed perspective now like a train wreck in his rearview mirror. The doomed eight-year project was already receding into the past. He looked out the narrow security window at the sun-sparkling palm fronds. They

171

waved at him sagely, affirming he was about to turn a corner in his life.

A spontaneous moment of pity for his subjects arose in that moment. How difficult they all had been, how thoroughly impossible, mired as they were in the wretchedness of their lives and backward ideas of business. He'd meant to honor them, empathize with them, plead their case to the academic universe. He'd even offered to help them, free of charge. They wanted no part of it. He'd been foolish – no question of that – but so had they. And now he was finished with every single one of them. He thought of Ava and sighed, then logged off the computer.

In the solace of that bittersweet surrender, he decided to blow off his second disciplinary meeting with Bertram and company. As he made his way across the school parking lot, he laughed again to himself, imagining the silly prick waiting around in the principal's office for him to arrive. They still didn't get it. They were still hanging tough. Good for them. When they finally figured it out, they'd send him off to teacher jail where he belonged. There he'd cozy up with his warm laptop in a cubicle and grind out the thesis or bust, all while racking up his miserable hourly wage. It was bound to happen just as he'd hallucinated it in Bertram's office. There was no other conceivable way. For now, though, he was headed home, his mind on a family of cats.

35

Though he slept well that night on the cold cement floor, a surge of dread woke him well before sunrise. He looked around in the dark, as though the source of that sense had arrived with the early morning shadows, the stillness out in the streets, or the dull silent fog that crept in overnight. There was nothing else to do in such a state but arise and get distracted by the workday's routines. He showered quickly, dressed for work, and went down to the refectory. It was only he and Javier, the spidery old Spaniard, facing each other across one of the long wooden tables as they so often did, the edges of their plastic breakfast trays up against one another. The old man toothlessly smacked away at his watery oats. It soon became unbearable. With most of his breakfast uneaten, Gil swallowed what remained of his coffee and headed out.

It was only six-thirty when he arrived at the detention center. He parked in the near-empty lot, passed the guards, and went through the main office doorway. The ceiling lights were on, but nobody else was there. Even the office secretary, Ms. Mott, hadn't yet arrived. How pleasant it was to sign in for work and check his mailbox without crossing any administrator. And no memo tucked into his timecard! Clearly Bertram hadn't gotten around to writing him up yet for dodging the previous afternoon's disciplinary meeting. Gil felt for the moment that he'd outsmarted the man where he lived. As he walked down the corridor to his classroom, he became aware that the unease he'd awoken with had worn off with the strengthening light of day. A sense of acuity remained. He had more than enough time to get all his lessons on the board and review his notes before the first-period students arrived. He even swept the floor, the amorous janitors not having bothered to do it lately. He sat at his desk and switched on the computer monitor, nudged the mouse to its usual position. As he reached for the power button on the desktop tower, the system awoke with a startling hiss. It was already on. He expected to see the login screen for his attendance chart or a page of notes from yesterday's last class. What shimmered to life instead was the unmistakable homepage of his website.

His reaction to the sight of it was something like cardiac arrest. Or had he simply forgotten to breathe? His chest tightened, his fingers tingled, his vision clouded. He felt as though he were slowly toppling over. The chair seemed to slide out from under him. Once those sensations faded he pored over a possible version of things he desperately hoped to believe in: In the ecstasy of the previous afternoon, he must have failed to log off before leaving. Except he knew that didn't happen. He painfully recalled closing out the browser and shutting it down. Someone else had been in the classroom. There was no way around it. That person had booted up the computer, visited the website, turned off the monitor, and left. It made no sense, yet it must have happened that way. He stood up and frantically paced, straining to imagine some other explanation. He shuffled through the events of the past day over and over again like playing cards in a trick deck. It only strengthened his madness. Kneading the sides of his skull with fisted knuckles, he cried out.

He checked his watch, the clock on the wall. Seven-forty-five. He had five minutes left to play with before the ten-minute bell, when guards led residents to classrooms for first period. He raced out the doorway and down the hall, past the chaotic stream of probationaries and up to LeTed Harris' office.

174

He hammered on the outside door. No answer. Of course not. LeTed would shamble in late, as usual. Or was he down in his dungeon? No time to find out. Gil went back down to his classroom and through the door to Wretchler's room. The old dog was sitting on a desk telling a dirty joke to the few probationaries already there. He turned his head and looked Gil up and down as he panicked in the open doorway.

"Sorry to interrupt, Mr. Wretchler. I just wondered if you happened to use my computer yesterday afternoon." He tried to mask his fear of the answer.

Wretchler tilted his head, as though tracing back through his memory. He finally admitted that, no, he had no recollection of doing so.

Gil tried the doorway on the other side of his room, the one that opened to Jeannie Lint's classroom. Hers was full of students. She was already passing around a bucket of the loquats that grew abundantly in her Altadena backyard.

"Ms. Lint, I'm sorry to bother –"

"Oh, it's no trouble, sweetie. Here, take a couple of these."

"That's okay, I was just –"

"Take one, at least, dear. They're wonderful! Better than a cup of coffee or tea. All the vitamins you need to start your day are all wrapped up in this tiny little fruit. Can you imagine?"

"No, thank you. I just need to –"

"Do you students know Mr. Crowell?" she asked the class. "This young man here…" She paused. "…is a fabulous, fabulous teacher. One of the great rising stars of Los Angeles Correctional Academy!"

"Suck a nut, Crowell!" someone yelled from the back.

"Hey," Jeannie Lint said. "There's no call for that. Now then, did everyone get a loquat? All right, let's take out our homework."

175

"Ms. Lint, I'm sorry to interrupt but I have to ask if you went into my classroom yesterday."

"Your classroom?"

"Correct."

"This room right here where you teach?"

"Yes, I'm afraid someone was on my computer yesterday afternoon or evening, I'm not sure which. It doesn't matter. Did you happen to use it?"

"Your computer?"

"Did you log onto my computer yesterday at any time?"

"Why would I do that, sweetie? I have my own computer right here. I'm pretty sure every teacher has their own computer, don't they?" She cracked up at the thought.

The sound of her laughter struck Gil like gunfire, staggering him back into the open door.

Throughout first period, the image of the website's homepage kept popping up in his mind. Nutrition break finally arrived. Three of his probationary students dallied insufferably in gathering up their materials. They gossiped all the while in their whiny little voices.

"Oh, come on," Gil said. "Move it, would you? I need to use the bathroom!"

One of his students, a hormonally challenged lump of flesh named Wilmer, began a nasal apology for the three of them.

"I don't need you to apologize!" Gil barked. "Get out of here!"

Without another word they scuttled to the door, Gil right behind them. He raced up the stairs two at a time to the computer lab. The door was wide open. LeTed was staring into a monitor, a cold piece of pizza outstretched in one hand.

"Excuse me," Gil said from the doorway. LeTed swiveled around. "Did you happen to go on the website from my classroom computer yesterday?" As soon as the words left his mouth, he witnessed their absurdity reflected in LeTed's

176

face. The young underpaid systems analyst looked back at him with stony-faced bewilderment, all while ruminating over the bite of pizza in his mouth.

"Never mind," Gil said weakly. "Sorry to bother you."

There was only one other far-fetched possibility left to hang on to. The custodians, Brandon Terry and Lee Banks, had been messing around in his classroom the previous night and happened upon the website while scrolling through his browser history. They checked it out for a laugh, got sidetracked by some hanky-panky, and neglected to log off. It was possible.

He laid low the rest of the school day, going through the motions of teaching, not leaving the classroom, dismissing students at the proper time. The final bell rang. He scampered over to the custodial office across the quad and knocked on the door. Outside the makeshift bungalow, waiting for someone to answer, he became aware of the starkness of the campus, with its razor-wire surroundings, windowless facades, and acres of asphalt terrain. Nobody answered. A search of the main building was in order.

His third appointed meeting with Bertram and company was scheduled for three-fifteen. There was no chance he would show up for that, yet the thought of running into Bertram while going up and down the hallways terrified him. As he searched for a janitor, he inched closer to accepting the only explanation that remained, indeed the only plausible version of events that ever truly existed, the one he had struggled mightily against reason to free from his mind: The unknown web prankster had been Bertram all along. He'd first entered the classroom to fetch Gil down to the meeting. Not seeing him there, he began snooping through computer files and recent URLs in search of anything damaging he could stick Gil with. *Stick it in and break it off.* Surely Bertram had been living off that ethos his entire career.

On the second floor of the main building, a wheelie bin was parked in the middle of the hallway, a sure sign one of the

177

custodians was working in a nearby classroom. Gil peered into open doorways until he spotted one sweeping up.

"Excuse me. I'm looking for Mr. Terry or Mr. Banks."

The old janitor rested his broom handle in the crook of his collar bone, straightened himself up painfully, wiped at his forehead. "They're not here tonight. Who are you?"

"Crowell. I teach downstairs. What do you mean they're not here tonight?"

"Tell me what part's got you confused and I'll think up another way of saying it."

"This is their night off?"

"One of them, yeah."

"Were they here last night?" Gil shifted uncomfortably like a child needing to pee.

"I believe, now let me see...." The man gripped the top of the broom handle and took another wipe at his forehead. It took so long for him to speak again that Gil wondered if he'd lost the question. "You know, I'm not sure about that," he finally said.

"Do you happen to know how I can get in touch with either of them? I'm a friend."

"A friend?"

"You know what I mean."

"I *believe*.... Hang on.... Brandon might be in school. I know that he did go back to school. He may be there tonight."

"What about tomorrow?" Gil asked.

"What about it?"

"Is he working tomorrow night?"

"You better check with the plant manager on that. His name is Mr. Bertram."

178

36

He arrived at work early again the next day, intending to avoid Bertram, Dr. Lee, or any other administrator. No memo was tucked into his timecard for failure to appear at the second and third disciplinary meetings; no random visitors came through the door; no omens appeared in the reflection of his classroom's security window. The current lull made no sense unless it was meant to inspire fear over what was in the offing. He thought of calling David Costa-Price, but decided on Brinda Bagchi instead.

"I've been thinking about you quite a bit lately, Gil. How are things?" The lilting Calcutta accent rattled through his cell phone speaker like notes on a familiar instrument.

"How are things? Good question," he said. "I was about to ask you."

"What's that supposed to mean?" she asked.

"I don't know," he said. "Sometimes I just begin speaking and let the words go where they will."

A silverfish crawled out of Frinkle's literary guide.

"How's the dissertation?"

"That's not the problem," he said.

"What is it then?"

Faced with an opening to come clean with the one person who could mitigate future damages, he dodged instead. "Just a little unsure of my sources is all." He knocked the insect to the floor.

"What is it now? You were so optimistic the last time we spoke."

"I can't seem to find that critical insight, that indescribable something on which the whole thesis might be supported." With the toe of his shoe, he prodded the creature in circles.

179

"I don't know what any of that means, Gil."

"Nor I. But most of the women down there are doing quite well, I can safely say. They're pretty comfortable in their skin, too. I haven't met a single one yet who's been raped, robbed, or had her face sliced open. I mean, there's still hope, but you see my dilemma? I've got nothing – nothing substantial or even interesting – to work with. They all seem to be well fed with plenty of money in the bank. Most are having little houses built in more desirable parts of the country. One started a tomato farm. She has eight people working for her. That's pretty good, huh? Yeah, they're doing a lot better than I am, you can be sure of that. What's more, my interactions have revealed them to be surprisingly boring and kind of bitchy. Should I weave that in somehow?"

"It took Colin Turnbull a magnificent effort to resist despising the Ik People. He managed to do some of his best work on them."

"This is different." He scooped up the silverfish with an office memo and cast it onto a set of novels to feed.

"How so?"

"Different place, different time, the whole gender issue, the politics of studying sex work within the academic constraints of the day, and I ain't no Colin Turnbull."

"Report on your findings and do it honestly. That's all you can do. They're agents of their own empowerment. What's wrong with that?"

"I get it, but will that be accepted coming from a straight white privileged male? And I use the word privileged in the conventional sense. I've been living hand-to-mouth for years."

"The whole thing will depend on your analysis, Gil. You have the background and the chops. You need to utilize them. I have to go. My sons are playing on the roof."

He ended the call as apprehensive as ever, staring at the screen of his cell phone as though waiting for a sign to appear

180

in the pixels. As it became clear none would, he scrolled through his list of contacts in search of some person on whom he could unburden himself. When he came to *Sub-Planner*, the substitute teacher assignment service, he decided to call in sick for the following day and go straight down to Tijuana. Surely Ava would have something to say about all this. At the very least, she'd toss off some good jokes at his expense.

He recognized in that moment she was the one person who might bring him back to reality. He could picture her bright smile laughing away his problems. The thought instantly soothed him. Such a woman was a magnificent thing, a natural wonder to behold.

It was all settled then. He'd drive down early before morning rush hour fueled by black coffee, powdered doughnuts, and a Johnny Winter tape he'd picked up at a Koenig House charity event. He'd get high with her, screw the night away, and completely forget the world according to Bertram for a couple glorious days. Sex and drugs and rock and roll. Properly administered, had they ever truly failed?

37

Mother Cat gazed down at him from the bed, her supercilious countenance seeming to question his very presence. Couldn't he see she'd taken over this space, that it was all hers now?

The night had slipped away in a blink. All the sleep he'd lost writing day and night over winter break must have finally crashed down on him. He took his time getting up and ready, not leaving for the border till after nine. He parked and crossed over. It was a slow day at the coffee shop on Constitución. It

181

looked like his sparring partner had the day off. He took a seat in the corner and tapped away on his laptop for eight hours straight. And that was it; the first draft was finished. One hundred and eighty-eight single-spaced pages. It wasn't much, but he had nothing left to give, no other notes to sort through. A few weeks of revising and he'd be sitting before the committee.

An elation swelled up in that moment, like a runner's high. He'd never run before in his life, but he could easily imagine running. That was the point. Indeed, it was his imagination that kept him from ever trying to do it. The sustained mental image of sweating profusely, his feet slamming into the pavement, the unbearable smog, the monotony of the passing city blocks.... He could make it all come so alive in his mind. But then, he could just as easily think of something else and the instant euphoria would kick in. That was how he felt in that moment, having completed the first draft of his thesis. He closed down the laptop and did some light stretching.

In his raised spirits, he crossed the street to a print shop and promptly ran off every page. Holding the warm stack proudly in hand, he breathed in the scent of the ink, ran his thumb along the manuscript's thick edges. It was almost like having a book, his very own after eight long years. He asked the man working the counter if he wouldn't mind binding the pages for him and putting a cover on it. Without answering, he took the pile, ran it through a machine, and handed it back.

Ava's shift began in less than an hour. There was nothing left to do but go to Placita's on Revolución for tacos and beer. Food never tasted so good, and the beer.... Had any poems ever been written about the sparkling golden sunshine that went into every pitcher of Mexican beer? He was in a different world now, far from any thoughts of Bertram. The man was only an idea anyhow, and not a particularly unique one. There was a Bertram in every workplace in America. The trick was to keep such a character out of one's head.

182

He went to Ava's post in front of Hotel Enva. She wasn't there. Either a client had already gotten to her or she was running behind. He took a walk down the Coahuila and spoke with a few girls who'd signed up for the website. Each greeted him with familiar aloofness, avoiding eye contact, answering questions with head-shakes and grunts. One girl didn't remember who he was. He ducked into a corner bar. The narrow steps led to a stuffy underground darkness. A six-piece outlaw *Norteño* outfit that called themselves *Los Chacales del Infierno* beat on their instruments and howled into the low tile ceiling. Copies of their latest CD hung from crisscrossing wires off the bar. He sat down and ordered another beer. An old sex worker with metal teeth and warts on her eyelids approached him for business. He waved her off. The music rattled every cell in his body. It was the sound of life itself properly lived. After tilting back the last swallow of beer, he headed up the stairs into the electric tangle of the scene.

There was some kind of local festival beginning on Niños Héroes. The end of the Coahuila was blocked off. Fireworks exploded as he approached Ava's post. She was leaning up against the hotel doorway, one high-heeled shoe hooked behind the other. They made eye contact across the alley. He held out his arms and did a little soft-shoe shuffle, crossing between taxis to the other side.

"What are you doing here?"

"I needed to get out of town. I may be in trouble."

"I thought maybe you came to see me."

"That wouldn't be so bad, would it?"

"I hope not."

"What were you reading just there?" he asked.

"Nothing."

"No, you were reading a book. You just put it in that bag."

She looked down at it.

"Yeah, that bag in your hand."

"I think you're confused."

He reached for the bag and a mock-struggle ensued. She laughed helplessly. He wrestled the bag from her and pulled out the book. A cop walked past.

"Nothing happening here, officer," Gil said in Spanish. The cop looked back at them, glowering at a scene he couldn't make any sense of. Gil held up the book and read aloud from the cover. "Applied Fiscal Planning."

"I got it at a used book store," she said, as though it called for an explanation.

"Can I invest a couple hours into your fiscal plans?"

"A couple hours? So you did come down to see me."

"If I admit it, do I still get the early-bird special?"

She leaned into him. "You won't even notice the cost."

"Vamos al cuarto," he said.

She took him by the hand up the circular iron stairs. On the wall by the street-side window was the room's only adornment, a faded black and white poster of Billie Holiday. Eyes closed, mouth open, she looked forever lost in a deliriously erotic moment.

He did what he came to do and finished with over an hour to spare. Gazing up through the birdshit-dappled skylight, he struggled against a shortness of breath to express his wonder at her. An homage of cringing inanities spluttered forth: She was the most beautiful woman he'd ever seen; she really knew what she was doing; she moved in mysterious ways….

She gave him a playful slap, took hold of his cheeks. "I'm a professional mister," she said, mirroring each of his contortions with her own scrunched-up face. "I should know a few things."

"Are you kidding?" he slurred through his disfigured mouth hole. She let go, allowing him to speak unencumbered. "No, you really are special. Forget it. You don't know what I'm talking about."

"Guys say all kinds of shit."

184

"Okay, but I mean it."

"It *was* good, wasn't it?" She lit up a joint.

He rolled onto his side to make eye contact. "So, you enjoyed it then?"

She paused before answering yes.

"Did you finish?"

"Of course."

He reached over to high-five her but it wasn't returned. She turned her eyes to the ceiling.

"How many times?" he asked.

"I think we're tied."

"Give me a signal next time. I get off on that."

"I'm not paid to put on a show." She exhaled a column of smoke toward the skylight. "If you were perceptive, you'd notice these things."

"But you say it was good?"

"Yes, it was," she said.

"Where do I rank?"

"What?"

"I just said this was the best sex of my life. Give me some idea where I stand."

"I said it was good. Don't push it." She closed her eyes.

"Oh, come on, I can take it."

"Top eighty or ninety."

"Top ninety?" he asked.

"I don't know, top five percent."

"That somehow made it worse."

"Only because you're in love with me." She shot him a glance.

"I don't think that's what it is."

She hit the joint again. "You'll get over it."

"I'm not *in love* with you, but there is something there, know what I mean?"

"Lust."

"You've never been in love?" he asked.

185

"What's the difference?"

"Seriously?"

"Yes." She handed him the joint. "Tell me about it."

"There's nothing to say about it. It's just a feeling."

"Top five percent doesn't cut it?"

"It has nothing to do with data, thank god."

A siren screamed outside, drowning out the rhythms of a nearby dance club.

"You can't explain it because it isn't real," she said.

"You're honestly telling me you've never been in love?"

"It's human nature," she said. "The man and the woman fall in love, as you say, until the baby comes. Then it's transferred there. It has to be that way or nobody would go through the trouble of raising one."

"That's a pretty harsh assessment. You'd make a good sociobiologist."

"A good what?"

"People who don't believe in love."

She shrugged. "If I'm wrong, prove it."

"How can you be sure you're right if you've never been in love?"

"Exactly," she said.

"Exactly what? It's a question."

She rolled on top of him, seized him by the shoulders. Her heavy raven locks enveloped his head like a curtain. "I've never experienced it because it isn't real." She made a goofy open-mouthed face, wagging her head from side to side as she leaned into him.

"What a miserable thought," he said. "You're a miserable person."

"You're only saying that because *you're* miserable." She took another hit off the joint.

"True," he said. "But there's room for both of us."

186

She laughed. "Now if you can also admit you're in love with me…"

"Like I said, I don't think so. Give me another hit off that joint. Maybe I'll change my mind."

"What's wrong with *like*? That's what I want to know."

"Like?" he asked.

"Yeah, as in, I *like* you. Without the… everything else." She widened her eyes, inviting him to counter.

"I can go along with that. Tell me more about it."

"That's it," she said.

"Want me to tell you a secret?"

"You're going to anyway."

"Most women have nothing I'm interested in."

She pinched together a strand of hair, holding the end up as though threading a needle, then rolled onto her side and poked it into his ear.

"Hey." He pushed her off. "I'm serious."

"Me too. And I seriously think you have issues with women."

"You really think that's what I'm saying? You missed the point entirely."

"Yeah, you're all over the place. If it makes you feel better, most men aren't worth anything, either." She put out the joint on the cement floor.

"I'm saying you're different. You have something. Don't get defensive."

"What makes me so different when you're paying me by the hour?"

"I already said I can't explain it. It's personal. It has nothing to do with class or profession."

"That's how people convince themselves they're in love. Then time passes and the fog clears, and they go on to the next one."

"You don't get it, but that's okay. I'm too drunk to argue."

187

She took hold of his face again, compressing the flesh noseward, then released it back to its natural form.

"Just please understand that I don't want anything from you," he said. "I'm not looking for a relationship on the streets of Tijuana."

"What's that supposed to mean?" she asked.

"You know what it means."

"No, tell me."

"You really think I would date a sex worker?"

"You just said it has nothing to do with profession."

"Okay, well, I'm not looking to date anyone."

"It sounded superior."

"Well, that's not how I meant it," he said. "What I meant is I'm not looking for a partner who fucks five strangers a day."

"Then it does have something to do with profession." She rolled out of bed to get dressed.

The spareness of the room, bled of all color in the darkness, accentuated the lines of her naked backside as she moved among the shadows. An explosion from the outdoor festival lit up the window. Billie Holiday, in a sudden change of expression, took it like a shot to the back. An awkward silence dragged on.

"Look, if I misspoke then I'm sorry," he said. "It's only how it came out. I'm so stressed out right now I should probably be medicated or at least on a lot more alcohol. Also, I don't have enough experience to speak with any authority on this subject. Who knows, maybe I haven't been in love either."

She turned around and gave him that smile, absent its usual radiance. "It's all right. We're almost out of time is all."

38

Wrenched with distress and clashing emotions, he walked the three miles up to Ava's house in the hills. He went by the cops, the *taxistas,* the side-walking street dealers, the colorful lights and pulsing rhythms of the all-night dance halls. He passed the young couples promenading up and down Revolución, the heavily-rouged faces of party girls strutting the sidewalks in their plastic heels and tight dresses, the swaggering *caballeros* in high-collared shirts, their brilliantined black hair and shined shoes snappily matching.

By the time he arrived at her house, he was exhausted. He went around back to the garage room, opened the door, and flipped the light switch to the sight of Lupita and some john, banging away *al estilo perrito* right there on the cold hard floor.

"Jesus fuck." He snapped off the light and stepped out.

Lupita's voice rang after him. "Gil!" A moment later she appeared in the open doorframe in all her glory. "It's all right, Papa," she purred. "We were just finishing up."

He turned around. "No, it's definitely not all right. I'll find a hotel."

"Unless you want to …" She left the rest of that proposal hanging in the cool night air alongside her prodigious cock and balls.

"I'm not up for it, Lupe," he said.

"If you'll just give us a few minutes then…"

"I'll be in the house. Take your time."

As soon as he entered, the silence enveloped him. The muted hum of the kitchen refrigerator traveled freely to the front room, where it mixed with the tics and clattering of the

189

ceiling fan. He poked his head into the barely furnished bathroom, then a hallway closet, unsure what he was looking for. A thrilling tingle flushed across his scalp as he took the first step on the staircase. The floorboards creaked. He removed his shoes. With one hand braced on the banister, the other on the wall, he took the next two steps barefoot. He looked up to the darkness at the top of the stairs, climbed another step, then another, till he was surrounded by doorways. He edged into an open room and flipped the wall switch. An unmade bed, a number of stuffed animals, a pile of laundry on the floor. He went back into the common space and tried one of the closed doors. Locked. Another opened onto an empty room. The mattress was stripped and the dresser empty. A large black suitcase squatted by the door. He stepped back, closed up, and went through another open doorway to a bathroom. Inside the medicine cabinet were rubbing alcohol, a box of condoms, and nine different containers of skin cream. He took a leak, flushed, and went back into the hallway. One more room.

The door was closed but unlocked. He stepped into what could only be described as a hundred-square-foot library. Countless books loomed over him, filling two walls from floor to ceiling. He drew himself to their bindings: *The Age of Religious Wars; La Ruta de Hernán Cortés; Autobiography of a Yogi; La Sucesion Presidencial; Notes from the Underground; Estudios Escogidos; Human Variation: Races, Types, and Ethnic Groups; Great Essays in Science; México en 1554; Familiar Trees of North America; Visitador de México; The Mind and its Control; Guía: Museo Nacional de Arte.*

He opened a notebook on the cinder block nightstand. There were no confessions of desire, celebrations of self, or painstaking reflections. It was, rather, a graphic journal of fantastical whimsy: animals cavorting across elaborately multi-tiered cityscapes, convoluted patterns spiraling off the page, effete-looking men laboring in Rube Goldberg workspaces,

190

goat-headed stormtroopers, radially-symmetric aliens, super-heroic women with dragon-like wings....

A sound from downstairs. He put the notebook back and stepped out, too astounded by what he had seen to recall if the door had been open or closed. He pulled it shut and went down. Lupita was in the hallway, arms akimbo.

"I, uh … Somebody was in that bathroom so I had to go upstairs." He stepped into his shoes.

"Oh, I don't give a shit about that."

"In that case, allow me to reprise my apology for the intrusion. I should have knocked. Obviously, I had no idea anyone was in there."

"And I had no idea you were coming. Miss Thing didn't say a word. What's her fucking problem anyway?"

"No, that's also on me," he said, going into the front room. She followed. "I just asked her a couple hours ago." He flopped down on the sofa and pulled the newly printed manuscript from his backpack. "It was wrong of me to –"

Lupita put a thick manicured finger to her lips, silencing him, and took the dissertation from his hands. "You finished already?"

"It's just a draft. I'm already seeing mistakes."

"Yes, but it's something, isn't it?"

"True," he said, at a loss to add anything more.

"Is there a chapter on us?"

"Who?"

"The trans workers."

"I was focusing on women here but –"

"And I'm not a woman?" she asked, vamping.

"Ah, you got me there."

"You're going to have to make that up to me, *Papacito*."

"You know, I may return one day and –"

191

"Listen to me. There's a club off the Coahuila where I started dancing a couple nights a week. Take me down and buy me a drink."

"Oh, I don't know. I've been drinking and smoking weed for the past four hours. I'm pretty beat up."

"Now, Gil, you just scared the hell out of me a minute ago. And what about that poor boy? He went ice cold. Who knows how that might affect our future relations, you know?"

"I hadn't thought about that."

"Maybe this will pick things up." She waved a small plastic packet in his face.

He stood up and reached for it, held it to the light. "Unless I'm mistaken, that's what they call cocaine." He handed it back to her.

She laughed. "You're not mistaken. Except around here they call it *co-ca-EE-nuh*."

He ran his hands through his hair, walked to the far wall, shimmied back around and squared up to her. "It's been a long time since I've done anything like that and it was a most memorably bad experience when I did."

"Well, this stuff is as pure as the driven snow," she said. "One of the local kingpins is a regular of mine. I'm linked in, you might say."

Gil sat down again, surrendered a nod. "Maybe just a sliver," he said.

Thirty minutes later they were in the backseat of a taxi, headed for the colored lights. Lupita's arm was looped around his, her head cocked back. She stroked her extensions. He stared bug-eyed out the window into the passing darkness trying to figure out what he was doing there and when the night would end.

39

El Jugador Alegre was the festive new gay bar on the outer edge of Zona Norte. With Lupita on his arm, Gil stepped across the faux drawbridge connecting the sidewalk to the bar's fortress gate. The energy inside the place was almost nerve-damaging: driving rhythms of Nineties electronica, a wall-to-wall light show, the gropes and perfumed scents of passing revelers. An image of a rakishly winking skull and crossbones was debossed into wooden pillars and glass doors. Aesthetic influences ranged from magical realism to Anglo-Saxon architecture so that any leather-clad biker pirate or Renaissance drag princess would become instantly absorbed in the scene upon entering. No matter who you were, who you thought you were, or who you were afraid you might be, you fit right in and felt welcome at El Jugador Alegre.

A small group was getting up from a table next to the dance floor, providing Gil and Lupita a place to sit down. She ordered a Sex-on-the-Beach, Gil a double rum on the rocks. She pointed to the caged dancers hanging from the ceiling. "That's what I do on Tuesday and Thursday nights."

"Looks like a workout. Any benefits?"

"A nice break from trick or treat plus it keeps my ass in shape."

Gil mustered a smile, but faltered slightly when a line of naked men paraded down the bar top. They spun their gear clockwise, then counterclockwise, in perfect unison. Cheers erupted from those at the bar.

"I'm going to the bathroom," he said. "Let me know if I miss anything."

The multicolored strobe lights disoriented his progress through the space. He felt dizzy and slightly nauseous, the rum twisting its way through his intestines. He pushed open the

193

washroom door. Lights were flashing even in there. They bounced off the mirrored walls, stalls, and ceiling. He looked down and observed colored reflections of his urine stream off in four different directions. A hangover was coming on. His head pounded to the rhythm of the music. He raised his aching eyes from the patch of ice he'd been targeting.

There, in the mirrored wall, passed a figure so completely out of context that a shot of adrenaline charged through Gil's limbs. His member retreated into his pants like the head of a frightened turtle. From an opened stall door Scott Bertram had marched to the sinks on the other side of the washroom, rinsed his hands, wiped them over his bald head, and left.

Gil took hold of the top of the urinal and steadied himself with a couple deep breaths. He would not vomit, he told himself. He would not freak out. The thing to do now was walk out the restroom the same way he'd come in and make a beeline for the drawbridge. He went over the plan again, nodding at the strobing reflection of himself in the mirror. After turning around, he placed one foot in front of the other and headed for the door. A train of bodies was entering. Gil yielded the right of way, then slipped back into the maddening throng. Head down, just keep walking, he told himself. A hundred feet to go. He shifted his eyes to scan the room. One hand shielded his face. Bertram appeared again at the edge of the dance floor. Their eyes met. That's it, Gil thought. It's over. Nothing else to do but keep moving.

"Gil! Over here!" It was Lupita, her face strobed out and beaming in the colored lights. She waved and yelled across the pounding dance music and the roar of two hundred voices. No more than fifteen feet from where Bertram stood, she would not stop Gil from leaving. In thinking it only once, he resolved it to be true. If necessary he would lower his shoulder, block her right and juke left. True, she was taller and stronger than Gil and surely possessed a longer penis, but none of that mattered

194

now. He would knock her on her shapely ass if it came to it. That spirit of being ready for anything got him through the crush of bodies and out the door.

He climbed into the nearest cab. In a vehicle motoring away from Bertram, he should have felt safe, but his panic was all-pervading. At one point, he actually looked out the rear window to see if anyone was following, but it was all splotched gray, the flash blindness from the club's light show still fresh upon his retinas. When a pair of headlights lit up the vehicle's cabin following a turn in the road, he was overcome with vertigo and put the seat back. At Ava's, he handed the driver a hundred-peso note and told him to wait. He rushed into the house and grabbed his backpack off the floor. When he returned, the cabbie was leaning against the hood of the taxi inhaling something through a narrow glass tube.

"You've chosen this moment to smoke crack?" Gil asked in Spanish.

"It's just a weed pipe," the driver replied. "Want some?"

"No, I do not. Please get in the cab and head for the border. And do not breathe through that thing along the way."

There was no need for such haste but then, why was he crossing into the States at such an hour? And what precisely was the great threat in having seen Bertram? It was all the misfirings of an overworked brain intent on solving a problem of its own creation.

The driver made a few attempts at small talk, meaning to connect with Gil over his disgust with everyone and everything he drove past. Gil made no response, and the driver turned up the radio. At the border he handed over another hundred-peso note and got out.

"It's a hundred and fifty, amigo." The cabbie held out his hand.

"Let's call it even." Gil slammed the door behind him. "*La propina no está incluida,*" he called over his shoulder, trotting off.

There was no line, per se, just a steady stream of people crossing over. He handed his passport to the Immigration and Customs officer.

"Where you going tonight?"

"LA."

"Anything to declare."

"No."

"You seem nervous," the officer said. "Everything all right?"

"Cab driver tried to shake me down."

"Why don't you open that backpack."

Impatient to unzip it, Gil caught the slider on the fabric, jamming it halfway. Rather than take a moment to separate the material, he grabbed both sides of the pack and yanked them apart, destroying the zipper in the process.

"Why'd you do that?" the officer asked.

"Look, I'm in a rush. Inspect what you need to inspect, and let's get it over with."

Without so much as a peek inside, the officer slid the backpack across the smooth aluminum counter top. "Have a nice night."

40

It was a little after midnight when he reached the Isuzu Gemini hatchback. Following Newton's law of conservation of fear, his relief at the sight of the car morphed into a panic that he'd somehow lost the keys. He set the backpack on the sidewalk and rummaged through the outer pocket. There they were, right where he'd placed them. Perhaps some order had been restored to the universe. He got in and started the engine. Waiting for the windshield to defog, he tried to recall with some measure of reasonableness whatever it was that had happened back at the club. He pulled away from the curb and turned down San Ysidro to the freeway entrance ramp. There was no traffic and very little high-mast lighting, leaving that stretch of highway with a dark abandoned look. He switched to the Five North. The steady rev of the engine calmed him somewhat. In the rearview, he saw the distant mountain of lights on the other side of the border. Lost in that luminous field was the last eight years of his life, and now Scott Bertram along with them. He gave the car a little more gas, as though increasing the distance between himself and the past, and turned on the radio. The local alternative station was in the middle of its early morning trip-hop hour. The watery rhythms washed over him in sync with the hum of the engine. *Everything was going to be all right,* he thought. It was something Norm would say to the other men in the Koenig House refectory whenever they finished eating.

"Everything is going to be all right," Gil said aloud to himself. The music responded with an ecstatic moan. He laughed, and a vision of Ava's face lit up the night sky. The comfort of that image was just what he needed. The madness of an ill-at-ease mind, he thought, and laughed again, though more softly this time. He rolled down the window and let in the cool night air....

Red, white, and blue lights filled the cabin of the Gemini, reflecting off the windshield. The terror of the dance club flashed back, and he almost drove off the road. The lights grew brighter as the patrol car got closer, but it did not speed past him as he'd expected; it settled in a few feet off his bumper. Lights spun off the Gemini's tattered cloth ceiling. The loudspeaker came on. While the highway had been dark, the Palm Street exit ramp was pitch black. He remained seated, trying to recall the last time he had been pulled over. A lone patrolman approached the driver-side door.

"License, insurance, and registration."

"Good evening – or morning. Your choice. Unfortunately, I don't have the registration and insurance card handy. This vehicle was recently vandalized as you can see from the broken glove box and passenger seat. Those documents were stolen along with some other things. I do have a current driver's license, however."

The cop retreated to the squad car for what seemed like a lunch break. Gil looked back through the rearview mirror. The cop appeared to be writing the whole time. What was he doing, journaling the experience? He finally got out and reapproached the Gemini.

"Whose car is this?"

"Mine," Gil said.

"I just ran the plates and they aren't in the system. You bought this car yourself?"

"No, it was left to me by my deceased father, but was more or less stolen a few months back."

"Vandalized or stolen?"

"Both, at different times. It was stolen then recovered and later vandalized."

"And you never noticed the plates had been changed?"

"Something like that."

198

The officer looked down in the one hand at the citations he'd spent the last fifteen minutes composing. He seemed to be weighing his interest in the matter. "I'm going to cut you a deal," he said. "I've had a long night. Shift ends in an hour, and I'd like to get home to my wife and newborn. Lucky for you, I'm not in the mood to prolong this."

Gil looked up at the officer through the open window, trying to make some sense of his words. "Got to get back to the family, I can appreciate that. I have a few cats myself, so…."

"Okay, listen, I can take you downtown and book you on a 4-8-7 or just tow this thing off the road and call it a wash. Got someone to pick you up?"

"You're talking about taking the car?" Gil asked, his face falling.

"Impounding it. You can sort it all out with the courts on Monday morning if you're able to come up with the title or registration."

"There isn't a third option?" Gil asked.

"Oh, sure."

"Well, let's have it then."

"I can arrest you *and* impound the vehicle," the cop said.

"That's not what I had in mind."

"What did you have in mind?"

"Driving back to LA and sorting it all out there." His expression meant to frame the good sense behind this overture. "You have my name and information. Just give me the tickets and track it all online. I'll go to court and pay it off Monday morning, like you said. If I don't follow through, you can put out a warrant for my arrest."

"No, you're way off base. You can surrender the vehicle now or go to the station in handcuffs. I'm being generous."

Taking that as an insult, Gil snatched his backpack off the passenger seat, removed the keys from the ignition block, and got out. The officer handed him a pen. Gil used the hood of

199

the car to sign the citations and gave everything back to the cop, who separated Gil's copies with one hand, while jotting something down with the other.

"You know who else was very good at documenting things?" Gil asked as he stuffed the citations into his backpack. "Soviet prison guards. After murdering the prisoners, they'd list the cause of death as alimentary dystrophy. That's the medical term for starvation. Pretty clever, huh?"

"I don't think we're there, yet."

"Ah, *yet*!" Gil exclaimed, walking backward and gesturing wildly. "Did you catch that everyone? *Yet,* the officer says!" He turned around to trek the weedy growth of the exit ramp to Palm Avenue, the destroyed backpack slung over his shoulder.

41

If a person is drunk enough or simply homeless, crashing beneath Imperial Pier allows for a good night's sleep. There's a nice level stretch of beach that's quite dry unless the tide rolls in before dawn. Nature's alarm clock, the wharf rats call it. But Gil was sober as a Sunday school teacher when he dropped to the sand at two thirty AM, and still far from homeless. He took his raggedy UC San Diego sweatshirt out of his backpack, pulled it over his head, and drew the pack in as a pillow. In his exhaustion, he was able to retreat from the society of voices in his head, each demanding his full attention. One of them exhorted, "When you ain't got nothing, you got nothing to lose." The parallel dullness of those lines made Gil laugh. He still had plenty to lose, he told himself, and pulled the pack in even tighter.

The waves crashed into the farthest pylons, followed by a rolling hush as their remains flowed back out to sea. A sliver of moon peeked through the wooden slats of the pier overhead. The stench of beached kelp sweetened the heavy air. He was just drifting off to sleep when he felt a sharp poke between his shoulder blades. A wiry figure holding a cane stood above him.

"What the fuck?"

"You're trespassing, sir, on my premises. Kindly move it along."

In the shadow of the pier – and through the dryness of his contact lenses – he couldn't make out the face, nor did he see any point in arguing over a patch of sand. He crawled down the beach. A glance at his watch. Three AM. If he could just get a few hours of sleep before the sun came up, he'd figure out his next move in the morning.

"Got a light?"

Gil looked over. It was the same character who'd poked him in the back. "Do I have a light? Is that what you asked?"

"Ah, begging your pardon. May I, with all the customary prostration befitting such an entreaty, humbly trouble you for a goddamn filthy match?"

Gil could see now in the full light of the moon the man who'd taken his space below the pier. "Sunshine? Is that you?"

"Come again?"

"Never mind."

"And how about that match, governor?"

"I don't have any matches."

201

"Very well, O Keeper of the Sacred Ignition. In such a circumstance, might I receive a complimentary spark from your gold-plated lighter?"

"Sorry, no."

The scrawny tramp grumbled something to himself while fussing over his belongings. He flopped over motionless and a moment later was snoring like an angry elephant seal.

Gil rose up, grabbed the backpack, and wandered a hundred or so yards farther down the beach. A steady breeze blew up from the sea, and he soon grew cold. He never did quite fall asleep, but dipped in and out of a dream in which he was simultaneously falling and drowning. When the sun rose, it immediately warmed the air, making any kind of rest impossible. He brushed off the sand fleas and went up the beach to a doughnut shop, trailing sand from his hair and clothes as he went.

He was the only customer. Some great old jazz was playing, but the young girl working the counter kept talking over it. She had somehow gotten the impression that he wanted to have a long, astoundingly one-sided conversation. In the middle of the incoherent monologue, she let out a burst of laughter. He sat looking out the window while she carried on with clueless abandon. He could neither tune out her voice nor make any sense of it. Still, he remained quiet out of some sense of decorum, despite very much wanting her to shut up. *I could be coupled to such a woman. I could go through this baffling ritual every morning. After seven years I would be married to the sound of that voice, not the woman producing it.*

"What's this music?" he finally asked.

She said something, but he couldn't understand.

"The music? Do you know the name of the song or the bandleader?"

She mentioned a music-streaming service and ducked into the deli case.

He walked up to the counter. "I'm sorry but I have to find out who's on that other horn. I can hear Dizzy all right, but who's he trading fours with? Is that Clifford Brown?"

She pulled her head out and looked up at him. He might as well have been asking her to juggle a dozen doughnut holes.

To stay or not stay in San Diego. It wasn't even a question. He'd lost touch with all his friends from the old UCSD days and had no money to pay the impound and storage fees on the Gemini. In his present condition, he couldn't imagine plea bargaining with a rigidly humorless justice of the highways who'd been banging the gavel in traffic court the past twenty years. No, he now realized he'd gotten off easy the previous night. That kind of luck wasn't likely to carry over to a Monday morning hearing.

He bought a thirty-four-dollar Amtrak ticket to LA and spent the next three hours seated opposite twin manic Jesus freaks, who amused him with their gravely worded revelations of the end of the world. Beyond their identical appearance, they each had the same tattoo of a delirious-looking savior on the left shoulder. There was no sense in debating these two. Best to just let them run till they run out of gas. What's more, the rational accounts of the universe Gil had been studying the past eight years were wearing thinner by the day. Sitting in an overly air-conditioned train car with a frosty breeze blowing down the back of his neck, he was actually warmed by the pair's descriptions of a fiery hell. The thing to do now was listen. Pay attention and enjoy the show.

As the train neared LA, Gil took his turn. "Can either of you boys recall any experience with reincarnation?"

No, that was nonsense.

"Actually, it's quite real. I wouldn't want to rile you up too much with my own stories, but I've listened patiently to you, haven't I?"

They couldn't argue with that.

203

"What would you say if I told you I've lived many past lives, going back as far as the first known humans? I can almost remember swinging from vines, but not quite, know what I mean?"

The two stared back at him, saucer-eyed. It was the first time the whole trip they hadn't said anything.

"I didn't want to bring this up till I knew it was safe." He turned around to be sure no one else was listening. "I even lived one of my past lives during the time of your savior, if you can believe it. Who knows, maybe that was the thing that brought us together today. Now, I didn't know the guy personally, mind you, but I heard a lot about him. Mostly good stuff."

He looked up to make eye contact and see how he was doing, then turned an unsuppressed laugh into a cough. "I'm sorry," he said, shaking it off. "The centuries have added up." He excused himself to switch cars, coughing all the way.

42

When he got off the city bus Monday morning, the news crews were already staked out at Los Angeles Correctional Academy. He crossed Washington Boulevard, wondering if a skateboarding student had finally been struck by a commuter.

Or perhaps the custodial union followed through on its delayed threat to strike. No, it was nothing like that. They were there for him.

"Mr. Crowell, will you be making a statement today?"

"From where did you recruit these girls?"

"Were you working with a gang or a group of partners?"

While he had no precise sense what they were asking, he knew enough to plow through the phalanx of TV cameras and foam-covered microphones pointed at him like daggers. A few probationary students stood off to the side. One of them, a girl reporting for the journalism class, elbowed the pros out of her way.

"What is it like, Mr. Crowell, to be the center of so much attention?"

He passed security at the main entrance and went into the nearest men's staff restroom, taking shelter inside a stall. With a wad of toilet paper, he mopped up the previous user's errant urine droplets and reached for a seat cover. The dispenser was empty. The stall door was busted open such that it wouldn't stay closed. To keep it from swinging open, he had to hold it shut with an outstretched hand while doing his business.

Seated there with eyes shut, his left arm extended to the door, he tried to picture how the rest of the day would unfold. At some point, they would send him to district headquarters downtown. That much was certain. But before that –

Suddenly two hard knocks came from outside the stall. Each was forcible enough to jolt the door slightly open, even with Gil bracing it shut from the inside.

"*Ocupado!*" Gil called out.

"Crowell, I know you're in there. Open up."

"Bertram?"

"What are you doing here, Crowell?"

"I'll leave that to your imagination."

"You've been fired, and that means you must leave the premises immediately." Bertram tried pushing the door open.

"Are you crazy? I'm using the toilet!"

"Out of here this instant!"

Using his overdeveloped upper-body strength, Bertram easily overcame the pressure Gil placed on the door from the inside. With his pants still down around his knees, Gil shot off the toilet seat and tackled Bertram to the tile floor. The two men wrestled around in the viscous filth, tumbling toward the urinals. Bertram was bigger and much stronger than him, but Gil – with his bare ass and balls flopping about – was fighting with something like pride, though clearly not that.

A newly hired teacher from Ghana entered the men's room. It had perhaps been his intention to take a quick leak before his first-period class.

"Excuse me, gentlemen," he said, stepping away from the tangled bodies. "Is this some kind of lovers' quarrel?" Neither wrestler acknowledged the question, so the dapper African raised his voice. "Gentlemen, stop this at once!"

That worked. Like most half-hearted warriors, both men took the first opportunity to quit. Each let go of the other at the same moment and got to his feet. Bertram's characteristically pink face went from purple to red as blood coursed back up his neck. Remarkably, his black plastic-framed glasses never fell off. Gil leaned forward to pull up his trousers. Each man went to opposite corners of the bathroom, taking hold of whatever he could for support: a sink for Bertram, a wall-mounted hand dryer for Gil. The sound of deep labored breathing filled the air. They cast agonized glances at one another off the mirrors. Bertram staggered to the wall.

"Is that toilet paper you have on your head?" the Ghanaian asked Bertram.

"What?" Bertram turned around to face the mirror squarely.

"Behind your ear," the Ghanaian said. "No, the other ear. All right, now listen, both of you." He sharpened his tone. "I don't know what that was, and between the three of us, I'd

206

rather not find out. I'm new here and not about to get mixed up in the politics of this place."

"Oh, you'd rather not get mixed up in them, huh?" Gil asked, his speech halting sporadically as he gathered his breath. "You'd prefer not to know how the administration barges into toilet stalls while teachers are relieving themselves? No, because then you'd be a witness to a crime, wouldn't you?"

"That's a distortion of facts," Bertram said, turning around. "This man is trespassing."

"Trespassing!" Gil repeated. "I work here, you bald-headed fart!"

"Watch your language," Bertram said. "Title Nine laws are in effect, even here in the restroom. This is no sanctuary from them, believe me. I keep up on the Ed Code."

"The Ed Code!" Gil exclaimed. "Oh, my *god*! Are you crazy?" He bent forward, took hold of his knees.

"You no longer work here," Bertram said. "You're breaking the law just by being here."

"I saw you in Tijuana, buddy!" Gil jabbed his finger in Bertram's direction. "You, a married man, in the gayest bar in town. Busted!"

"What are you talking about?" Bertram asked.

"*You*! I'm talking about *you*! Friday night at El Jugador Alegre with the spinning dicks swinging down the bar top and the coked-out drag queens dancing in cages and *you* in the middle of it all! That's what I'm talking about! That's what I'm talking about!" He strutted across the floor tiles in a pathetic little victory dance.

"My wife and I were in Palm Springs all weekend racing a tandem bicycle for charity." Bertram jutted out his chin. "We finished in the top third and raised five hundred dollars for canine distemper."

"Listen to this guy," Gil said to the Ghanaian. "Palm Springs he's talking about. A bike race for charity. Can you believe this?" But in that instant an aperture of doubt opened in

207

his mind. "And what do you mean I'm *fired*?" he asked. "What about the union? Teacher jail? Due process? Hello!"

"What are *you* talking about?" Bertram asked, gaining poise with each recovered breath. "None of those protections apply to you. You're probationary. Tenure takes three years."

"What?"

"You had no rights in this labor exchange. You march when we tell you to march, and your marching days are over. Now it's time to march on out of here before I call the police."

"You must be mistaken."

"No, Crowell. That's the best part. I'm not mistaken because I don't make those kinds of mistakes."

"Gentlemen," the Ghanaian interrupted. "I have to teach my French class. Can you two manage to continue this without resorting to violence?"

"French class?" Bertram said. "What French class do you teach here, sir? We hired you for English."

"Ms. Mott said she needed someone to fill in on a first-period French class," the Ghanaian said.

"Is that right? And they speak French in Africa?" Bertram asked. "I thought they spoke English."

"I do speak English. I'm speaking it now. I also speak five other languages."

"Five other languages? Let me hear some French."

"*Qu'est-ce que tu veux que je dise?*"

"What's that supposed to mean?"

"What do you want me to say?" the Ghanaian replied.

Bertram shrugged. "Just tell me what it means."

"That's what it means."

Gil stepped between them. "Okay, while you two figure out your comedy routine, I'll be finishing up in the stall."

"Those toilets are for employees only," Bertram said, his arm outstretched to block the way. "I already told you that."

"And don't forget what I told you," the Ghanaian said to Bertram. "I'm the only witness here, like the man said. Let him finish his business." As Gil re-entered the stall, the Ghanaian turned and walked out the men's room door.

"While you're waiting," Gil called out from his reclaimed seat on the throne, "you can prepare a copy of my termination papers, something I can fax over to the union."

"That was already sent out," Bertram replied, "by certified mail. I took care of it Thursday afternoon, so you must have signed for it by now."

"I signed nothing, Bertram. I was out of town this weekend. Present me with another copy."

"Ah, yes," Bertram said. "Down in Tijuana, pimping your filthy whores."

Gil came out of the stall, buckling up. "What did you say?" he asked, over the sound of the flushing toilet.

"Your whores, Crowell. The very creatures that did you in. Yeah, it was the website. Nice work." He gave his best icy smile, but on such a face it looked more like frozen dough.

"Let me tell you something about filthy whores, pal. There's not a single one down there who couldn't do your job blindfolded, but you'd last about twelve seconds trying to do theirs. No, you just keep sucking off the city tit, Bertram. Call your meetings, write your memos, drum up new ways to rationalize your sinecure. You're worthless, and everybody knows it."

"Sinecure?" Bertram repeated.

"Yeah, you like that word, Mister I-used-to-teach-literature-till-I-found-my-true-calling-in-administration? Look it up in the dictionary while you fill out my pink slip. There should be a thumbnail of your fat red face next to the definition. Now get out of my way. I have to wash my hands."

Bertram nodded at Gil's reflection in the mirror. "That was a tight little speech, Crowell. Al Pacino would be proud. But you're still fired, and that's my last word on the subject."

As Gil headed down the main corridor to Bertram's office, the first-period tardy bell rang. The student bodies plodded to their dreaded destinations. Through a grated window, he could see the news crews shuffling back to their wonky vans on Washington Boulevard. Just then a loud pop shot through the air. Nobody reacted at first. A couple seconds later came another. That's when the screaming and running began.

"You nitwit, give me that!" It was Wretchler, there in the middle of it all on the main corridor, noticeably taller than most of the students. He had a frightened-looking youth pinned against the lockers and was removing a small pistol from his hand, what looked to be no more than a toy. Twenty feet farther down the hall was Bertram, spinning around on the floor as he had in the men's room, this time in a solo performance. Blood spilled out the back of his leg. Gil raced up to him.

"Get him!" Bertram called out in agony, pointing at Gil. "Man is armed! Armed and trespassing!"

Wretchler approached from the other side. "It wasn't Crowell, goddamn you. It was this blockhead." He held the student's arm. "I've got him now and the gun, so just pipe down, Bertram. And get over to the side before somebody slips on your blood."

Dr. Lee came down the hallway from the other direction. The news crews were falling all over themselves to keep up. She recognized at once what had happened. "Mr. Wretchler, take this student to grief counseling, please. We have on-site services, psychosocial workers, for these types of flareups," she stated for the cameras. "Los Angeles Correctional Academy is unique in that regard. We specialize in the finest facilities, counselors, and treatments available. Many of these youths," she continued, "are simply misunderstood. Terribly misunderstood and misguided. While our job as educators –"

"It's Crowell!" Bertram howled up from the floor. "Get him out of here!"

Dr. Lee turned away from the news crews and looked down at Bertram, then Gil standing beside him. The cameras followed her eyes. "Yes, Mr. Bertram, we're taking care of everything. Mr. Crow, why are you here? You've been fired. Didn't you send him the papers, Mr. Bertram?"

"Of course I sent them!"

"Security!" she called down the hall. "Security! Emergency!"

One of the school's armed guards came around a corner in the hallway, stepping around Bertram. "Officer Steckel, please remove Mr. Crow from the campus at once. Excuse me," she said to the cameras. "Where was I?" Another guard arrived, then another.

"Are you insane?" Gil asked. "There's a man on the floor with a bullet in his ass and you're carrying on about district policy?"

"Get him out of here!" Bertram yelped. "Trespassing! Armed and dangerous! Call the police!"

"We're getting him out now," Dr. Lee said. "Please just be still, Mr. Bertram. Another officer is on the way."

But she didn't need to say any of that. The security guards had already seized Gil by the elbows and begun dragging him down the hallway to the main entrance. The news crews and Dr. Lee trailed behind while Bertram writhed away on the floor like an acid head making snow angels.

Walking away from the facility, Gil passed three ambulances and fourteen cop cars. It looked like LAPD had it under control. There wasn't anything to do but go back to his room at the Koenig House and decompress. At the bus stop, a young man kept sidelonging Gil. Finally, he sauntered over, wagging a finger. "Hey, aren't you – aren't you that guy that was on the news the other night?"

"I don't think so," Gil said.

211

"Yeah, you're the high school pimp." The kid looked around, as though searching for someone to share in his discovery. "That's fucking awesome man. Like in that TV show, right?"

"I don't know."

"That TV show with the high school math teacher who pimped out all the girls on the diving team. You never saw that?"

"No."

"Oh, that was a great show, but they shut it down after four episodes. The best stuff always gets canceled."

"I don't own a TV so I wouldn't have seen it. I'm also not a teacher. Little footnote."

The kid's face fell. With nothing left to say, he drifted back to the other side of the bus stop. He continued looking over at Gil, then came back with a recharged sense of urgency. "Well, maybe they'll make a TV show out of you now, huh? Have you thought about that?"

"Thought about what?"

"Ah, come on man. You had your face all over the news, right? Maybe they'll make a reality TV show out of it. This is America, right?"

"Yeah, I don't know what you're talking about. Can I just catch the bus? You're starting to creep me out a little."

"Oh, right," the kid said with a smirk. "Laying low, huh?" He laughed to himself. "Sorry, I've just never met anyone famous before."

"Let's give it a rest."

But for all the bold impropriety, his fellow bus rider's account of things had not been mistaken. When Gil got back to the house later that morning, Norm greeted him at the front door as he came up the steps of the entranceway.

"Seen any TV news, son?"

"I've heard a few things. What's the damage?"

212

"Check it out for yourself. I have it right here on my laptop."

"...behind me here on Washington Boulevard where a high school teacher has been fired for allegedly running a cyber-brothel. The teacher's name is Gilmore Crowell, and what they're saying he did here at Los Angeles Correctional Academy was an outrageous violation of the public trust. Operated out of an English classroom of this juvenile detention facility was a prostitution website, if you can believe it. The question on everyone's mind tonight is whether Crowell was recruiting high school girls enrolled here. That certainly seems possible and – some would say – highly plausible. While we cannot yet confirm or deny anything that may or may not have happened, this entrepreneurial English teacher is out of at least one job tonight, Paul. Back to you in the studio."

43

Anthro-999 – the dissertation workshop informally known as Slug-out – held its first class of the spring semester that evening at six-fifteen. Gil took the Number Twenty-One bus down Wilshire Boulevard to the edge of campus. It was already dark with threadbare clouds woven across an El Greco sky. From his drop-off point at the south kiosk, he wound down the herring-brick footpath past the medical center, through the espaliered archway separating the planetarium from the natatorium, and angled across the geometric lawns of the bursar's complex. In front of the library, a pack of frat boys merrily trampled the Indian hawthorn shrubs. A bevy of gulls bewailed the cruel chain-link cage of the loading dock dumpster. And from an open dorm window Eminem blustered to the beats of untreated self-absorption. All the evident signs of foreshadowing from Frinkle's literary guide seemed to be taking shape.

As he approached the social sciences building, Gil's heart began to surge. He tried slowing things down with some deep breathing as he went up to the anthro floor. It was then that it hit him: There was little chance his academic career would survive the scandal. He imagined in his vulnerable state that he must have created the website as a means of self-sabotage. After all when one really got down to the essential business of human nature, the will to fail was equal to the will to succeed. With success came pride and that reinforced ego, which led to danger. With failure came truth, the cold hard truth of self-knowledge: Either he was not good enough to get a PhD or he didn't think he was good enough. What was the difference? Maybe there was a third option of which he was scarcely aware, like believing he was above and beyond it all. Just as he had despised his parents' values, had he also come to despise his own? Did he unconsciously seek to dismiss and destroy everything he believed in because that's *who he was*, the person he was genetically constituted to be? It was a losing mindset but in such a world success was for suckers, those who believed they were special and thus entitled to it, too foolish to realize what they studied wasn't worth anyone's time and that was why nobody read their insufferable dissertation. Or was that the mad thought process of a damaged mind, one that studied sex workers instead of tibia variation in early hominins? He caught

214

himself before slipping too far down that dark slope. No, he loved learning; he loved science; he loved people. Well, in theory at least.

Srinivas Chakrabarti, Wilson James, and Ebby were huddled in their usual spot out in the hallway, discussing something with far too much enthusiasm. Their energy level dropped as Gil approached until they simply stopped talking altogether and just stared at him.

"Innocent till proven guilty," Gil said with a lifeless laugh, intending to cut through the first lines of awkwardness. His opening wasn't returned and a moment of silence followed.

"When has that ever been true?" Wilson finally asked.

"Here we go," Ebby said, stepping back. "Black man gonna set everybody straight."

"Take it easy," Srinivas said to Wilson. "Let's not get ahead of the investigation."

"Investigation?" Wilson asked. "What are you talking about? This is the court of public opinion, bro. Ain't no burden of proof to hurdle. The skankiest skanks from Skanktown have brought down governors, senators, even Tiger Woods."

"Oh, listen to this," Ebby said, walking away, only to turn right back around and rejoin the huddle.

"Ever watched the evening news?" Wilson asked. "They closed with this shit the other night like it was a community interest story. How could any career survive that?" He turned to Gil. "I'm only bringing it up 'cause I care. Otherwise, I'd be clowning like these two." He took him by the shoulders, brought his face down to his level. "I'm surprised you even showed up tonight, but I get it. You're owning up."

"All right, let's try to think some positive thoughts," Srinivas said.

"Yeah?" Wilson said. "Should we say a team prayer, too?"

215

"Thank you for the warning, gentlemen," Gil said, "but I'm pretty sure I'll be all right." He heard himself say it but wasn't sure he believed.

"Spoken like an innocent man," Srinivas said.

"Or at least one wishing to appear innocent," Ebby added.

"All right, I'm going in now," Gil said.

"We're going to hold back a bit," Ebby said, patting Gil on the shoulder and pushing him forward.

As each semester of Slug-out included a new instructor and a handful of new Slugs – those taking the seats of the Alicia Cosgroves, the Magnus Wingates, and the Petra Solises of the department – the class began with the usual round-robin introductions. The new instructor kicked things off.

"Hello everybody, and if you'll just look up here a moment, I'll tell you a bit about myself." The lights dimmed, and an LCD projector lit up a screen hanging from the ceiling. A much larger brighter version of the instructor's head came to life. "Good evening," it said in a deeper register, "and welcome to Anthropology-999."

Gil closed his eyes, exhaled through a thin part in his lips. Academic limbo, that's what this was. Was it grandiose to imagine himself the world's most inept anthropologist? Logically, there had to be a worst of everything, didn't there? The worst president, worst actor, worst dishwasher. Somewhere the world's worst brain surgeon carved into somebody's skull; the worst rocket scientist drafted a new missile.

"My published name is J. Arch Schwartz so if you're tracking me down on the Internet, you can start there. My real name is Jonathan Scerzinski. Friends call me Jack." The giant distorted screen version of Jonathan Scerzinski's illuminated head looked down on them.

Someone laughed. The real-life Jonathan Scerzinski had already retreated to a corner of the seminar room to whisper into

216

his cell phone. Gil wiped the sweat from his hands to his hair, down his neck, and into his beard. The projection continued:

"My scholarly interests are around the subject of think tanks," it said with a shrug. "How they're conceived and raised; how they come of age and become American centers, councils, and institutes in their own right; how they mature, reproduce, and eventually pass on as we all do – some taking their rightful place in history, others fading away never to be heard from again."

Real-life Jonathan Scerzinski spun around, turned off his phone with one hand and paused the video with a remote device in the other. He nodded at the lifeless-looking Slug to his left. "Shall we begin with you then?"

"Do I speak to you or the screen?" the Slug asked.

"Ideally you could speak to all of us." Jonathan Scerzinski gestured toward everyone seated around the seminar table. "Start by telling us who you are."

"Prescott Clutterbuck, paleopathology, Mesoamerican civilization."

"Thank you, Prescott. Would you like to say anything about the progress of your work?"

Prescott wagged his head no.

"Okay, well, thank you then," Jonathan Scerzinski said. "We'll look forward to hearing more from you. Would you like to continue?" He smiled oafishly at the young woman seated next in line around the seminar table.

"Cynthia Kaufman is my name. It is both my real name and my published name. The title of my master's thesis is Landscape of Flesh: Tantric Sects of the Kangra District, 1902 to 1948. Now half price on Amazon. I intend to continue the line of inquiry through the dissertation." She began rummaging through her handbag.

"Very interesting, Cynthia. And what happened in 1948?"

"That's when my study ends."

217

Candace Beswick eyed Gil from the far end of the table, her tongue slathering across her incisors. Gil nervously tapped out the rhythm of Miles Davis' *So What* on the edge of his chair.

Jonathan Scerzinksi nodded at the next Slug in line. "Would you like to continue then?"

"Hello, yes. I'm Daphne Minster-Farrand. So, I think of myself primarily as a morphological linguist. My work penetrates the object of phallocentric domination within the overarching bisexual intercourse. But I'd like to probe something else tonight if I may. It regards this person," she said, pointing across the seminar table at Gil, "and what we've all been hearing about him the news."

"What have we all been hearing?" Jonathan Scerzinski asked. He looked from face to face.

"I'd like some clarity, as well," Candace said. She set her eyes on Gil while teething the longest, thickest highlighter anyone had ever seen.

"Has something happened I should know about?" Jonathan Scerzinski asked.

"It's this guy right here," Candace said, pointing a sparkly fingernail at Gil. "Let's give him a chance to explain himself."

"What exactly —" Jonathan Scerzinski began, but Candace cut him off with a raised hand.

"That's all right, Jack. I've got it under control. Explain yourself, Mr. Crowell. What have we all been hearing about you in the news recently?"

"Yes, do tell," Cynthia Kaufman added, "who you are, and why —"

"Objection!" Ebby called out, but when Wilson and Srinivas slid their chairs away, Ebby lowered his voice a couple octaves. "Excuse my interruption. Please continue."

Gil raised his eyes to the ceiling, took a breath. He looked to be inducing a trance, but the room was already filling

218

with pink cottony air, its foundation slipping away underneath him. The clock on the wall ticked off the seconds of silence. He braced himself on the tabletop and rose out of his chair. The young women of the class looked on with a single expression. Jonathan Scerzinski consulted his cell phone. Ebby, Wilson James, and Srinivas Chakrabarti lowered their eyes in deference to the moment's gravity. And Gilmore Crowell turned and walked out the door.

Having regained enough composure to ride an elevator to the ground floor, he retraced his path back to the bus stop on the edge of campus. The faces of the working poor returning from their daily labors beheld him from both sides of the bus aisle. He sat next to an old woman, who jerked her raggedy bags away. When her haunch barely touched Gil's, she slid closer to the window and looked out as though plotting her escape. A girl no more than five years old stared at him vacantly, as young children often do without any self-awareness. As the girl's mother noticed her fixation, she pulled her closer, lest Gil happen to seize the child as he got off the bus.

Every cultural anthro course he'd ever taken had romanticized the poor as the salt of the earth, the wretched product of unrestrained social forces. Yet here he was, absorbing their imagined fears and contempt. He desperately wanted to stand up and announce in perfect Spanish that he was one of them, a common man laid to waste by the same crooked system. Of course, he lacked the nerve to pull it off. Just as well; such a speech would be dismissed as outright lunacy. He slunk down at eye level with the pornographic graffiti on the seatback in front of him.

From out of nowhere, a backpack full of textbooks hit him on the side of the head. He could tell without turning around that someone standing in the aisle had been rocked off balance by the movements of the bus. When he looked up, he couldn't believe his eyes.

219

"Petra?"

She smirked, flipped the half-hawk locks away from her face. "How are you, Gil?"

"Seriously?"

"Why not?"

"Well, it's just that in the past forty-eight hours, I've had my car impounded, wrestled with my boss on the floor of a men's room, been fired from my teaching position, slandered in the local media, and publicly censured by my fellow Slugs in the graduate program. If I had a wife, I imagine she'd be home right now packing her bags."

"That's a damning report."

"I'm surprised you haven't heard anything."

"I don't have a TV."

"Yes, I remember," he said. "We used to lie around and talk about all the shows we hadn't seen. Those were good times. What's going on with you? Where are you going and why are you taking the MTA?"

"Just returning from the university while supporting our city's public transportation."

"I thought you finished your thesis. Didn't you tell me that?"

"Yes, I teach there now. Just started this semester. They brought me on as an adjunct on a couple survey classes." She held up an introductory text.

"An adjunct, wow. Just leap-frogged over the lecturers, huh? Well, congratulations, Petra. I'm happy for you."

"Don't say it if you don't mean it."

"Why wouldn't I mean it?"

"All right, thanks. I'm getting off here. Take my number, just in case."

"Pretty sure I have it already."

"No, it's a new number. Here." She handed him a business card.

220

"Petra Solis. Department of Anthropology. So, it really happens then. People actually move forward in life. I wish I could say this gives me hope but the timing would be wrong."

"You'll get through it, Gil."

"Just to be clear, you're not *giving-me-your-number* giving me your number, you're just giving me your number, right?"

"Don't give it too much thought."

She looked good, or maybe he was just horny. It was a surprise to feel anything sexual at the end of such a day. The body's systems weren't so unified after all. He transferred over to the Alvarado line. The faces there were even angrier and more defeated than on the first bus. The ride was short, however. He got off at the corner of Pico just past the Koenig House. It was close to nine. A single reporter was hanging around the entranceway, but no camera crew.

"Mr. Crowell, LA school reporter dot com."

"No comment." Gil cut past him and climbed the steps.

"The school shooting today at Los Angeles Correctional Academy. What are your thoughts?"

Gil paused in his attempt to get a key in the door, turned to face the reporter. "What are my thoughts on the school shooting?"

"Yes." The man held out his smartphone to record the response.

"I was mostly against it."

"Elaborate, please."

"Well, it gets in the way of learning, doesn't it?" Gil said.

"How do you mean exactly?"

"Gunfire is a distraction. There's the noise and all the blood. It sticks to the floor, stains the shoes. And the chaos that follows. The media, the vigils, the town halls. It has a real effect on a school's community. No, they need to work out the kinks before I can get on board."

221

"Who do you mean by *they?*"

"Whoever it is that's behind school shootings."

"Thank you, Mr. Crowell. And what about your own situation?"

"I'm less sure about that."

44

Gil entered his room, switched on the light. A stench of cat urine wafted over on the draft of the open door. He stepped out of his shoes and took a beer from the mini-fridge, then booted up the laptop. Search words: *high school, teacher, Los Angeles, pimp.* A story from the Times popped right up. No photo, just a four-paragraph single-column screed laid out like the police report in a small-town rag. The school shooting was farther down in the endless feed, a three-sentence paragraph with no mention of Bertram's condition. He wondered how the bowling-ball-headed blowhard was doing. And what of Wretchler and the teen shooter?

Aiming to bypass a round of morbid self-reflection, he sought distraction on the Internet. He did a Google search for Kelvin Masterson, an undergraduate roommate he'd lost touch with. The posted obituary of some other Kelvin Masterson appeared. Gil clicked the link to the online memorial and swiped through all seventy-six posted photos of this unknown individual's life. He lit a virtual candle in the dead man's honor and moved on to a dating site where he'd created an account months before. At the time, he didn't have the money for full access so he signed up for the free version, which allowed only a view of the subscribers. Nearly every woman stated her demands for a long-term relationship followed by marriage and children. Great care was put into the digital photos: bikinied on the beach, cleavaging in the garden, sluttied up at the office Christmas party.... He was moved by how desperate and unoriginal each entry appeared. This one posing on Sydney Harbor Bridge, that one at the Eiffel Tower, another at Niagara Falls. In each photo, the centerpiece was the outfit worn, not the travel landmark. The cozy home shots were visually shrill. And then the out-and-abouts: posturing on Rodeo Drive, rollerblading the Venice boardwalk, jet-skiing the slate gray waters of the South Bay.... Not a single candid exposure. His mind wandered to the men's entries. Surely they were dumber, cruder, and more obvious.

He snapped shut the laptop and cried. Not a blubbering breakdown, but a tear came to his eye just the same. Was he lamenting all the lonely people of the world, their misguided direction and imbecilic mating skills? No, but for a moment he thought so. There must be a clinical term for denying one's pain in order to vicariously process someone else's. If not, some grad student was working on it. He caught himself again in the throes of his cynicism, acknowledged the complete exhaustion he'd been living with the last several weeks, the lost sleep and adrenal overload. The resulting scattershot neurotransmissions conjured up all sorts of irrational projections and emotional extremes. His mind returned to his so-called anthropology career. After tonight, surely it was finished. Another voice said maybe not, a lone defender of the world's volatility. Ava's face came to mind, the last look she'd given him at the hotel. So out of character. It appeared to take on new meaning, a foresighted goodbye perhaps, though of this he was also unsure.

A weary glance from Mother Cat set him straight. It informed him that he'd only been feeling sorry for himself and his lost time. Lying there in her cardboard nursery with three kittens sucking the life out of her, she bluntly judged him a crackpot and a fraud.

"Oh, get lost, would you?" he called down to her. "You're so distant and controlling. A dog would be more understanding. Try to be more like a dog."

She absorbed this domestic abuse with grace, flashing him her best needle-toothed yawn.

He took from his jeans the business card Petra Solis had handed him, studied it for several minutes, and spun it out the open window to the dumpster below. It suddenly became clear why the women on the dating site had professed such guileless demands for a lockdown relationship. It was both self-preservation and what civil society expected. What kind of man pursues a woman openly trolling for sex? Most, of course, but therein lies the rub: She only wants one. A list of demands filters out the scum.

The phone buzzed off the floor, derailing that mad tangent. He picked it up, checked the caller ID. It was Rex. He let it continue buzzing. If it buzzed all the way to voicemail, it meant the big bum wanted something. If it ended after a few buzzes, then he was just checking in. It went to five buzzes and the outgoing message began. The call quickly ended. He waited, staring at the phone. It buzzed again, and he took it.

"How can I help you?"

"How can you help *me*?" Rex chuckled. "That's a good one."

"Figure of speech. What do you want?"

"Take it easy. Just wondering how you're holding up."

"Yeah, you'd like to know, wouldn't you?" Gil said.

"Well, of course, why not? I mean, this is crazy, isn't it? I can't even grasp how you're dealing with it."

"Thanks for your concern."

"You got talk radio beating down your door? You can make a lot of money off this if you play it right. Have you gone over that yet with an agent?"

"No and no."

"Good," Rex said. "Wait for the book offers, and make sure you get a six-figure advance."

"I can only imagine you're out of your drug-addled mind, but sure, why not?"

"How's that?"

"I've spent the last eight years – that's one fourth of my life – becoming a scholar, not some fly-by-night operator."

"A scholar of prostitutes."

"Correct, and I'm not about to trade that in for some cable news notoriety."

"It's a funny world," Rex said.

"No, it isn't."

"Funny strange, I mean. Listen to this. I met a chick who teaches at the junior college out here. Totally into astrology going back to the Mayans and the Babylonians. You wouldn't believe how complex this stuff is. She tells me the other day that Mercury is in retrograde, whatever the hell that's supposed to mean. At first, I thought she was jabbering on, right? But then I saw your whole trip on the news and –"

"No, you don't."

"What?"

"Don't call up here with some horoscope horseshit some woman laid down after a couple lines of blow. Not tonight you don't."

"What's gotten into you?"

"You're seriously asking that right now? Want me to hang up?"

"I take it back. Figure of speech, right?"

"Look, I don't have time for this," Gil said. "Thanks for checking in."

"No, wait –"

"If you're so concerned, you can loan me a few hundred dollars."

"A few hundred dollars?"

"Make it an even grand."

"Dude, you know I don't have that kind of scratch lying around. The little I have is tied up in mutual funds and money market accounts. The penalties for withdrawal –"

"All right, I'm hanging up now."

"You know what you ought to do?" Rex asked.

Gil flipped the phone closed, sending the call to oblivion.

45

Low-end news crews staked out the Koenig House the following morning. They came up with the sun and stayed till mid-afternoon. The manager, Claudia, would bark Spanish obscenities at them while she dumped her dirty mop bucket down the front steps. They'd back away as the suds sloshed forward, then reconvene once she'd closed the door. Like a cloud of gnats, they could only be scattered a moment, always returning to formation.

Most of her simmering rage was directed at Gil. He sensed it as she scrambled his eggs in the mornings, batted down goulash at lunch, and ran her vacuum over his heels in the afternoons. For well over a year, he'd been practically invisible.

Rarely taking meals, always off at the university or up in his room. Now he was just *there* like some kind of vagrant – scandalized, disheveled, and looking more unemployable every day.

He took to furtively coming and going through his bedroom window, scaling up the security bars to get in and jumping down on the plastic lid of the dumpster departing. Leaving early each morning, he bound through the backyards to Eleventh Street and took the long way across to the doughnut shop at Alvarado and Pico. From there, he gulped coffee, ate powdered doughnuts, and looked out the huge plate glass window at the clueless reporters on the other side of the street. All the while he tinkered with the dissertation, fleshing out case studies and slipping a bit of shit into the mix for good measure. Afternoons he walked the streets of Westlake, inevitably crashing on the lawns of MacArthur Park.

He got to know some of the more presentable class of homeless, those with unbloodied faces who still had shoes on their feet. Also, the regular day crew, including the bearded dragon dealer, the megaphonic preacher woman, and a charismatic young dope freak who shot up in the tunnel beneath Wilshire Boulevard.

One time, as he was sketching the splashing patterns of mud-colored ducks in the reservoir, an Asian woman with a wide-brimmed hat and matching hygienic mask handed him a greasy two-dollar bill. He took it in hand, turning it over warily. When he looked up, she was gone. She'd mistaken him for one of the park residents. Another time, an old tramp asked if a heap of trash belonged to Gil. Following his failure to answer, the street-wise transient rifled through the pile.

When one of his former students passed by, he wondered why it hadn't happened sooner. Her name slipped his mind, but the face he placed to third period: a smart girl who had taken her assignments and probation seriously. She was with her mother and much younger brother.

"Crowell!" she called out, her eyes lighting up at the sight of him.

"Hello," he responded demurely.

"Are you all right, Crowell?" She looked down at him with his sunburned skin and ratty beard. She seemed to be forming a conception of her disgraced teacher out of the juvenile detention setting.

"Yes, thank you. How are you?"

"Good. This is my mother."

"Nice to meet you," Gil said. He reached up to take the woman's hand. She looked down at him, clearly unaware who he was.

"A lot of people have been talking about you at school, Crowell," the girl said with obvious amusement.

"I'm sorry," Gil said. "I've forgotten your name."

"Amelia."

"Amelia," he repeated. "Isn't that funny, I was about to say Madeline and now I'm wondering if I've ever known a Madeline."

At a lack of attention, her younger brother began writhing figure eights through and around his mother's legs, swinging from her arms to accelerate the turns. She can't smack him, Gil thought. Not with all these bicycle cops circling around.

"So what happened, Crowell?" Amelia asked.

"You probably know better than I," he replied. "Why, what have you heard?"

"Prostituting students, possession of pornography, corruption of minors, trespassing –"

"Trespassing, huh?" He removed a twig from his beard. "No, none of those things happened, at least not the way they're telling it. The truth is always far less compelling, I'm afraid. I do have a loose link to a community of sex workers. That's about as far as it goes." He looked up at the mother to see how much of this she was following. "I studied them for a few years

228

in Tijuana. You know, like we studied literature in our English class?"

Amelia looked down at him. "Trying to figure out their character?"

"The character of the community, yes. Anyway, some people found that out and used it against me. I could have defended myself a little better. Truth is, I just didn't want to hang around a high school jailhouse much longer." He grinned up at them both a little defiantly.

"Our sub is insane," she said. "All he does is rip up newspapers and wave them around the classroom. He says there's government spies everywhere. On rooftops, in passing cars, coming out of computer screens. He even looks through our backpacks as we come through the door. He drives around in this beat-up old station wagon with a ladder strapped to the roof. I think he paints houses after school. Anyway, he hasn't graded anything yet. Come to think of it, he hasn't really assigned anything either."

"I've seen that fellow around. They'll probably make him principal before too long, though he sounds overqualified."

This offhand prophecy had a sudden impact on the little brother, who began wailing like a wounded monkey. He pulled his mother's arm in the direction he wanted her to take him.

"I've been thinking about you, Crowell," Amelia said. "I think your problem is that you're smart-stupid."

"What's that supposed to mean?"

"Smart-stupid?"

"Yeah."

"It's the opposite of stupid-smart," she said, "which is what I am. That's what my friends say anyway."

"Thanks for clarifying."

She hesitated, as though deciding whether to continue. "What I'm saying is you're really smart, Crowell. I mean, you *seem* really smart. And you know how to say things in a smart way, like, when you speak it really sounds like you know what

229

you're talking about. But looking at you now makes me think you don't have any good ideas about what to do with that intelligence, know what I mean?"

"Not really."

"You don't know how to get by in life. I mean, we learned in biology that intelligence is an evolutionary trait, and like, the ability to work with your environment. Mrs. Haremza was telling us that knowledge is only useful if it can be applied. Smart-stupid people are interested in facts and stuff but they can't manage their lives too well. They don't –"

"Yeah, I think I get it now," he said, cutting her off. He picked a dried leaf off the ground and mechanically crumbled it to dust. A stillness gripped them amid the sounds of the park. Even the younger brother seemed to sense it. He quietly rested his head on the cushion of his mother's thigh as though listening to something inside her that he modulated by sucking his thumb.

"There's a Buffalo Springfield song about that," Gil said, breaking the spell. "Before your time. Before mine too, actually, but that whole Laurel Canyon scene –"

"See, that's what I mean," Amelia said, "right there. You understand the idea, but you don't get that it's you I'm talking about."

After a few days, the motley news crews disappeared altogether, off to some fresher scandal. It was around this time that Claudia called Gil into her office to inform him that he had to get out.

"What am I supposed to do?" he asked. "I'm not even working."

"I understand," she said, meaning she understood the words he'd spoken. As for the homeless condition she was effectively placing him in, she couldn't have cared less.

"Can I at least get my security deposit back?" he asked.

"Thirty days after you move out following the inspection for damages."

230

"Damages?" he asked. "The floor is concrete, the walls are cinder blocks, and the window was broken when I moved in. What's to damage?"

"It's policy."

"Let's do it now then."

"It doesn't work that way," she said in the same voice she might have used to order a sandwich.

"How can I move out if I don't have anything to put down on a place? Can I at least have another month to get a job and gather some savings together? I'll be living on the streets if you kick me out now. I don't even have a car to sleep in."

"That's not something we deal with here. You have till the end of the month." She tilted her head toward the door.

That gave him five days. There were a number of things he could have done in that time had he known enough to simply do them, including flat out ignore her and let the eviction kick in. That would have trashed his credit for several years, but allowed him a couple months free rent to figure things out. He had some vague sense that the Catholic affiliations of the place codified it as a charity, thus permitting dispensations from the burden of renters' rights, but never took the time to look into it. And so, when the very legal-looking Violation of Terms of Tenancy notice appeared taped to his door a few days later, it achieved the desired effect.

He spent the intervening time trying to pass off Mother Cat and her kittens onto one of the old men. The subject confounded some, silenced others, and angered one.

"You're keeping five cats in your room, is that what you're saying?" old Brian asked one night at dinner.

"It didn't start out that way."

"But you're bringing in fleas and diseases and god only knows –"

"I'm not bringing in anything, Brian. They never replaced the window screen and that's what happens. You get a cat in your room. Next thing you know, there's four more."

231

The harsh defensiveness of his reply returned the others' eyes to their plates of food. The collective silence drove home the point: Nobody was about to care for those cats.

His final paycheck arrived the day before he moved out. He opened the envelope and studied the color printed paper, trying to draw some inspiration from the numerical figure inked into the "Net Pay" box. It was enough to get him out one door but not through the next, what with the first month's, last month's, and security deposit every room in the city required. And so, he took a pile of belongings down to the curb, moved Mother Cat's cardboard box next to the dumpster in back, and left the Koenig House with two backpacks of essentials. With no better idea, he got on a train and headed for the border.

46

"I'm here for the February retreat," he said to the buzz-cut woman in the ashram lobby. "I signed up yesterday, online."

"Namaste. You're a little early, though. The welcoming ceremony isn't until tomorrow at sunset."

"I hitchhiked down from Portland. Didn't expect such good luck getting rides. Could I possibly crash in the back tonight or…?"

"I think we can accommodate you." She looked at the computer screen. "Your name?"

"Gilmore Crowell." He set one of his backpacks on the floor. "Could you go over the escape clause, as well, just to be clear? I had a fear of cults as a child."

"This is nothing like that," she said. "It's a thirty-day retreat. If you're dissatisfied for any reason within the first week, you can get a full refund."

"That's a lot of lost meals for you, isn't it?" He handed over his credit card.

She shook her head. "People don't leave."

"Like Hotel California, huh?"

"I beg your pardon?" She broke from the computer screen to renew eye contact.

"Nothing," he said.

"You'll be in the singles quarters in Wave of Breath building, first floor, room 102. It's got a nice view of the coastline. Bath facilities are on the end. The rooms are simple but great for retreating. We ask there be no burning of candles or smoking in the rooms. On Sunday mornings, please strip your bunk of its linens, stuff it all into the pillow case, and leave it by the door. Sign this, please."

"Sounds kind of like what I'm used to." He took the pen in hand. "Okay if I go to my room now? I need a shower and maybe a nap."

"Absolutely. Here's your key. And this is a map of the grounds and schedule of events for the next couple days. They're still tidying up after last month's group so if a cleaning lady – excuse me, a cleaning *person* – enters your room, you'll understand."

He went across the grounds to the assigned building and found his room on the first floor. Except for an old black-and-white photo of a sheeted woman in Virasona pose, the walls were serenely blank. A military surplus bunkbed, an armchair, an old brass floor lamp, night stand, reed trash basket, a small window with wheat-colored drapes that felt as though they might well have been made out of wheat: These were the room's only furnishings. He put his packs down and squared off with the photo, tapping it level as he checked his reflection in the glass, then crashed back onto the steel-framed bunk. The mattress sank at the center, its springs creaking. He fixed his half-closed eyes to the underside of the bed above him. The

233

rectangles of crisscrossing wires supporting it began to pulse as he nodded off. Just then, the door opened.

"How's it hanging, partner?"

Gil shot upright.

"Ross Orbeck, Orbeck Contracting and Development. Now, see, I can't stop saying that, which means I'll probably never *fully* retire." His laugh was like an old eight-cylinder struggling to turn over. "This has been one hell of a vacation, though. Hey, I needed it."

Gil looked at him, speechless. Ross Orbeck was an older man, stubby, hatchet-faced, with a Texas accent and an easy manner. From the look of his clothing, he was either on safari or there to fix the water pipes.

"You're the cleaning person?" Gil asked.

"Did I wake you, son? My apologies."

"All right, but how did you get in here?"

"This key they give me. Pretty clever, huh?"

"You're saying..." Gil paused, brought his fingertips to his forehead. "The woman at the front desk said these rooms are singles."

"That just means we aren't married. To each other, I mean."

"What's the difference?" Gil's annoyance began to crack through.

"Well, for starters, they give us a second mattress. Looks like you already staked out the ground floor. Guess I'll be taking the loft." Ross Orbeck heaved one of his bags onto the upper mattress, then fell back into the armchair. He kicked out his heels and removed from another bag a bottle of Crown Royal scotch and a couple lowball glasses.

"I thought – didn't the last group just move out? The woman at the front –"

"A few of us are on the two-month plan," Ross explained. "Me, I signed up for one, then re-upped a couple days ago. Couldn't get enough of that ocean breeze." He

234

laughed again. "They moved me out of my room for some reason. You want to tell me your name, private, or am I going to have to read your mind?" He poured the glasses nearly full, handed one off.

Despite the blunt force trauma of first contact with Ross Orbeck, Gil was soon won over by the man. That didn't mean they started giving each other backrubs and blow jobs right away, but the charms of the senior Texan were mostly irresistible.

"That's some dangerous whiskey you got there, cattle man." Gil swirled what remained in his glass. "That what they serve where you're from?"

Ross raised his tumbler to the nineteenth-century mystic woman on the wall. "I got it from her over at the gift shop."

That line doubled Gil over, coughing and seizing like a man freshly maced. He rolled off the lower bunk, sputtering up from the floor, his cheeks flushed a sweaty crimson. "No, please..." He pulled himself halfway back to the mattress, then collapsed again spread eagle. "I'm gonna die if you say another..." But that was it. Caught in the middle of a sentence he couldn't finish for being too drunk to remember how it began, he slipped into unconsciousness.

It would take some time and a whole lot of effort to restart the afternoon after a binge session like that. Gil first had to figure out where he was, then noticed he was alone on the floor. He couldn't possibly have dreamed such a personage as Ross Orbeck, could he? Before taking that thought any further, he noticed his backpacks weren't where he'd placed them at the foot of the bunk. What's more, they were nowhere in sight. He shot up in a panic, looked around, but nothing. Had the old Confederate run off with them? The thought terrified him, what with all the newly-revised dissertation work he'd saved onto his hard drive. He charged outside.

235

There was old Ross, plain as the wart on a witch's nose. He'd taken the hard plastic armchair out to smoke a cigar and watch the sun set over the sea.

"You seen my backpacks?" Gil asked.

"Under the bunk."

"Any reason?"

"Just straightening up."

Gil went back inside to be sure the old-timer wasn't dragging out a prank, but the packs were right there, stuffed under the bed like the man said. He went back out the door.

"You all right?" Ross asked. "Need another drink?"

"I think not."

"Then put your ass in a seat and let's chew the fat a while. Cigar?"

"No, thank you, and, uh, you may not have noticed, but there's no other seats out here, Ross."

"Young man like you ought to be able to sit on the ground."

Gil lowered himself to the sandy grass and looked out to the golden sheet of sunlight glimmering on the Pacific.

Ross spoke into the horizon. "How's your love life, son? You got something waiting for you at home?"

"That's an interesting way of phrasing it."

"You came here for a reason, didn't you?"

"No, I'm just here to hang out for a week till I figure out my next move. No real plan to stay the whole month. Let's keep that between us."

"Well, if your ears are open you'll still learn something."

"Thanks for the warning."

"So, let's have it then." Ross stood up to fiddle with the pockets of his utility vest. "Got yourself a little lady?" He sat back down.

"Have I got myself a little lady?" Gil repeated. "I mean, she's bigger than a bread box."

But Ross Orbeck had suddenly turned serious and seemed not of a mind to engage in Gil's nonsense. "They're going to ask you at one of these sessions."

"If I have a little lady?"

"Might as well warm up to the idea."

"You're talking about my sex life?"

"Well, that's this month's theme, isn't it? Living through loving relationships. What did you do, walk in here blind off the highway?"

"Kind of, yeah."

"Well, son, that ain't what's happening so you better start getting real and the sooner the better. How's your woodpecker peckin'?

"Come on, Ross. I'm not seventy-one."

"What's that supposed to mean? My tool is as stiff as an ax handle. Wake up to it every morning. That's how I know it's time to get out of bed."

"What a relief," Gil said. "Here's hoping we don't return to the topic anytime soon."

"That could be a problem. See, we don't discuss these things and we're all mixed up as a result. You know what the ladies talk about when we're not around?"

"I have a few ideas."

"Vaginas."

"No, that doesn't sound right. There's not enough to say on the subject. It wouldn't add up to a conversation."

"Yet we think about it all day." He winked.

"Well then, I might not last till the end of the week," Gil said. He got up off the ground, brushed the sand off the back of his jeans. The sun dropped below the horizon, and the air turned chilly as it often does on the arid seacoast. "You said you're married. Shouldn't your wife be here?"

Ross took a puff off his cigar. "I'm not here for this month's theme, son. I came for last month's and just got stuck

237

on the place. Maybe you don't remember me saying that. You were a little messed up."

"And what was last month's theme?"

"The Lost Sacrament of Divorce."

"So, are you married or not or is it none of my business?"

"Barely. I'm getting ready to move on. It's not easy after forty-nine years."

Gil was silent. This was a different Ross Orbeck than the one he'd gotten drunk with a few hours before. He was unsure what to make of the man now, but that's how it went. You got to know someone, you came to like them, and then out of nowhere the fuller picture emerged and you had to go back and look them all over again. Every relationship involved constant revision. This is how we're wired, he thought, as he watched Ross gaze out to sea. "Good luck with that," he said finally.

"Good luck?" Ross repeated.

"I don't know, pal. Whatever it is you're supposed to say in these situations."

"I'm not sure luck has anything to do with it. All right, partner, your turn. What's going on?"

"Like I said, I'm not here to work on a relationship. I haven't had one in a while."

"That bad, huh?"

Something about Ross Orbeck's demeanor put Gil at ease. Before he knew it, he was opening up to the old troll.

"I'm kind of hung up on a sex worker at the moment." As the words left his mouth, they echoed back in his mind, affirming that he'd really said them.

"What?"

"What you'd likely call a prostitute."

"A whore?"

"Sex worker."

Ross took another puff off his cigar. "Makes me feel a little better about my own situation. Boy, we're on opposite ends of this thing, aren't we?"

"How's that?"

"Why, my wife's been with only one man. I've had only one woman. See how it's hard to move on? But a prostitute, I don't know. What makes you think, I mean –"

"I'm not sure, but she's magic. Unlike any woman I've ever met."

"She doesn't feel the same, though, does she? I mean, she couldn't, right?"

"No, of course not, but we seem to click in a way. She's smart, self-educated. She's one of a kind. It's hard to explain, but there's a connection there."

"And how much are you paying for that connection?"

"She's made the same point. I mean, she's aware of what's going on. Would I be happier if she were a nurse or an airline pilot? Sure. But maybe then she'd be a different person altogether, right? Can you just subtract something from a person and have them still be who they are?"

"Enough with the philosophy, son. There's a bigger issue here and it's you being hung up on a prostitute. It's like being in love with a cover girl. You may need help, and you might get it here."

"I don't think so," Gil said. "I'm aware how foolish the whole thing is. I'll move on just fine. That's always been my way."

"So, you understand it's a fantasy then?"

"Yeah, I don't have any illusions. It is what it is, as they say. You asked a question, I gave an answer. That's it. I guess you can fall for anyone if the connection is right."

"Tommyrot," Ross said. "That connection, those feelings, they take time. I just picked up on it myself last month." Gil didn't answer, and Ross got out of the hard plastic chair to face him straight. He removed the cigar from his

239

mouth. "Listen up and listen good, son. You're playing a tricky game with yourself." He growled the words like Burgess Meredith spiriting Rocky in the early rounds. "You're only young once, you hear what I'm saying? Don't waste it on a loose woman."

"A loose woman? What are you talking about?"

"Take some pride in yourself!" He spit a gob of phlegm into the Baja dust. A tense silence followed.

"That's what those sheeted celibates taught you last month, is it?"

"Celibates? Don't kid yourself. That freak Tonawanda who runs this place is a horn dog to the bone. One night I thought he was coming on to me till I remembered I drank that ayahuasca punch. It's that creepy personality of his, always smiling, know what I mean? I can't trust a fellow like that."

The welcoming ceremony was a spectacle. Tiki torches and incense and dancing children in white cotton clothing all spiraling down into a bowled slope of shoreline that formed a natural amphitheater. Lute and lyre filled the cool night air. A hundred or so congregants sat around on the sandy grass beaming breathlessly as a silk-sheeted man came into view. He held a glowing orb in front of him. A group of acolytes waving ostrich feathers escorted him down the stony path. As he passed, some kissed the ground he walked on. Others stroked his gray shoulder-length hair.

"Is that Kenny Loggins?" Gil asked.

"Who?" Ross said.

"This guy whose records my dad used to play."

"No, that's Swami Tonawanda," Ross answered, "the one I was telling you about. He's from Western New York but a lot of folks think he's Indian. I guess it's that Mexican sun."

Gil and Ross sat as far up the hillside as possible. They weren't completely isolated there – the venue being too small for that – but the location permitted Ross to smoke a cigar and

240

scratch his balls if the need arose. Gil stretched his back from side to side, unable to grasp how all the roads of his life had led to this.

Tonawanda was surprisingly engaging for a holy man. He opened up with some corny jokes about his Frisbee golf handicap, then moved on to a story about some socks he thought he'd lost. "Then I remembered I don't wear socks." Confused laughter resounded throughout the space. A reflective pause followed, and he got down to the present moment. "It is so very important that everyone remain grounded in their expectations of the retreat. Please take the time in your next meditation to expel any prejudicial notions and bad karma you may have brought down in your sports cars and luxury SUVs. Am I saying that right? S-U-Vs?"

"You must know this is nuts," Gil whispered to Ross.

"Just relax and have a good time with it," Ross said out of the side of his mouth. "I'm telling you, this is the greatest party you'll ever go to and it lasts all month. Hey, if you put a smile on your face, you might get laid. Some of these broads are kind of cute, aren't they? And tomorrow we got paintball."

Just then, Gil's phone vibrated in the seat of his pants. He checked the screen. It was Brinda Bagchi. Take the call? He couldn't decide. The phone kept buzzing. He finally got up and walked to where the arena flattened out.

"Hello?" he asked, as though unsure of the caller's identity.

"Gilmore Crowell, Brinda Bagchi." The familiar Calcutta accent was there, but the delightfully clattering cadence was gone. Her inclusion of both their last names in the greeting also startled him. After all these years, did she suddenly suspect he knew another Brinda? No, she was being formal for a reason. He detected a tremor in her voice as well, the kind that often presages bad news. He turned toward Swami Tonawanda in the center of the amphitheater's low stage. The jubilant holy man held up three fingers of one hand while folding the opposite foot into his groin. He began a one-legged hopping number with some of the white-cottony children. The others clapped and chanted along.

"Brinda, great to hear from you. I was getting ready to call, believe it or not. I've finally completed my dissertation. Just doing a little editing and some –"

"It's not happening." They both gave it the moment of silence it deserved. Gil looked out at the cold endless sea. How many people had drowned in those waters? "The department has terminated your candidacy."

"Terminated?" Gil repeated. The rat-a-tat-tat of the word startled him.

"Look, I did what I could with what you gave me, but De Goeuf and a couple others raised a real stink. They had to take a position and ultimately decided this couldn't go forward after the blaze you lit up around here."

"I suppose I was playing the fool to imagine a different outcome. You say you did what you could. Would you mind going over that?"

Either it was the way he'd asked or how the words hit her ear.

"Hey, this has left me in a mess, too," she snapped. "You don't think they interrogated me about my guidance? What I knew and when? I've spent the past two weeks trying to convince people I was out of the loop on this. I'm up for tenure at the end of the semester, understand? And where have you been since the shit hit the fan? I should think you would have called and made some effort to explain yourself – apologize even – but no. You've pissed off half the department and the other half already thought you're an asshole. This is a giant stain on a renowned university, where you were lucky enough to study and I'm lucky enough to work. Quite a bit of it has spilled onto my reputation, got it?"

In his years of working with her, he'd never heard Brinda speak that way before, could not recollect her ever uttering a single profanity.

"Well, uh," he stammered back, "I guess I can see your predicament then. Thank you for clarifying. I apologize and hope you're able to set things straight for yourself before the tenure review." He waited for her to reply, but only dead air followed. He checked the phone screen. The call had ended a full eighteen seconds before.

47

How did it go again? *Freedom's just another word for nothing left to cast into the Sea of Filth?* That didn't seem right. As he urinated off the edge of the bluff separating the ashram grounds from the Pacific, he recalled only that those popular verses had something to do with the promise of liberty following personal loss. He wasn't feeling it. Oddly enough, he was also not despairing. That was a surprise. If anything, he felt somewhat right-sized. Oh sure, all the cards had been finally laid down. Brinda's words were merely a formality. Whether the game had been rigged or not, he'd surely lost. And yet, there was a comforting, almost benumbing, resignation that came with losing. Was it the same feeling that surges through the oxygen-starved brain of the mountaineer, who quits the summit bid to collapse deathward into the icy slope? If so, was that the point of those deceptively melancholy lyrics?

He had force-marched himself through the past few weeks on a steady stream of cortisol only to arrive at this moment. The worst possible world had finally declared itself, his anthro career good as over. And yet here he was, upright and breathing despite it all. He continued to retain his acquired knowledge, however dubious its worth. His wits and physical well-being, to whatever degree he'd possessed them, remained intact. And as Ross Orbeck pointed out, he could still get an erection. Those were things to value. To hope now that some compensatory wisdom might flood forth in the wake of this ordeal would be downright outlandish.

The rocks at the littoral edge stared up at him, as though daring him to leap. He spat down on them. All that he'd feared *had* happened, *had* come true, and in a strange way *had* floated out to sea with the distant chants of Swami's enthralled believers. He was going to live through this after all. The thing to do now was go back to his military-style bunk, take stock of himself and begin charting the next course of action. At least, that's what he told himself in the moment. He spent the next three hours walking some darker thoughts around the Frisbee golf course. As he reached the barracks, he spotted Ross Orbeck seated out front, hairy gut overhanging the bath towel around his waist. He had the bottle of Crown Royal and was looking out over the star-lit sky.

"What happened? You look like the rat the snake swallowed."

"Kind of how I feel," Gil said.

"You missed a heck of a feast. Lot of good wine. They even had some kind of barbecued lizard. Not bad."

244

"I wasn't in the mood for lizard tonight, Ross. On another subject, my anthropology career – if I can even call it that with a straight face – is officially over." He flashed a fake smile. "The woman who'd been mentoring me the past eight years was kind enough to give me notice this evening."

Ross looked over, slack-jawed. He got up from the plastic chair. "Take a load off, partner." He tapped the chair for Gil to sit down. "Tell Papa all about it."

After a few false starts, Gil opened up. He told the story of his ethnographic field work: his years of failure getting the sex workers to confide in him; securing the teaching position at the juvenile detention center; his decision to pay the girls for their time; the fatalistic night of transgression, when he slept with one of them; the doomed website idea; and finally, the daffy scandal that brought the whole thing tumbling down. Through it all, Ross massaged his shoulders, tsk-tsking at the pity the tale produced in him.

"That was you, huh?" Ross asked.

"You heard about it?" He suddenly regretted opening up to the old-timer. He could have unloaded all this on Ava.

"Of course I heard about it," Ross said. "Read all about it on the computer. Couple weeks back, right?"

"Yeah."

"Well, Jiminy Cracker. You got a talent for screwing things up, don't you?" And then that laugh, like he was choking on a bong hit.

A sheeted monk walked past. He nodded uncertainly at the sight of half-naked Ross massaging Gil from behind.

"It helps to know this amuses you, Ross."

"Oh, come on. You'll be laughing about it yourself before you leave this place."

"Eight years of grad study and nothing to show for it? Sure you understood that part? And what about Bagchi not standing up for me? That's the least she could have done, isn't it?"

245

Ross stopped massaging. "How was she supposed to do that?"

"Plead my case to the dean of natural and social sciences? Give me a chance to defend myself before the committee? Explain to the almighty gatekeepers that I was doing something meaningful?"

"You say you didn't tell her about the website. Was that a good idea? I mean, you got to turn your eyeballs around on this, son."

The smell of a nearby campfire passed through, inciting a false memory of bygone wholesomeness.

"She was the one person I had in my corner, you know, who knew I meant well."

"And I haven't had a good night's sleep since Janis Joplin died. What of it? Let it go and come work for me. I need a good PR man."

"I don't think so. No offense, Ross, but I'm not ready to sell hardware door-to-door or whatever it is you do."

"Contracting and development. Never mind, I wasn't serious." He dug his fingers into Gil's neck.

"Just more bullshit, huh?"

"Now, what's that supposed to mean?"

"Everything you've said since you first opened your mouth."

Ross removed his hands and circled in front of Gil. "It will work itself out, boy. You got to believe that."

"Yeah, I told myself the same thing a few hours back. It sounded good at the time. It's also a pat dismissal of everything I've worked toward my whole adult life. No, it won't work itself out, Ross. What will happen is I'll turn around and start at square one in a different direction." The primal sound of drums and distant chanting came on, though he couldn't tell from where. "There's no way of knowing how long it will take to get where I'm going next. And on the subject of bullshit, you're not divorcing your wife so let's stop kidding ourselves and get it all out in the open like you said yourself yesterday."

"Now listen, I understand you're down, kid. I really do, but –"

"I'm just being honest about where we're both at. You stayed here an extra month because you didn't like what you heard last month. Now after fifty years of marriage, you're trying to figure out what a relationship is supposed to be. Sorry, but it's kind of pathetic."

Ross stared at Gil as though readying to punch him in the face. "Forty-nine years."

"Admit I'm right."

Ross removed the cigar from his mouth and stepped forward. "Give me back the chair." Gil glared at him a moment hoping to produce some extra tension, then slowly got to his feet. Ross elbowed him in passing and sat down. "Where to begin?" He stretched out his arms to the moonlit sea. "I missed out on my youth, partner." He brought his hands in, clapped his gut.

"You're really going to open with that?"

"My wild oats. I never sowed 'em."

"Santa didn't fill your stocking with pussy? Welcome to the club, pal."

"I'm talking about life, you little shit. I've never lived it. I went straight from my mama's tit to my wife's. Shoot, I'd never been out of Texas till they shipped me off to Korea."

"Well, it's a big state. And if you didn't get laid in Korea that's on you. You want to sow your wild oats, is that what you're saying?"

"Look, this is personal. I've only had one piece of ass my whole life, like I told you. Think about it. I don't even know if what I've got is any good."

"She's seventy years old. Cut her some slack."

"I mean I got nothing to compare her to," Ross said.

"We're still talking about pussy?"

247

"Yeah."

"They're pretty much all the same, Ross."

"Come on, you're just saying that. There's different size dicks, there's different size pussies."

"Look, man. I've had twelve, maybe fourteen, total. I'm telling you, they're pretty much all the same. It's not worth talking about. Well, no, I take that back. I did try an extra-large once. It may have been a double XL."

"And what if I got an extra-large and didn't even know it all these years?"

"No, you'd have known."

"Goddamnit!" Ross got up from the chair, spiked his cigar into the sand.

"You really want to get laid? Is that what you're trying to tell me? Because if you do, I know where to go."

Ross cocked his chin, stepped into Gil's space. "What are you talking about now?"

"Sowing your wild oats."

"Oh, please."

"Do you want to or not?" Gil asked. "Don't even answer. I'll just take you. Trust me, it'll solve everything."

"You're off your rocker."

"No, you're going to get laid, and that's all there is to it. Come on, let's get out of here."

"Hold up, cowboy. I'm a good Christian man. Cheating is out of the question."

"You were about to divorce her last month, weren't you? What's the difference?"

"There is a difference."

"Explain it."

"One path is honest."

"And the other leaves a loving wife of fifty years in the Texas dust."

Ross stared him down. "Forty-nine."

"Listen to me, you old son of a bitch. We're going to Tijuana *right now* and you're going to get laid. I don't want to hear another word about it. I have just the woman for you. She'll change your life. She'll make you feel like a young man again, all full of wild oats. You can bang her for the next month if you've got the money. How does that sound? It would beat hanging around this lunatic asylum." He could see a new look coming across Ross' face, one that showed he was considering it. "Then you drive back to Texas and live out your golden years with Agnes or Beatrice or Doris or –"

"Joyce," Ross said.

"All right, Joyce," Gil repeated. "Poor miserable Joyce, who's put up with all your bullshit for the last half century. And she doesn't have to know a single thing about it, understand?"

"It's dishonest," Ross said.

"Well, of course it's dishonest, but it isn't cruel. See the difference? Now, you can leave your loving wife of forty-nine years because you're full of dopey regrets or you can screw a thirty-year-old beauty and save your marriage. What's it going to be?"

"Those are my options, huh?" Ross stared down at his empty hands.

"Yeah, that's about it."

Next morning, they broke their fast in the Assembly Lodge on freshly sliced melon and cream of hemp seed. The first class of the day was titled "Reunifying Our Yokes," in which participants were grouped by table according to gender and sexual orientation. Gil and Ross sat at the end of one table with Gil slouching toward the nearest exit. Swamis directed each group with questions on three-by-five cards.

"Your significant other sends a text message informing you she's been in a car accident. How do you respond?" one swami asked.

No one from Ross and Gil's table answered.

249

"Don't be shy," the swami prodded. "We're all here to open our hearts and minds."

"I think I should ask if she needs a ride," someone offered.

"Incorrect," the swami replied.

"The insurance card is in the glove compartment," another said.

"Is it, now?" the swami asked. "So, she's driving your car then? Another wrong answer. I want you to really search your highest selves now. This is your wife or girlfriend we're talking about. This is the woman you love. Okay now, she's been in a car accident. Do you understand the emotional significance of that?"

More silence.

"*Are you all right and what can I do?*" the swami read off the back of the card. "Always be thinking of her, you see? Let's try another. Your lover has just informed you she's spending the weekend with friends. How do you respond?"

"Does my wife know?" someone asked.

Gil rolled his eyes over to Ross.

"Now?" Ross asked. He stuck his fork into a wedge of papaya.

"I can't sit through much more of this. We went over everything last night. It's time."

"Just a couple more questions. I want to finish my coffee."

At a lull in the exercise, they slipped out and headed back to their shared room at the Wave of Breath building. Ross sorted through one of his bags.

"How long is this going to take?"

"Plan on the whole day," Gil said. "Think of it as a break from all this spiritual nonsense. We'll be back in time for vespers or whatever they call it."

"So, sundown then?"

"Sure. And look, try to relax."

"I am relaxed. I'm figuring out what to bring."

"If you have your wallet, you're all set. We'll meet up afterward and eat some tacos or something, maybe catch an afternoon strip show."

They left in Ross' enormous pick-up, kicking up dust and gravel as they wound their way down the drive to the *carretera*. Except for Gil's directions, the two hardly spoke.

"You all right?" he finally asked. "I mean, you're ready to do this, aren't you?"

Ross shaped his mouth to speak but no words came out.

"Ross, you there?"

"Yeah, I was just thinking about something."

"What is it?"

"Just how messed up I was after the war." He lit a cigar, powered down the window.

"You really have to go there now? You're about to get laid."

"Hear me out. I've never told this to anyone before, not even my wife. I'm not sure why I'm telling you, but I am."

"All right," Gil said. "Let's have it."

"When I got back from Korea, it had been so long since I'd been laid that I started to wonder if maybe I was gay. You know, homosexual." He shot Gil a side glance. "That ever happened to you?"

"Have I ever wondered if I was gay?" Gil asked.

"Yeah."

"No, but there's still time."

"Anyway," Ross continued, "I spoke to someone about it at the VA."

"Yeah? What did they tell you?"

"Well, this guy was a social worker or something, a psychologist maybe. Is there a difference?"

"Sort of, go on."

"One of those guys that help vets deal with the war, that kind of thing."

251

Gil pounded his thighs. "All right, so what did he say? I mean, are you gay or not? We're on our way to a brothel. I can't stand the suspense."

"What did he say?"

"Oh, my god. Are you in the middle of a story right now or just pulling out random memories?"

"No, he asked me some questions."

Gil smacked the dash. "Questions to figure out if you're gay?"

"Yeah."

Another pause.

"Well, what was the result, buster?" Gil asked.

"He said I wasn't gay."

"And how did he figure that out, or don't I want to know?"

"He asked if I ever looked at a man and thought he was handsome."

"You answered no to that?"

"No, I answered yes." Ross took a puff off his cigar, blew the smoke out the window.

"You really don't know how to tell a story, do you? Then what happened, captain?"

"He asked me if I'd ever turned around on the street to check out a guy's ass."

"How'd that one go?"

"I said I never had, and then he told me I wasn't gay."

Gil scoffed. "All right, whatever. I suppose that's as good an ending as any. That is the end, correct?"

"Then I went to a diner and had some pie."

Gil looked out the window at the rolling desert hills. "You like those diner waitresses, huh? With the tied-up hair and the knee-length skirts? Switching subjects a moment – unless you still want to talk about being gay – are you ready to do it with a woman whose legs are so long it takes her five minutes just to pull down her panties?"

252

Ross looked over at Gil. "You may be talking me into it."

"You want to pick something up on the way? A little blue pill to be on the safe side?"

"Don't you need a prescription for that?"

"Not in Mexico."

"All right, maybe that's a good idea. You got any johnnies?"

"Condoms?" Gil asked.

"Yeah."

"Don't worry about that. She'll have all the johnnies you need."

They continued down the *carretera* in silence, passing rusty warehouses, isolated gas stations, department stores out in the middle of nowhere; random radio towers and forty-foot-tall signs for Walmart, Oxxo, Pemex. They took an exit to the southern edge of the city, went down a side street into the hills, and stopped at a pharmacy.

Ross suddenly panicked, as though he'd dropped some hot ash onto his lap.

"What's wrong?" Gil asked.

"Nothing. I just got a bad feeling."

"You're nervous, man. You're about to have sex with a beautiful woman. Can you just keep your focus on that for two hours?"

"No, this is something else," Ross said. "I'm going to pull over a minute."

"If you think it'll help."

Ross parked in the shade of a tree. He removed the bottle of Crown Royal from his bag, took a hit, and threw his head back into the headrest. He swung the bottle in Gil's direction. "Want any?"

"No, let's go."

They pulled up to Ava's and parked behind an old camper out on the street. One of the women from the house was arguing with someone inside the camper. Gil got out of the truck. He saw Ava in cut-offs and a tank top up at the house, her arms raised up into the door frame. She'd been watching the squabble out front, but when she made eye contact with Gil her face opened up. She trotted down to the sidewalk. Ross got out of the truck, shuffled over.

"¿*Cómo estás?*" Gil asked.

Ava gave him a hug. "How's it going? You just checking up on me or what?"

"This is my friend, Ross. I was wondering if you could do him a favor. He's willing to pay for a couple hours if you can help him out today."

Ava took a step back. "Help him out?" She looked Gil up and down.

"Well, what is it, baby? Is it a bad time?"

"A bad time?" she repeated. "Yeah, I'd say it's a bad time. This is my home. You bring a stranger to my home to do business?"

"Should we meet up at the Coahuila or…?"

"Who do you think you are, my pimp?" Her face trembled.

"This wasn't any of my idea, ma'am," Ross said. "Come on, son. Let's get out of here."

"Wait," Gil said. "I'm still a little confused. Did I say something wrong? I mean –"

"Oh, you're definitely confused," Ava said. "This is how little you respect me?"

"All right, look, I'm not very good at this, evidently. If I misunderstood something, or if I asked in the wrong way, or if I should have said something I didn't –"

It struck like a bolt of lightning from the sky, a right cross to the jaw. It was a remarkable punch in all aspects: speed, power, accuracy, and follow through. He never saw it coming. Defenseless against the sudden jolt, he toppled over instantly, sprawled in the gutter between the curb and the camper like a broken sack of trash.

48

There are a number of jobs open to a master of anthropology: bone digger, dirt sifter, shelf stocker, snake milker, corn husker, file clerk, life coach, soils consultant, paper boy, soda jerk, riverboat barker, human resource specialist, yoga teacher-trainer, and assistant manager of McDonalds. Gil became a sales rep in the kitchens department at Home Depot.

He spent hours each day studying the variety of refrigerators, stoves, and countertops, learned about faucets and flooring and faux-wood paneling and the merits of each brand of cabinetry. This type came with a lifetime warranty, that kind with free installation, another had child safety latches. He perused manuals on marketing strategy and customer service and personal hygiene and got to wear an orange vest and a name tag for the first time in his life. His supervisor was a twenty-two-year-old with an afro-mullet, pierced eyelid, and a tattoo of a '54 Chevy on his throat. His name was DeMaximus Wiley. Wiley was a patient man with sense enough to see that Gil, with his master's in anthropology, must have just recovered from one of life's terrible falls. He gave him plenty of space to adapt to where he'd landed, there on the cement floor at Home Depot. DeMaximus would check up on Gil from time to time to see how things were going. Though most of their communication was nonverbal, they understood each other well enough. Somehow Gil managed to sell a lot of kitchen products. Go figure.

He took a room in a duplex just beneath the Harbor and Santa Monica Freeway interchange, a few blocks from the old Koenig House. Four generations of a Salvadorean family lived on the first floor, while the upstairs had individual rooms for rent. The woman who owned the building had just renovated the upper floor. Gil was one of two tenants she'd rented to in the new space. The first was a divorced man who was almost never home. For a time, this permitted the illusion that Gil was living by himself. A couple weeks passed and a lovely Colombian dancer moved in. Gil would see her in the middle of the night – he stumbling, she floating across the floor – as they went to and from the only bathroom. The fourth tenant was a young Marine whose room was adjacent to Gil's. His hobbies included death metal music and casting empty beer bottles out his room's window to the Eighth Street pavement below. The fifth bedroom remained vacant.

Gil didn't start work until ten AM, which gave him a good chunk of time to sit out on the porch of his new home with a cup of coffee in hand, observing the morning routines of his new neighborhood: noisy yellow buses shuttling children to school, working men off to whatever labors occupied them, professional women striding the sidewalk to the downtown high-rises. All of this flowed at street level under the roaring complex of the overhanging freeways. Around nine o'clock, two toddlers who lived in the downstairs unit came out onto the porch, armed with a dirty stuffed dinosaur and a plastic truck. They orbited Gil with these objects outstretched in hand. The truck and dinosaur could not only fly equally well, each performed outlandish air stunts while passing mere inches from Gil's head. They also made the same sputtering noise. It was quite a show, though he could handle only a few minutes of it before needing to head off to work.

In the back of the garage, he found an ancient women's bicycle with a wire basket affixed to the handlebars. No one seemed to care that he started riding it. It was in such rough shape – coated with grime and spider webs through the spokes – that he didn't need to lock it up at work. It was late spring, and he would often ride it around MacArthur Park in the sunlit evening hours, observing the ducks and paddle boats on the man-made lake. With the fading light of dusk, he watched the surrounding scene give up its color to the advancing darkness, nature's most time-honored act. On days off he holed up in his room and read public library books about self-improvement or self-acceptance or self-renewal as the scent of *tamales* rose up from the floor below and the sound of death metal music pounded his wall. He imagined these books were authored by people doing quite well with their lives. They were so hypnotically written that he almost couldn't put them down, though their real value was in taking his mind off his troubles.

Given the frequency of southern California scandals, whatever had happened at Los Angeles Correctional Academy could not remain long in the public eye. That was good news for a man who rode a women's bicycle on the busy downtown streets. From time to time, a Home Depot customer would hold their attention a moment too long on Gil's face. Once, the woman behind the sneeze guard of a ninety-nine cent Chinese buffet suggested he looked familiar.

"You been on TV?" she asked. "You can give picture for wall?" She gestured behind the cash register at dozens of signed head shots. Gil did not recognize a single one of these handsome characters, but then again, he hadn't watched television in eight years. "All these famous people, they come here, they eat here," the woman said proudly.

"No, I've never been on TV," he lied. "Although, it doesn't surprise me that famous people eat here. It's good food and it only costs ninety-nine cents."

She beamed back at him.

Another time, while reading a book about recovering the essential self from the clutches of the egoic mind, he heard a hollow explosion of glass below in the street. A moment later, a

257

short muscular fellow pushed through Gil's bedroom door. It was the Marine.

"Hey, I just figured out where I know you from."

"You didn't see the sign?" Gil asked.

"What sign?"

"On the door."

"There's no sign on this door."

"All right, then I haven't put it up yet. What it says, though – if you're interested – is that enlisted men must knock before entering. You understand the good sense behind that, don't you?"

"Sure, but hey, weren't you on the news a while back for setting that brush fire in Ventura County?"

"You mean Orange County?"

"Was it Orange County?" the Marine asked.

"Yes, but I didn't set that blaze. I did consider it more than once, however. Sometimes when I wake up in the middle of the night, I think maybe I really *did* set it. You must have picked up on that."

"How do you mean?"

"Ever heard of the collective unconscious?"

"No, you want a beer?"

"Okay, but first let me tell you about the collective unconscious."

"I'll get the beers."

49

Any reasonable person would think losing the family chihuahua would be cause for celebration, yet there was the color photo of Sparky's vicious little face plastered to the glass door of Joe's Coffee Shop. Three-hundred-dollar reward. Contact details inside. Since he needed the money and had the day off to cycle around the streets of LA, Gil went in for a cup. He'd keep an eye out for the dog as the day wore on.

It was one of those coffee shops that couldn't just sell coffee. It did multiple duty as an art gallery, a vintage clothing boutique, a neo-Bolshevik home office. Music piped through the ceiling speakers. *Whiskey with your water, or sugar with your tea. What are these crazy questions they're asking of me?* There were nineteen different coffee blends, all with race horse names like "Winter's Atlas," "Alluring Notes," "Sylvan Shadow," and so forth. One was called "Old Black Joe."

"Seems pretty racist," Gil said to the young woman behind the counter.

"I don't know, I just work here." She turned around to steam some milk.

"Yeah, and the Nazis just worked here, too, right?"

"What's that?" she asked over her shoulder.

"That upstart faction that blamed the German economy on skinny little baristas."

"Meaning what?"

"How should I know. Do I look like a Nazi?"

"Look, uh, you can either order or leave." She gestured to someone in the back.

"Fine, give me a cup of Old Black Joe. With a name like that, it's got to be good."

He paid for the coffee and went over to the bay window in the front of the narrow shop. Two nattily bearded young men whose expensive footwear belied their homeless appearance were playing the board game Troke in a corner.

"My mother was very good at that game," Gil said. "She was good at all games, actually. I used to play her sometimes when I was a boy. One day I started beating her at checkers and all the rest of them. I was so proud of myself. I thought I was getting better, but that wasn't it. She'd gotten sick and her game skills deteriorated with the illness. It was a really sad thing to witness. She died a couple years later."

"Do I know you?" one of the hipsters asked.

"I doubt it," Gil said. "But I was famous for about fifteen seconds so...."

"Put up twenty bucks and you can play the winner of this game."

"I'll pass," Gil said.

"Scared?"

"Broke. And I never play on another man's board."

He turned around. A woman as old as original sin sat at a black iron table beside them. She whispered something to the steam rising off her tea cup. Gil took an empty chair from her table, pulled it to the side and sat down. He sipped his coffee and quickly sketched the people he saw pass the bay window. Each image had its own title: *Urban peasant woman pushing baby stroller of recyclables. Yelping teenage youths on diminutive bikes. Elderly man fixated on quarreling sparrows in hellstrip jacaranda.*

His cell phone buzzed. He silenced it and checked the screen. A Tijuana number.

"Bueno."

The caller identified herself as Professor Lopez, chair of the anthro department at the Autonomous University, Baja

California. She had received Gil's paper. She had read it. She shared it with a few of her colleagues, who also looked it over. They discussed it briefly at a recent department meeting. They were reaching out to him now.

Someone tapped his shoulder. He turned around, the phone still up against his ear. A middle-aged black woman looked down at him. She pulled up a chair, sat back to front.

"I'm Cheryl, the manager. Did you have something to say about Nazis?"

He silenced her with a raised finger and stood up. "Sorry, Professor Lopez. I didn't catch that last part." He picked up his things and stepped outside.

Professor Lopez repeated her invitation to Gil: Would he like to come down to the university to discuss his work?

"How did you get hold of my paper?"

"We assumed you'd sent it," she said. "Your name and phone number were on the cover."

"That's right. I sent out a bunch out of them," he lied. "The last couple months have been a real blur."

"That's the academic world, isn't it?" she said.

"I can see that now."

He looked through the glass door of the coffee shop. Cheryl-the-manager had retreated to the kitchen. With ballpoint in hand, he scratched a Hitler moustache under the runaway chihuahua's nose, then rode up the street to the Koenig House.

"What are you doing here?" It was Claudia, hosing off the front steps.

"Delivering some heart medication to Norm he asked me to pick up."

"I'll take it to him."

"He specifically asked me to bring it."

"You're not entering this building."

"What did I do to you? I'm still trying to figure it out. You've got ex-cons living here, drug addicts, alcoholic

261

psychopaths, a guy who couldn't hit the toilet bowl with a bowel movement if his life depended on it. A news crew shows up on the sidewalk for a few days, and that's the thing that bends you out of shape?"

"Leave or I call the police."

"I'm on a public sidewalk."

She pulled out her cell phone.

He waved her off and rode around the block, slinking through the backyards of the apartment buildings behind the house. He climbed up onto the dumpster as he'd done so many times before and looked into his old room. Still vacant. Norm's was the next one over. He took hold of a downspout and pulled himself onto the security bars. His head just cleared the lower reaches of the window frame, allowing him a view in. The window was open, but he couldn't reach the glass. He rapped on the frame and brought his face to the screen. Norm soundly napped in the center of the barely-furnished room.

"Norm, wake up."

No answer.

"Hey man, it's Gil. Wake up. I need help."

Norm began to snore, as though blocking out the disturbance. A different approach was needed so Gil began to sing.

"Whenever I see your smiling face, I have to smile myself because I love you. Yes, I do ...."

"Huh, what?" Norm straightened up, looked out the window. "Oh, what the –" He reached under the bed and pulled out a fire extinguisher.

"Hey relax, man. It's me, Gil."

That's when he felt the needle-like claws of Mother Cat climbing up his right leg. It was either yield to the pain or freak out and fall to the pavement. He clung tightly to the drainpipe as she made her way up his shirt.

"What's going on?" Norm's face was now up against the window.

262

"Can you unlatch the security bars and let me in?"

"No, it's impossible to put back."

By this time, Mother Cat was firmly affixed to Gil's torso. He couldn't remove her without losing his balance. One of her kittens was also on its way up. Though its claws were much sharper, they weren't long enough to penetrate much past the denim pant leg.

"Can you meet me out front then? If I stand here any longer, I'm going to fall."

He sidled over to the top of the dumpster again, where he detached Mother Cat and her kitten. He tossed them down and circled around to the front of the building again. Claudia was gone, her task of watering the entranceway completed. Norm opened the front door and, shielding his eyes from the outside light, looked down at Gil.

"Hey, man, you got a suit?" Gil asked.

"What?"

"A suit of clothes, like a matching jacket and pants?"

"I'm a Buddhist. Why would I have a suit?"

"I don't know, but I'm desperate. I got a job interview and no money. I was thinking we were the same size so…"

"I may have something. Hang on."

When Norm returned, he was holding up two articles of clothing, one in each hand.

"Dude, that's purple. You own a purple suit?"

"Is it purple or lavender?" Norm asked.

"No, lavender is a plant. That's a purple suit you got there."

"It's also a color, like orange is also a color."

"Isn't that what they called a leisure suit back in the day?" Gil asked. "My grandfather used to wear them."

"I don't know, but it's a suit. Interested?"

"Bell bottoms and wide lapels… I don't know. Where'd you get that thing, anyway?"

263

"I think I wore it to a wedding years ago. They handed them out. I was part of the procession or whatever it's called. You know, like everyone had the same costume."

"Yeah, it's called a wedding party, Norm. Sounds like you were on the groom's side."

"That's right, my brother's wedding. His first." He brought his hand to his jawline. "Is that possible?"

"Sure it's okay if I borrow it?"

"You can burn it for all I care. Just don't breathe in the fumes. It's pure polyester." He handed it down from the doorway.

Norm didn't have a necktie or a pair of matching dress shoes, but Gil easily acquired them at a thrift shop on Pico. And so, with his purple suit, lemon shirt, striped vermillion necktie, and white penny loafers, he headed back down to TJ on the train. For once, the long commute did not weigh on him like an eight-hundred-pound boulder. He looked out the train window. There was a freshness in the air. The sky was nearly smogless, the ocean cobalt blue. He crossed the border and took a friendly cab ride to Otay Centenario at the edge of the Autonomous University campus. It looked like an Orange County office park stranded in the middle of the desert. He pulled himself out of the cab, tipped the driver, and looked around. The campus was already barren, following the May dismissal of students. The corridors of the anthropology building were barely lit. He passed wall upon wall of displayed relics and handiworks, Olmec statues and stone Aztec calendars, even a balsa wood replica of the ceremonial center of El Tajín.

These objects took him back to his undergraduate summers in Mexico City, when he would wander the anthro museum all day, endlessly enchanted by Classic Veracruzean culture. His view of things had been so pure and unpoliticized then. However unfulfilling life seemed to be, his love of learning always pulled him through. He sensed standing there among the artifacts that he could no longer experience that love, that view of things. The remembrance of them lived on, but the person who made the memories no longer truly existed.

He went through the main office door of the department. Professor Lopez greeted him. She was a short, moon-faced woman, whose manner quickly put Gil at ease. The loose skin around her neck and eyes suggested she was closer to the end of her career than the beginning, yet there was a cheerful vibrancy about her. She led him into an adjoining room with a high pyramidal ceiling lit by triangular windows of red and gold glass. Books lined the walls. Pigeons cooed in the rafters. A scholarly cloister. He met two other professors, both male, one young, one much older. They looked distant, as though under some enjoinder to let Professor Lopez run the meeting.

"Mr. Crowell, this is Juan Vargas, a recent addition to our department, and this gentleman to my left is Professor Emeritus Roberto Rangel, who ran things around here for a number of years. He's given that up now to spend more time doing what he really loves, which is taking long afternoon naps."

Polite laughter and handshakes.

"We've all read your paper. Is it a dissertation or monograph or…?"

"My doctoral thesis," Gil stated. He felt a bit guarded to be uncovering the subject of so much recent disaster. "Actually, what you have there is a working draft. I've since done a lot of editing. If you're interested, I can present you a revised copy. I brought one down."

"Fascinating, isn't it?" she said.

"I found it to be," he said. "I can't estimate its academic value, but –"

"Oh, I think it has tremendous value," she said. "Has anything like this been done before?" She looked over at her colleagues, whose wan faces matched their level of interest.

"Sustaining an eight-year gaze on a community of sex workers?" He'd been practicing that line.

"Is that how you put it?" she asked.

Vargas and Rangel exchanged smirks.

"I'm a little unsure why you invited me here," Gil said. "Is there anything I can help you with, something I can offer the department?"

"What is your current status?" Professor Lopez asked. "I imagine you've been offered a position in the States."

"No," Gil said. "As a matter of fact, I haven't completed the doctorate. I've had some hang-ups along the way regarding methodology. I've learned the hard way to be up front about these things."

"Well, hopefully it all gets straightened out." She got up to take some Perrier bottles off a cart in the corner and handed them around. "What was it about your methods that caused such a stir? You weren't sleeping with the girls now, were you?" She mugged, horrified.

Vargas and Rangel shared in the folly of this remark, their polite chuckles growing louder and wilder until they were both guffawing so violently that the floor seemed to shake. It didn't end. One would stop laughing for a moment to catch his breath, and the other would start up again. That's when the bright triangular windows of the room began to warp and unfurl, leaking hazy air. Gauzy as gossamer, fibrous as spider webs, diaphanous as a hippie's skirt, the slightly pinkish fog thickened among them. Gil took hold of his chair, just as the seat rocked backward. He hung on, white-knuckling it till the laughter subsided, the floor reasserted itself, and the fog began to fade.

He cleared his throat. "I did sleep with a few of them, yes."

Each looked over at him with bugged eyes and trembling lips, breathless as beached flounder. The punchline never came.

Gil shrugged. The unbearable silence continued until broken by Professor Lopez.

266

"Fascinating." She looked up at one of the colored windows. "To cross the threshold of the liminal veil, am I right? How else could you deconstruct the objectified body's material play, to separate the labial winks from the blinks, as Geertz might have put it, yes?"

"I don't know about that," Gil said. "I've read everything he wrote at least twice. I never saw a labia wink or blink. Nor did I imagine that sleeping with sex workers would advance any line of inquiry. I just messed up one day and kept at it."

"Well, you proved yourself wrong," Professor Lopez said, her head high as she flipped through the manuscript. She looked over at her colleagues for support. None came. Having finally come to rest following their shared bouts of laughter, both Vargas and Rangel kept a safe, if wide-eyed, distance from whatever remained of the interview. Gil started to get up. Professor Lopez grabbed his wrist and pulled him back to a seated position. "But you were able to determine the social factors that shaped and supported their lives. What more could anyone ask of such a study? You could not have learned those things that you wrote of here with such precision and clarity had you not slept with a few of them. I mean, come on."

"Sorry to disappoint you," Gil said.

"Who's disappointed? I'm madly inspired by your courage. There's so little of it anymore. Everybody's writing what they think they're supposed to write, saying what they think they're supposed to say. Whatever gets them their thesis, their tenure, their book deal."

"Courage, you say? I've spent my whole life bending the rules to get by. Twisting some things, skipping over others, taking shortcuts that turned out to be endless dead ends."

"Well, were they endless or were they dead ends, *mijo*? You can't have it both ways. Work with me now. I'm trying to help you out here. Can't you see that?"

267

"I can see it and I thank you, but the only reason I traveled down this path was out of laziness. My parents were attorneys who worked all the time. When I went to college I took a good look at my professors. It seemed like they had it all figured out. Teach a couple classes and spend the rest of the time reading with your feet on a desk. That was the life I wanted and I took the easiest route to get there. Well, I thought it would be easy. My mistake."

"*¡Déjate de mamadas!*"

"Look, I'd rather tell it to you straight now than suffer for it later. I even kind of fell for one of the sex workers, if you can believe it. A clever young woman, I should say. If she'd been born to a different family, who knows where she would have ended up. I'm rambling now. My apologies for wasting your time."

Vargas and Rangel exchanged another smirk. Gil suddenly recognized he could never work there. He'd inevitably be fired for smashing Perrier bottles over their heads. Would Professor Lopez sweep up the glass?

Someone coughed into the crook of their elbow. Somebody else looked at their watch. Professor Rangel stood up stiffly and farted, then headed for the door.

"Okay," Professor Lopez said. "Thank you for coming down."

"Not at all," Gil said. "It was an education."

50

Wandering back out into the concrete desert, he quickly figured out that hailing a taxi there was a far more enterprising task than being dropped off by one. He looked up and down the surrounding boulevards. The cars and trucks rumbled past. He climbed aboard a pickle-green city bus that, judging from its exhaust, was running on coal. He sat down among the *abuelas* and the chickens and the ecstatic chatter of youth and rocked and rolled his way to the municipal bus station. From there, he took a splitting headache back to Zona Norte for what he hoped would be the very last time.

It was a simple plan. Meet up with Ava wherever she was, apologize for his unconscionable crassness, thank her for sending out the dissertation, and get out of town. Cross the border and rebuild from scratch. Sell real estate or car stereos; learn the fine art of bartending; get a certificate in financial planning; teach karate to the thriving suburban preschool demographic; paint his face and juggle fire in the middle of an intersection; what difference did it make? A job is a job is a job. After balancing the pros and cons of each, one sucked just as much as the next. That was the real American Dream, the one you don't wake up from. The homeless must have figured this out long ago: Don't have children, do as little work as possible, and keep expenses down to whatever the universe provides. It was the best way to keep from getting fat, too. There'd be good days and bad, to be sure, but even a bad day homeless in Los Angeles meant hanging out warm and sunny in one of the world's richest cities. Starving was out of the question. There were those who shook their heads at that lifestyle, others who pitied it, but they were wracked with student debt, hooked on scrips, priced out of the housing market, and downloading e-books on living in the moment. He wasn't there yet, but he'd keep his options open. In the meantime, he was getting out of a cab below the magnificent chrome arch at Revolución and First.

He walked down the sidewalk in his purple suit, lemon shirt, striped vermillion necktie, and white penny loafers. Rip-roaring *rancheras* cried out from the open saloons. The stench of the Tijuana River floated over on the breeze. A few of the girls eyed him. One reached out. He kept on walking down to Ava's post, the same place he'd spied her nine months before, leaning back on one leg, picking the paint off her fingernails. A girl grabbed him. It was more than a simple tug on the sleeve. She said something in Spanish and screamed. Another girl came over, then another. This is it, he thought. Whatever's happening, I'm fucked. He looked around, wondering how to escape, but soon there were twenty girls surrounding him, then thirty, each grabbing at him and jabbering away.

Ava emerged from the back of the swarm. "It's the website. It exploded a couple months back. The girls who signed on have been killing it. I'm making twice as much as before. You been advertising or what?" She flashed him that radiant smile.

"No such thing as bad publicity, I guess."

The girls continued to crowd him, each one cutting in front of another.

"What am I supposed to do?" he asked Ava over the commotion.

"Get their names and numbers," she called back.

He forced himself out of the pit of pressing bodies. "I just wanted to talk to you for a minute, you know, about what happened and all."

"Okay, but don't pass this up. There's another two hundred where they came from. If you charged a monthly fee, you'd be rich in no time." He stood there, too shocked to speak.

270

They surrounded him again. All of a sudden, Ava whistled. "All right," she called out in Spanish. "Everybody get in line or you don't get on the website." She reached into his backpack for something to write on and pulled out the dissertation, stuck a pen in his hand.

"Hey, come on," he said. "It was never about this for me. I'm no pimp."

"You want me to do this for you?" she asked. "I don't know what's going on in the States right now, but around here this is the kind of money you don't let slip through your fingers."

"You could do it, too, couldn't you? I mean you're already kind of bossy."

"Listen," she said. "I'm sorry about what happened. You caught me at a bad time."

"Yeah, it was a bad time for both of us."

She lowered her eyes to the sidewalk. "I meant to tell you about this before. I just wasn't sure –"

"No, it's all right. I actually came down to debrief on that very incident. With the hope of moving on from it, I should add."

"I'm talking about the website. Do you want to talk about it, too? Maybe I can help you or we can help each other."

"Are you trying to ask me to lunch, Ava?"

"I think maybe I am," she said. "And my real name is Aurora. You can call me that."

"The rising sun." He thought back to Frinkle's literary guide. "I like the symbolism. You sure it's not too soon for us to be having lunch together?"

She looked at her cell phone. "I've got twelve-fifty-seven."

And so, they headed up Revolución, arm in arm, with thirty-some high-heeled streetwalkers in line behind them. As they waited to cross the street, his cell phone buzzed.

"Is this Gilmore Crowell?"

271

"That depends who this is."

"Los Angeles Police Department. We've recovered a stolen vehicle."

"Yeah? And you're sure it's mine?"

"If you're Gilmore Crowell, I'm sure. They found it in San Diego County. The tags were fake and the VIN had been removed, but they put it into the system by make and model. Since yours was the only Isuzu Gemini hatchback stolen in the last ten years, they figured it must belong to you."

"Is that right?"

"CHP pulled over some guy speeding up the Interstate Five a while back. Whoever this character was, he had your license. I guess you must have left it inside the vehicle when it got jacked. When the guy didn't show up to court, we figured it must have been stolen. And for that same reason, he must not have been you."

"What are the odds?" Gil asked.

"Some good old-fashioned police work paid off in your favor."

"Makes perfect sense, officer, but I doubt I'm going to be in LA anytime soon."

"Got someone to pick it up? All they need is a valid driver's license. We can do the paperwork right now over the phone."

"I think I may have just the guy. You got a pen?"

"Well, I'm a police officer sitting at a desk in a police station. What do you think?"

"Great. Hang on a second." Gil took out his wallet and removed a business card. "His name is Scott Bertram. Ready for the number?"

If you liked this book,
do the author a favor
and post a review.
Thanks for reading!

Made in the USA
Las Vegas, NV
12 June 2023

73300274R00163